D0761914

CATHERINE CAVENDISH

IN DARKNESS, SHADOWS BREATHE

This is a **FLAME TREE PRESS** book

FLAME TREE PRESS
6 Melbray Mews, London, SW6 3NS, UK
flametreepress.com

US sales, distribution and warehouse:
Simon & Schuster
simonandschuster.biz

UK distribution and warehouse:
Marston Book Services Ltd
marston.co.uk

Thanks to the Flame Tree Press team, including:
Taylor Bentley, Frances Bodiam, Federica Ciaravella, Don D'Auria,
Chris Herbert, Josie Karani, Molly Rosevear, Mike Spender,
Cat Taylor, Maria Tissot, Nick Wells, Gillian Whitaker.

The cover is created by Flame Tree Studio with
thanks to Nik Keevil and Shutterstock.com.
The font families used are Avenir and Bembo.

Flame Tree Press is an imprint of Flame Tree Publishing Ltd
flametreepublishing.com

A copy of the CIP data for this book is available from the British Library and the Library of Congress.

HB ISBN: 978-1-78758-553-9
US PB ISBN: 978-1-78758-551-5
UK PB ISBN: 978-1-78758-552-2
ebook ISBN: 978-1-78758-554-6

Printed and bound in Great Britain by Clays Ltd, Elcograf S.p.A.

CATHERINE CAVENDISH

IN DARKNESS, SHADOWS BREATHE

FLAME TREE PRESS
London & New York

For Colin, who made it all possible

PART ONE
IN DARKNESS...

PROLOGUE

Dr. Oliver Franklyn washed the young woman's blood off his hands, staining the water vivid scarlet. "The spirit needs a permanent home. The work is almost complete. We followed her direction and all is ready for her."

Arabella Marsden lifted the unconscious woman's chin and let it fall, watching the trickle of blood slick down the side of her head, onto her cheek. She wiped it away with an already gore-sodden cloth. No more followed it. Carol Shaughnessy was quite, quite dead. "You said the spirit would enter her at the point of death and that she would rally. I see no sign of life in this woman."

Dr. Franklyn dried his hands and rolled down his sleeves. He lifted the girl's wrist and felt for her pulse. "Have patience, Arabella. The power we are dealing with has her own way of working. She is the One and the Many and has lived a thousand, ten thousand times. We must be guided by her. We have pledged to serve her."

"I'm worried. Ever since we entered into this...arrangement... we have ceded more and more control to her. It was better before."

Dr. Franklyn gripped Arabella's arm. "Don't say that. Don't even think it. We were about to be exposed. We would have gone to prison, or even worse. Do you really want to know what it's like to be hanged? Because I'm damned well certain I don't. We were on the verge of a breakthrough. Probably the greatest scientific breakthrough of the century. We were about to find the true source of the soul. All our experiments...all the years of work. They would have been for nothing if the spirit hadn't come, protected us and removed the danger."

"But the price—"

"Is worth paying. I would do it again."

Arabella scratched her throat. "I can still feel her inside me. I thought she would have gone over by now."

"Give her time. She has been doing this for millennia. Ever since she was cast out and set to roam, in desperate need of a host. She has gone from body to body. This time she will have a permanent home. One who will not age or die. One who will endure, recharging herself every natural lifespan, with no memory of previous years, merely a set of false memories to satisfy the humanity left in her."

A flicker caught Arabella's eye. "It's working. Look. I saw her finger move and...I can feel *her.* The spirit of the One and the Many. She's leaving...."

She staggered backward with the momentum as the spirit wrenched itself out of her body. She and Dr. Franklyn stared wide-eyed at the charcoal mist, swirling around the still figure of the woman who had been Carol Shaughnessy. It mingled briefly with a silvery light that seemed to draw itself out of the dead woman.

"Her soul is departing," Dr. Franklyn whispered. "And now the One and the Many will give life to the corpse."

The light spun and ascended. It vanished from sight as the mist cloaked the body in the chair.

The woman's head slowly rose from its slumped position. Her fingers flexed. Her skin grew pinker as blood once again flowed through her veins.

"It is done," Dr. Franklyn said.

Arabella nodded and sank down onto a nearby chair. "I was but a temporary vessel and now *she* has gone, I feel empty."

"Be thankful that the spirit has her new home."

Arabella nodded. In the chair, the woman's eyelids flickered and she opened her eyes, showing no recognition, only fear and panic. She squirmed, straining against her bonds.

"Who are you? Where am I? What are you doing to me?"

The doctor smiled. "It is as the spirit promised. She has no memory of who she was. We have succeeded."

CHAPTER ONE

Her footsteps echoed along the gloomy corridor. An antiquated light flickered overhead, illuminating the peeling walls and dirt-encrusted tiles in brief, almost surreal flashes. Carol Shaughnessy's breath quickened as her heart rate increased. She glanced nervously around her. How had she come to this place? One minute she was asleep in her bed and the next....

She had no idea why, only that she must keep walking, keep moving forward. Surely this corridor led somewhere, but her feet merely took her farther and farther into a building she didn't recognize. A building where she appeared to be the only inhabitant. Meanwhile, the sound of her footsteps seemed to grow louder.

A door slammed. She stopped. Listened. Somewhere, not too far away, the tapping of shoes on stone. Approaching. Getting louder. She peered into the darkness. Nothing but the flickering light. And then—

A face rose up out of the gloom. Pressed close. Almost touching her. Penetrating eyes. A woman's face.

A face of madness.

Carol screamed.

* * *

She shot out of bed. Every nerve heightened, her breath struggling in short gasps. It hadn't been real. A nightmare to end all nightmares but that was all. So why couldn't she stop shaking?

It's not happening. It didn't happen.

Trembling uncontrollably, she staggered down the freshly carpeted hall to the kitchen. She opened one of the glass-fronted oak cabinets that lined the walls, only to be faced with stacks of gleaming china she would never use; she would be too frightened of chipping a cup. Carol closed the cupboard. The cheap mugs and plates she had brought with her would suffice for her needs. But where had she put them? She had only moved in today and with so few of her own things to unpack, how could she have forgotten? But the luxury of this place overwhelmed her.

She peered through the glass door of the second cupboard. There, an array of lead crystal glassware glittered and sparkled. That lot would have set her back at least a month's wages, probably more. The third cupboard, more sparsely filled than the previous two, contained her own tableware. At last! She settled on a chunky tumbler that had cost her a few pence in a charity shop a few weeks earlier and grasped it in both her trembling hands, concentrating on not dropping it.

Carol half-filled the glass with water, downed it, then topped it up. The cold drink revived her and she took deep breaths, holding each one for five seconds before releasing it. That was supposed to help when you had a panic attack, wasn't it? Though she couldn't remember where she had heard that.

Gradually her heartbeat slowed to normal and she made her way through the double glass doors into the spacious living room. The central heating had gone off a few hours earlier, leaving a distinct chill in the room, so she moved over to the fireplace and lit the gas fire. Not wanting a bright light, she settled for two wall lamps and sat on the edge of the comfortable, and no doubt expensive, settee.

Such a lovely apartment. Small as it was, it had not only a fully fitted bathroom, but also a smaller one, comprising a toilet, washbowl and shower, accessible through – and designed for the sole use of the occupants of – the master bedroom. A proper 'en suite bathroom'. Carol had never lived anywhere this fancy and had really fallen on her feet here. Not that she could ever afford to buy anywhere remotely like it or even rent one, except that this arrangement was different. Even if it could only be for a limited time. The owners were in Dubai on a six-month contract. They would return and that would be that. In the meantime all she had to pay was a peppercorn rent in return for maintaining the apartment and all its contents in the perfect condition she had found them.

Feeling calmer, Carol became more aware of the increasing chill in the room. She set her glass down on a coaster on a small table and retrieved her dressing gown from the bedroom. Wrapping it around her, slippers warming her chilled feet, she settled back and sipped more of the refreshing water.

Six months would be long enough. Long enough to decide whether she wanted to stay in this town at any rate. If it worked out, she could look for somewhere a bit more permanent. Permanent. Now *that* was a novel concept. She let her mind wander where it willed. Back to her childhood in one foster home after another, until.... No. Best not to dwell on that bit. Anyway, there were always so many gaps in her memory and sometimes she seemed to remember things she couldn't possibly. Things that had happened to another version of her, in another time and place. But how was that possible? No. She had a vivid imagination and particularly realistic dreams, nothing more.

Fast forward to age sixteen. Out in the world on her own and already old enough to know that trusting anyone inevitably led to disappointment, hurt and sadness. She had never forgotten *that* lesson. In fact, as she sat in this quiet, spotless room with its white walls and expensive furnishings, she realized she couldn't name one person she *did* trust. Not after.... There had been a school-friend, many years ago now. Becca had betrayed her, and taunted her for being an orphan with no knowledge of either of her parents.

No, she was better off on her own. This way no one could get too close. Besides, she was never really alone. Not *really*. There was always...well, *she* was always somewhere on the edge of her vision. Just out of sight. Was it her in the dreams? An extension of herself perhaps, or some form of alternative consciousness. Carol smiled to herself. Where on earth had she come up with that load of pretentious-sounding twaddle?

The figure, entity or whatever it was, never fully showed herself but Carol sensed her as a female. And one firmly attached to her as well. She existed in shadow, or at least most of her did.

It had always been that way. Over the years, Carol had imagined her as being an older woman, a sort of fairy godmother, or grandmother. Did having such an ethereal companion make her different or did other people have someone like that? Her schoolfriend Becca hadn't – or so she claimed. Confiding her secret to the girl had merely set her off on a new wave of taunts. She could hear the familiar sneering voice in her head.

You're crazy. Everyone says so. You're only called Carol because you were found at Christmas. You haven't got a name of your own. They had to give one to you. Crazy Carol No Name. Crazy Carol No Name....

The other kids would pick up the chant. Carol slammed her hands against her ears, trying to block off the noise in her head. Still it came, louder and louder, dragging itself up from the past like some unwelcome specter.

Crazy Carol No Name
Crazy Carol No Name
Crazy Carol—

A sudden noise. Like plastic snapping. A crackling, like static electricity.

The shadow flickered at the corner of her eye.

She was back.

⋆ ⋆ ⋆

When Carol awoke, she had no recollection of getting back to bed although clearly she must have. It didn't feel as if she had even slept, but the alarm had woken her.

Carol showered, dressed, dried her fine, dark blonde hair and put on black trousers and a gray sweater. She would cover this with her tabard when she got to work at the supermarket. This week she was on the checkouts but other times she would serve on the bakery, deli or fish counters, or behind the customer service desk. Carol welcomed the variety. She had worked there a month and her boss seemed happy with her progress. Moving around as much as she had in her life, she had become used to picking things up quickly and getting on with it. In her private, honest moments she recognized she would prefer not to work with food that stared back at her, so the fish counter had become her least favorite.

As usual, she arrived at work in plenty of time and her line manager, Sarah, greeted her. "Hi, Carol, how's the new flat?"

Carol liked her. Not enough to get to know her socially or anything but she found her pleasant, easy to get on with and she didn't pester her. Carol appreciated that. Being left to get on with it was exactly how she liked to work. She wouldn't let her boss down. "It's lovely, thanks."

"Waverley Court is a beautiful place to live."

"I'm very lucky, but I can only stay there six months."

"Enjoy. Make the most of it while you can. You never know, if they're happy with you, they may let you stay there again if they get another contract abroad."

Carol smiled. Stranger things had happened. Mostly to her.

She hopped up onto the swivel chair and logged in to her till. Within seconds, the first customer was emptying the contents of a trolley onto her conveyor belt.

"Good morning," Carol said automatically, remembering to smile.

"Hello, dear. That's a happy face to brighten up my day."

"Thank you." Carol scanned item after item, ensuring she placed the items within reach of the customer, an elderly woman of, she gauged, around eighty. This was not a supermarket that attempted to break speed records for scanning and chucking items at the customers. Any such attempt would bring the normally affable Sarah down on her like a pile of smashed concrete.

The woman paid cash. Carol waited while she fumbled in her bag for her purse and fiddled with the clasp. The queue was lengthening and a few people were shuffling their feet and glaring impatiently at the customer before pointedly examining their watches. The woman saw them and became even more flustered. She thrust the purse at Carol, who made eye contact with her for the first time.

I know her. I've seen her before. Can't remember where, or when….

The woman was speaking. "Will you do it please, dear? My

arthritis is playing me up today and I can't seem to open the wretched thing."

"Don't worry," Carol said, focusing once more on the job in hand. "I've got it." She opened the purse and handed it back to the customer, who dropped it on the floor. Coins scattered and a few people in the queue darted after them, picking them up. Someone muttered something about 'old biddies' who 'shouldn't be let out on their own'.

Carol left her position and came around to join the hunt for the scattered cash when Sarah appeared as if from nowhere.

"It's okay, Carol. I've got this." She collected the coins from the more helpful customers. The grumbler had joined another queue.

"Oh dear," the woman said, tears beginning to spill over her eyelids. "I'm so sorry. How embarrassing."

"Don't worry," Carol said. "It could happen to anyone." *I wish I could remember where I knew you from.* But the woman gave no sign of recognition.

Sarah pressed Carol's bell for assistance and summoned more staff to the checkouts.

"Would you like me to sort the money out for you?" Carol asked.

The customer looked as if Carol had just offered to save her life. "Oh would you, dear? That's so kind of you."

Carol counted out the cash, making sure the customer could see she was only taking out what she needed to cover the cost of the goods. She was aware of Sarah's eyes on her and met her gaze. Sarah smiled.

"Here's a little for your trouble," the customer said, handing Carol a five-pound note.

"Oh no, please, that's not necessary. I couldn't possibly…."

But the woman had already moved away, wheeling her shopping trolley toward the exit. Obviously she couldn't get out of there fast enough. The customer had given no indication that she recognized Carol so she must have been mistaken. Odd though.

Sarah touched her arm. "You handled that well. She'll tell all her friends how helpful you were."

"I couldn't take her money. She didn't look that well off and, besides, it's not allowed for staff to accept tips."

"Oh you'd be surprised. Sometimes it's the ones who look the poorest that have the most. How about you put it in the charity collection box?" She indicated a plastic bucket at the end of Carol's station.

Carol picked up the note, folded it and shoved it into the slit on top of the bucket.

"There you go. Cancer Research will benefit from your excellent customer service."

Carol returned Sarah's smile and served her next customer.

* * *

The rest of her shift passed uneventfully until it came time to hang her tabard up in her locker and walk the short distance home. With no plans for the evening, as usual, Carol settled in front of the television. A soap opera that had been running far longer than Carol's twenty-eight years on the planet droned on, its characters mixed up in increasingly bizarre plots that bore little, if any, relation to real life. It seemed every time she switched on, the pub in it had changed hands. Their solicitors appeared to have a passport to fast track every kind of property law for each of their supposedly impoverished clients. Impoverished! That was a laugh. Most of them had plenty of spare cash. They were always skipping off on foreign holidays or going out for meals in the local fancy bistro two or three times a week.

Her patience exhausted, Carol switched channels. A quiz show. The questions so absurdly simple as to make, "Who wrote Beethoven's Ninth Symphony?" look intellectual.

She switched channels again. A rom-com. Half an hour later, Carol had figured out the entire last hour of it, including the impossibly beautiful couple reuniting again after a series of predictable traumas. The credits would roll while they sat together, watching the setting sun on a Caribbean beach. The End.

Carol yawned and switched off the television. Lack of sleep last night was catching up on her. Maybe an early night. She made to stand up.

Out of nowhere, the familiar shadow flitted across the edge of her sight.

This time, she almost saw her face.

CHAPTER TWO

Shadows flickered in the bedroom. Where the fitted wardrobes should have been, a whitewashed wall had appeared, with a painted dark stripe running lengthwise halfway down it.

Carol sat up in bed, hunched, knees under her chin, staring at the impossible sight. Shadows moved within shadows. Moonlight filtered through the curtains, but there were no trees or shrubs outside tall enough to cast such shapes. Besides, where had the furniture gone?

Silence.

Only the sound of Carol's own breathing punctured the heavy atmosphere.

She wasn't asleep. The shadows had momentarily unnerved her, but she had come to bed and almost immediately dropped off. Something had woken her, and now this….

Carol reached for the lamp, her hands trembling. If she put it on, what would she see? Only one way to find out. She held her breath and pressed the switch.

The bulb flashed once and then out.

Damn it.

Now she would have to get out of bed, go to the far wall by the door that she couldn't even see anymore, and switch on the main light.

Sweat broke out on her palms. She rubbed them on the duvet cover.

Still the shadows swirled. Carol could make out figures. Women, dressed in Victorian clothes. Or could that be a trick of the light? Like sitting in front of an open fire and seeing angels dancing in the flames. Her imagination was playing tricks on her, making her brain create impossible images.

An urgent sensation in her bladder. She needed the bathroom

and would have to get up. Taking a deep breath, she thrust the duvet aside. Her feet found her slippers, she dashed across the room, and clicked on the light switch.

The room flooded with the glow from a dozen halogen bulbs implanted in the ceiling, almost like fairy lights but far brighter.

There were the fitted wardrobes, and the door, slightly ajar. Strange she couldn't see it from the bed. Even in the gloom, with only pale moonlight, she should have been able to make it out. She reminded herself this was only her second night in this apartment and she had yet to become entirely familiar with all its aspects.

Carol made her way to the en suite bathroom and used the toilet. As she switched off the light a sudden movement distracted her. The scurrying, yet indistinct, figure she had seen countless times all her life. Strangely familiar and always tantalizingly close, yet out of reach. But it had never hurt her before, so why should it now?

She crossed the hall and went into the kitchen. Rummaging under the sink, she found a small box of bulbs. Most were only suitable for the overhead lights in the living room, bedrooms and hall but she finally located one to fit the bedside lamp, returned to her room – and stopped dead in her tracks.

The lights were off.

Had she switched them off and forgotten? Carol tentatively touched the switch and applied the slightest pressure. Once again, light flooded the room. No shadows. Nowhere for anything to hide. She realized she had been holding her breath and exhaled, moved swiftly over to the bedside table and changed the bulb, dropping the dead one into the wastebasket beside the bed. When she pressed the switch this time, it worked. By now though, Carol was wide awake.

A mug of tea would be comforting. She returned to the kitchen and poured cold water into the kettle. A few minutes later, she carried her tea into the living room and stood by the glass doors that led out onto the driveway sweeping up from the main road. Dawn was on the horizon. Pink-tinged clouds and a pale, reluctant sun cast a faint, grayish light across the grounds of

Waverley Court, where a patch of well-maintained and nurtured grass nudged up against a neatly trimmed hedge. Beyond that, another patch of grass – slightly less well maintained – led onto a car park belonging to the Royal and Waverley Hospital. Beyond that sprawling building stood the Gothic red brick of the university with its impressive, ornate clock tower. The agent had told her that, back in Victorian times, the whole area had comprised a couple of upmarket streets built in the eighteenth century, the hospital adjoining the old workhouse and asylum, and a large cemetery.

Carol checked her watch. Quarter past six. No point going back to bed. She would have to be up in less than an hour anyway. Might as well start now.

She took her mug back to the kitchen and rinsed it before making her way to the en suite for her shower. Her thoughts occupied, she wasn't prepared for the sight that greeted her in the bedroom.

All the wardrobe doors were open and her clothes strewn across the floor. Carol stood and stared, not believing her eyes.

"Who's there?" she called, at the same time terrified someone might answer.

Nothing.

From the en suite came the unmistakable sound of running water. She dashed in to find the shower at full pelt, already filling the room with steam. But it couldn't do that. For one thing, the flat wasn't cold enough. The shower was thermostatically controlled at a constant temperature and the central heating had come on. Somehow, the thermostat had been changed, and quite dramatically at that.

Carol reached into the shower, careful to avoid the scalding cascade. She turned it off and leaned back against the sink for a moment, trying to calm herself and steady her racing heartbeat. As she returned to the bedroom, a sudden sharp pain shot through her abdomen and she doubled over, gripping the bed for support.

The pain subsided and stopped as fast as it had started. Carol concentrated on breathing steadily before she dared straighten up.

When she did, she felt a presence behind her, a split second before she toppled over onto the floor.

Someone had pushed her. Shoved her in the small of her back. A vicious, deliberate act, but she could see no one.

Carol curled into a fetal position, scared to move off the floor.

Footsteps. She could feel someone walking around on the soft pile of the carpet.

Please don't hurt me. Please....

They seemed to be moving closer toward her.

Go away. Just go...away....

She caught her breath. The footsteps had stopped. She could smell tobacco. And spearmint.

Something stirred in her memory.

She looked out of her eyes as a child. Barely thirteen and newly fostered for the fourth time. She remembered the family. It wasn't that the Sinclairs were bad people. They were unlucky. Unlucky to have a vile son like Jonah. She could hear his whiny voice now, feel his hot breath on her cheek, smell the mix of illicit tobacco and the spearmint chewing gum meant to conceal his smoking habit from his parents.

"Come on, Carol. You know you want it. Little slut like you. You want it so bad."

"Get away from me. I'll tell your parents."

But all that had achieved was to anger him. "What do you think they'll do, bitch? Do you think they'll believe you over their own son? Their own blue-eyed, perfect son?"

His laugh was as cruel as his actions. He tore her dress, ripped her knickers and forced himself inside her. It had hurt. Hurt worse than anything. Anything...until that sudden pain a few minutes ago.

Jonah had been right. His parents hadn't believed her and it had only made things worse. They turned against her and she heard them whispering when they thought she couldn't hear.

"There's bad blood there...a bad influence on Jonah...we need to send her back...."

He raped her again and again over the next month. Carol kept quiet. She didn't even scream or struggle anymore when he violated her. She just wept silent tears as she mopped herself up, cleaning his disgusting semen off and out of her body. She winced when she lowered herself gently into the hot bath water, watching the thin trail of blood turn the water a pale pink.

Carol had run away from that foster home and pleaded not to be sent anywhere else. She refused to tell them why. And they had asked her. Time and again they had tried to get her to talk. Maybe they guessed. But she wouldn't – couldn't – tell them about Jonah. If she did she knew he would find a way to get at her, harm her. Maybe even worse.... He had said so.

They kept her in the Children's Home until she was sixteen – the only place she felt safe. The only place she had ever felt safe.

Tears flowed as she lay alone on the bedroom floor in the beautiful surroundings of Waverley Court. Why could she never rid herself of her past, and why did it always feel as if it had happened to someone else? Someone else who shared her body, mind and memories, but chose to hide in the shadows. And Jonah? What had happened to him?

A series of flashing images rushed through her brain. A cold, rain-swept night and a damp, dirty cellar. In her raised hand, a carving knife dripped blood. Jonah's terrified face as he cowered on the filthy floor. A rat crawled over his feet and scurried away into a dark corner.

"Don't...don't...." His voice a whimper. A stupid, childish whimper, while anger raged within her.

"Too late," she had heard herself say before she brought the knife down again, again, again, obliterating his face until not even his own mother would recognize him. Slicing, chopping, scything out revenge for the pain and misery he had caused her. Strength she knew came from elsewhere drove her on. Pleasure overrode all other emotions. Blood. So much blood.

And then it was over. She was free of him at last.

Her mind jolted her back to the present. Had it really happened? Had she killed Jonah? She had no memory of getting out of that cellar. Surely she would have been covered in his blood – and worse. The police would have caught her. She racked her brains but could find nothing to draw on. So it was just a dream then.

Out there, somewhere, he still lived and breathed, so she must keep one step ahead. But those images felt so real.

Tears wet against her cheeks, she opened her eyes and slowly sat up. Her clothes still lay around her but she was alone. Using the bed to steady herself, she stood. Her legs wobbled and she half-staggered to the bathroom.

She checked the shower. It was set for the correct temperature so whatever had altered it hadn't meant to harm her, merely to scare the life out of her. Well, they had certainly succeeded in doing that. Carol slipped off her nightshirt and stepped into the cubicle, closing the glass door behind her.

* * *

"Your eyes are ever so red, Carol. Haven't you been sleeping?" Sarah's concerned look almost reduced Carol to tears again. She fought to control her voice.

"I had a bad night. Just a silly nightmare, but a really vivid one. I'll be all right." Sarah nodded, smiled and moved on.

Carol's work day began. Nothing eventful. One customer insisted on holding up her line while he ranted about the price of apples. Carol said, "yes" and "no", and hoped they were in the right places. Eventually the bombastic pensioner caught the frustrated glares of the other customers and shuffled off, still grumbling.

"Honestly, some people." A young mother with talon-like acrylic nails piled disposable diapers, pizzas and an assortment of tins of spaghetti hoops, baked beans and macaroni cheese onto the conveyor. "As if it's your fault."

Carol smiled at her. "It takes all sorts, I suppose."

"Yes, I suppose." The woman pushed back her bright blonde hair, enhanced with obvious extensions. The tot in the child's seat of the trolley gurgled and dropped a small plush toy rabbit on the floor. Her mother retrieved it, her fluorescent-pink nails flashing. "Here you are, Ariana." She handed the toy back to the child, who instantly started chewing its ear. "No, don't do that. It's been on the floor." The child ignored her and carried on gnawing.

With some difficulty, the woman extracted notes from her purse. Carol watched her and wondered how she could do anything with those nails in the way.

Carol handed over the customer's change, placing it in the palm of her hand so she wouldn't have to struggle to pick it up. Was it really worth all the effort? The woman smiled with her Botoxed lips and blinked her false eyelashes. She would be attractive if it wasn't for all the work she had had done.

"Thanks. Have a good day." The customer wheeled the child and her shopping away, teetering on six-inch heels. For the first time, the child caught Carol's eye, screwed her eyes up, opened her mouth and bawled. The woman quickened her step, nearly tripping over in the process.

"She'll do herself a mischief in them shoes," the next customer said.

Carol smiled. Her thoughts exactly.

* * *

At the end of her shift, Carol could barely keep her eyes open. Lack of sleep, and crying, had made them sting as if she had bathed them in salt water. At least tomorrow was her day off. It didn't matter what time she got up. But the thought of returning to the flat suddenly didn't seem as appealing as it had before the events of the early morning. The first thing she would have to do was tidy all her clothes away. As she inserted her key in the door, she prayed she wasn't coming home to anything worse than a messy bedroom.

She breathed a sigh of relief at the peaceful warmth that greeted her and made her way to the kitchen, where she extracted a pizza from her carrier bag and placed it on the draining board.

In the bedroom, the mess she had left behind awaited her and she spent the next few minutes folding, and hanging up her clothes. There weren't too many. Carol had never had much spare cash or been particularly interested in fashion and she rarely wore makeup. Most of her clothes were practical and comfortable.

Picking up her last sweater, she discovered an old leather-bound book she couldn't remember seeing before. Yet there it was, lying in plain sight on the floor. Before her clothes had ended up all over the place, she would have been bound to see it, surely, so where had it come from? She flicked through the yellowing pages. Some sort of diary. Maybe it belonged to the people who owned this flat? It certainly wasn't hers so she had no business reading it.

She closed it and tucked it in the drawer with her sweaters.

When she had finished sorting out her room, she switched on the oven to warm up ready for the pizza, which she later ate while watching the television news. Political infighting, a corruption scandal. Job losses. Enough to send anyone into a depression. She switched off the television and finished her meal.

After she washed up, she put her phone on charge and booted up her tablet. Her email provided the usual junk and she had long since deleted her Facebook account. What was the point when she didn't have any friends to connect with? Maybe that thought should have made her sad or lonely but it didn't.

A scratching noise disturbed her introspective thoughts. It came from the double glass doors that led outside.

Carol felt a twinge of apprehension but she mustn't give in to it. She forced herself to stand and pace steadily to the other side of the room. The reflection of the light inside made it almost impossible to see anything outside in the dark. Maybe it had been a cat. Pets weren't allowed in the complex but that wouldn't stop a determined feline from ambling across the grounds.

On impulse, she unlocked the doors and opened them. Outside, the concrete felt cold through the thin soles of her slippers. Security lights illuminated the driveway. No sign of anyone – human or animal. A slight breeze rustled the leaves of some nearby shrubs. It had turned into a fine, chilly night and Carol felt the urge to stroll around the grounds. She hadn't done so since she arrived and it was a fascinating place, given its history, even if the present building only dated from around twenty years earlier.

She retreated into the warmth of the living room, locked the double doors and removed her slippers, reminding herself she must wash the soles or risk staining the oatmeal carpet. For now though, she left them on the kitchen floor and grabbed her coat and shoes from the hall cupboard.

After locking her front door behind her, she tucked the key safely into her coat pocket, ready to explore her surroundings.

She pulled open the communal front entrance door and stepped out. Skirting around a couple of neat flower beds where no weed would dare to make an appearance, she followed the line of security lights under an archway, hearing nothing but the echo of her footsteps. A large wall plaque drew her attention, but the surrounding murkiness made it impossible to read. She reached for the phone in her pocket and switched on the flashlight.

Waverley Workhouse and Asylum. For the benefit of the poor and the feeble of mind. This foundation stone was laid by Alderman Grover Warren, May 18th 1859.

A rush of cold air ruffled her hair and she tucked a stray strand behind her ear before switching off the flash.

So this was the older part of the complex. Where she now lived had been bombed to destruction during World War Two and subsequently rebuilt twice since, but this red brick Gothic edifice, which also housed luxury dwellings, had somehow escaped the attention of the Luftwaffe. Restoration at the same time the newer apartments were built had been carried out with some sensitivity and at least a nod to the architectural Gothic revival opulence of the nineteenth century.

Carol continued her walk, emerging from the archway, seeing no one. The eerie silence seemed to her as if it was waiting for something to disturb it. Nothing did.

Circumnavigating the quadrangle, within which shrubs, a Japanese-style water garden and wooden bridge had been constructed, Carol felt an inner peace mount inside her. This would be a truly lovely place to settle down, not that she would ever be able to do so. Once her six months were up she would be off to some measly one-bedroom flat above a backstreet convenience store or fast food outlet. Even then she would probably have to fork out more than she currently did.

So much for inner peace.

Carol pushed the unwelcome thoughts out of her mind. Arriving back at the archway, she retraced her steps through it, but as she entered, everything changed. *She* changed.

In a second, she was looking at the world through someone else's eyes. Except…. It *was* her, but not as she was now.

She rubbed her eyes, trying to focus, and failing. Everything around her undulated and lost substance, stretching, contracting as if time itself was bending. The light grew brighter, then faded. She almost lost her balance and grabbed the wall for support. At first it seemed to resist her attempts to grasp it. She felt the cool bricks beneath her fingers and then she didn't. It had all changed. Now she felt fabric. She was inside a building and clutching floor-length, dark blue velvet drapes and seeing the room through a mist. Old-fashioned, heavy Victorian furniture surrounded her. Dark wood. Mahogany perhaps.

Someone rushed toward her. A tall, dark-haired man. Yelling, angry and out of control.

"I'll teach you your place, woman. You will obey me. Do you hear? You will obey *me*."

The heavy blow sent Carol reeling. Her jaw screamed pain. She fell to her knees.

"You will never defy me again. Ever. You are *my* wife and you will do as *I* say. *Only* as I say."

Another blow set her ears ringing. She tasted blood, spat it out, and the world buzzed in her ears, turning everything black.

She could only have been out for seconds. When she came to, she had somehow returned to the archway where the strangeness had all begun. She struggled to her feet, feeling her jaw. It ached a little, but surely not as it would have done if she really had been attacked as badly as she thought.

Carol shook her head in an attempt to clear out the fuzziness and unreality. What the hell had just happened?

She made her way back to the apartment, stopping for a while to stare over at the lights of the Royal and Waverley Hospital.

Into her mind flashed an image. Rows of iron beds lined up against the walls, neatly spaced and each with an archaic overhead lamp. Women in Victorian nurses' uniforms. Others dressed in drab brown, much-mended dresses, sleeves rolled up to their elbows, scrubbing the floor with brushes they dipped regularly in galvanized buckets of hot water. Carol felt the strongest urge to get down on her hands and knees and join them, almost as if she belonged there.

The image flashed off as quickly as it had come into her mind and the familiar figures sped across her peripheral vision.

Carol returned to her apartment and locked the door behind her. In the kitchen, she reached into one of the wall cupboards and took out a bottle of Scotch, which had been on special offer at the supermarket this week. She poured a large swig into a glass, topped up with ice and Coke and gulped it down, grateful for the rush it gave her.

She poured another and took it into the living room. It wasn't even nine o'clock but tiredness engulfed her. Lack of sleep had a lot to answer for. Maybe that's why she had experienced that weird hallucination under the archway.

Another scratching at the double doors. Carol stood and went over. The drapes were still drawn open. She made to pull them shut but something caught her eye. Something that shouldn't have been there. A piece of white paper, partially snagged on a small, thorny bush outside.

She unlocked and opened the double doors and peered down at the shrub. The sheet of paper didn't look like a piece of rubbish. It had been neatly folded and positioned as if it had been deliberately spiked onto the small bush. Lifting it off, she took care not to tear it. In her hand, it seemed old and appeared slightly foxed. Carol went back inside and locked the doors, before returning to the settee, where she unfolded her prize.

Lines of a poem, written in copperplate script:

In darkness, shadows breathe
Though the earth be still, with graves,
The mourning yearn for solace
And the dead shall hear their cry,
Sending spirits on winged flight,
To comfort and console,

But one among them bides behind,
Her soul of ebony and granite,
The fires of life long since quenched,
Replaced with voids of emptiness.
In darkness, shadows breathe
And death their only reward.
(Lydia Warren Carmody, 1856-1891)

That name. Warren. The same as the alderman who had laid the foundation stone. Coincidence? Maybe, but somehow Carol couldn't bring herself to believe so.

More scratching noises. Carol put the sheet of paper aside and returned to the doors.

And screamed.

Pressed against the glass was a young girl whose ghostly white face and huge eyes stared at her, mouth partially open, hands also pressed, palms flat, against the panes.

Carol shook uncontrollably and backed away but couldn't tear her gaze away from the terrifying sight. The girl wore a white, ankle-length shift. Her irises shone black and huge in the strange light. Her expression took the form of a silent scream, until her mouth gradually closed.

Her lips moved. *You're next....* The girl stepped back into the shadows and vanished.

Carol yanked the curtains shut and retreated to the settee. She lay, curled into a ball, fist in her mouth to keep her from screaming. She couldn't have seen that. It must have been some trick of the light or a hallucination. Sleep deprivation could do that. But it had only been a couple of nights....

Sleep. She must sleep. She forced her eyes shut, breathed deeply until her exhausted mind let go and she drifted off.

★ ★ ★

When she awoke, morning sunlight streamed through the chinks in the hastily drawn curtains. Carol rose, stiff and sore from the settee. It seemed she had barely moved an inch all night.

In the daylight, her nocturnal experiences paled and became unimportant, a product of a befuddled brain. That's all it was.

She wandered into the bathroom and drew herself a deep, hot bath, lacing it with a generous amount of bubble bath. Steam coated the mirror and Carol sank into the welcoming suds.

When she emerged ten minutes later, she wrapped herself in a big, fluffy white towel also generously provided by the owners. Luxury. She could take any amount of this. Carol felt pampered for once, not a sensation she had ever been accustomed to.

Drying her hair with another towel, she glanced at the mirror and froze. Condensation dripped from spidery letters, written in an old-fashioned hand.

You're next.

Her heart pounded. She raced out into the bedroom and quickly dressed in the same trousers and sweater she had worn yesterday. When she dared return to the bathroom, the steam had cleared. The mirror was clean. No words remained – if they had even been there in the first place.

Carol grabbed her tablet and sat at the small bistro table in the dining area of the kitchen. She searched for 'Royal and Waverley Hospital' and was rewarded by a whole plethora of NHS-related sites. She must narrow it down to the history of the place and her part of it in particular.

Searching for 'Waverley Workhouse history' proved a little more fruitful. Here she discovered photographs of the original workhouse, the asylum and of the old hospital itself. She even found a layout of how the massive complex had looked late in the nineteenth century.

She was able to pinpoint fairly accurately, or so it seemed, the location of her apartment. It had most certainly been built on the site of the hospital. She altered her search to try and locate Alderman Grover Warren. Surely not a common combination of names. She found a couple of obtuse references and a newspaper report of the laying of the foundation stone. No photographs.

Deciding on a cup of coffee, she stood and immediately bent double, clinging on to the table as an agonizing pain knifed through her belly exactly as before. She concentrated on breathing, calm, steadying breaths, as the pain gradually subsided.

It passed and she sat down again, praying it didn't return. There was nothing for it. If this happened again, she would have to go to the doctor. Pain like this couldn't be normal. She had never suffered badly with menstrual cramps and in any case her period wasn't due for another week or so. Furthermore, the pain seemed to have traveled. It had moved more to the right rather than centered and it seemed higher up her abdomen.

The intercom buzzed.

Carol made her way carefully out into the hall, peered at the screen and picked up the receiver. She could see no one. Maybe they were standing in the wrong place, out of shot.

"Hello?" she called.

The face filled the screen.

With a yell, Carol jumped back.

The girl from last night had returned.

CHAPTER THREE

Carol had no idea how long she stood there, cowering in her hall, not daring to move. Over and over, her mind churned. Who was that child and why was she tormenting her? Who was putting her up to it? Overriding all of her thoughts came the distinct impression she knew this girl from somewhere, or that some part of her did, which made no sense at all. But she couldn't rid herself of the conviction. She went over everyone she knew, past and present, from every place she had ever lived. One advantage about keeping yourself to yourself was that you didn't tend to make enemies. Especially if you never stayed more than a few months or a couple of years in the same place.

She came up with no one.

Finally, Carol began to get angry. For once she was living a dream, in a beautiful apartment in the right part of town. But someone wasn't content to see her happy even for an instant. No, they had to do their level best to wreck it. But they couldn't if she wouldn't let them, could they?

"Bring it on," she said to the walls. "Do your worst. I'm ready for you."

One last glance at the intercom screen. Empty. From now on, she would ignore scratching at the windows or doors and she wouldn't answer the intercom unless she was expecting someone – or a delivery. She resolved to remove the latter. She would simply buy everything she needed in the shops and not order anything online anymore.

Taking back control. It felt such a relief. She could get on with enjoying her life here for the short time she could.

In the living room, she glimpsed a piece of paper sticking out from under the settee. The poem. She had forgotten all about it and it must have fallen down there. She bent and retrieved it.

The author – Lydia Warren Carmody – who was she? Carol searched for her on her tablet. No entries. But something niggled her. For some reason, she couldn't leave it there. She had to find out more about the woman and maybe then she would understand why doing so seemed so important.

★ ★ ★

Days passed uneventfully and Carol allowed herself to relax a little. She established a comfortable routine and made a few trips to the library searching for information on the elusive Lydia Warren Carmody. She was more successful on Grover Warren, who had indeed been a prominent citizen in his time. She learned that he did have a daughter named Lydia, born in 1856. He had trained as a doctor and had lived and operated private consulting rooms in nearby Maupasson Street. Carol took a stroll round there one evening after work as the sun sank low in the sky. She stared up at the impressive Georgian terraced house. Elegant. This would never have been a home for anyone below middle class and fairly affluent. Today, houses like this sold for a small fortune, if they weren't converted into apartments. Judging by the array of doorbells, such had been the fate of number seventy-three. The front door boasted a high-gloss black sheen and brightly polished brass door knocker.

Carol imagined Grover Warren alighting from a Hansom cab and mounting the steps to his front door. A butler would have opened it for him, taken his hat and gloves, and helped him off with his cloak. All very civilized.

In a downstairs window, a young woman peered out at her from behind a net curtain. She was frowning, clearly suspicious as to what was attracting such earnest attention from a total stranger. Carol forced a slight smile and moved away, continuing down the quiet street.

A BMW approached from the opposite direction. It seemed too modern and out of place. There should have been horses and carriages, fashionable Georgian or Victorian people strolling up and down. Maybe an occasional child rolling a hoop with a stick, an excited puppy at his heels.

The sun had sunk below the horizon and shadows were lengthening. Carol's peaceful reverie had made her lose track of the time. She turned and retraced her steps back down Maupasson Street, pausing outside number seventy-three one more time and shivering as a sudden chill passed through her. Carol hugged herself and quickened her pace. Soon she reached Blenheim Road where Waverley Court was situated.

Back home again, she made coffee and toast. Unusually for her she had eaten her main meal at lunchtime so a snack was all she fancied. Kicking her shoes off, Carol remembered the need to keep the impractically colored carpet pristine, and placed them in the hall cupboard, swapping them for slippers.

She sauntered into her bedroom and changed into a pair of comfortable tracksuit bottoms and a sloppy T-shirt. Back in the living room, she grabbed the TV remote and switched on, putting her feet up on a leather-upholstered footstool.

Her phone rang. She rummaged in her bag and found it. Private number. She hesitated and answered it.

"Hello?"

At first, silence greeted her, followed by a little crackling static. Then a voice. A raspy, female voice, sounding as if it was coming from far away.

"You're next…."

The phone went dead. Carol was left staring at it in disbelief. She threw it across the settee as if it had burned her.

No, she must have misheard. It was a wrong number. Someone had activated their phone while it lay in their pocket. The old models were like that. You could so easily set them off dialing the last number they had called. But nobody had an old phone like that anymore, did they? Even if they did, who called her anyway? Hardly anyone had her number.

Carol tried to concentrate on the television. Anything to take her mind off what had just happened. The program didn't help. Some inane comedy that didn't hit any funny bone of hers. She realized she had neglected to draw the curtains and immediately rectified that. The last thing she needed was to see that awful child's face again.

She checked the front door. Locked, bolted and the chain on. No one would be getting in there in a hurry, and if the intercom buzzed? It could carry on buzzing. She wasn't answering her door tonight, or any other time for that matter. She had made up her mind, hadn't she?

After washing up her coffee mug and plate, she tidied them away and returned to the living room.

The comedy had finished and a film had begun. An old black and white horror. *Night of the Demon.* Carol recognized it from many years earlier. She settled herself down to watch, as the room gradually grew darker.

She realized what was happening when the advertisement break came on and she glanced up at the ceiling to see a bulb pop. Looking around, she saw it was only the latest. Three more had blown. No wonder it had grown so dark in there. What were the odds of that happening all at once? Unless there was something wrong with the wiring. Nothing for it. She would have to change the bulbs.

Carol located a box containing half a dozen of them and stood on the stepladder. Replacing them didn't take long and, thankfully, the new bulbs worked, but she would have to replenish the dwindling supplies tomorrow.

Back to the film. The demon pounded through the wood, emerging from a cloud of supernatural smoke. A pretty wobbly monster to be sure, but it worked better than if it had benefited from today's CGI tinkering. Old-school horror. When she had first seen this film it had sent her scurrying under her duvet, and she still found it unnerving. Maybe that was because it was in black and white. The grainy monochrome made it altogether more sinister than color. Hitchcock had known this. That was one reason *Psycho* and some of his other films were not in color.

The film ended. Bedtime and Carol's head barely touched the pillow before she fell asleep.

* * *

Once again, she came to in someone else's body, seeing what they saw, with no sense of being able to escape. She felt trapped there. Imprisoned in time and space. Her body ached from the blows the man had inflicted on her and it seemed only hours had passed since that awful beating, but in amongst the pain and fear, another emotion was growing. It built up strength with every breath she inhaled; anger, a determination to avenge herself for the treatment he had meted out to her. The same raging anger she had experienced when those images of herself murdering Jonah had come into her mind.

She lay on the floor of that Victorian parlor – or maybe a drawing room? Yes, it was too big to call a parlor. All those ornaments crammed onto the mantelpiece. The woman whose body she occupied hated them too. She wanted to smash the lot. None of them were hers anyway. They all belonged to *him*.

The door opened and the man she recognized from her previous encounter strode in. He stared at her in contempt. "Get up from there. You look ridiculous."

Carol didn't move or flinch. She concentrated on staring at him, knowing from his expression that he could read the naked hatred in her gaze.

"Defy me, would you?" He hauled her to her feet.

She shook him off and he grabbed hold of her hair, dragging her across the room. The pain screamed through her scalp. At any moment he would pull her hair out by the roots. She spied a vicious and substantial-looking letter opener, shaped like a mini sword, lying on a nearby desk. If she could just twist out of his hold, maybe she could reach it. She squirmed but that merely served to anger him further. He threw her across the room, where she hit her hip hard on the piano, setting the instrument off in a cacophony of jarring bass and treble. More pain shot through her, fueling her anger.

Her rage boiled over. He would pay for this even if she had to kill him. Never in her life had she ever felt such white-hot fury. The man momentarily had his back toward her while he calmly reached for cigarettes and a lighter. It gave her time enough. She lurched forward, grabbed the letter opener and plunged it deep into the back of his neck.

He let out a yell and fell to his knees, scattering the cigarettes across the floor. He twisted round to look at her and she stabbed him through the eye. Blood poured through the ruined eye socket. He raised his hands but she stabbed them too. Spurred on by some irresistible force within, she took out his other eye.

He rolled around on the floor, yelling and screaming in agony. Blood spattered the carpet, furniture, her dress. She watched it, conscious that the other presence in her body was seeing what she saw, with no passion or emotion, only sheer, naked hatred. Hatred so overwhelming, it chilled her bones. Her body was out of her control now. Time and again she slammed the letter opener into the man's face and neck. No will of hers could stop it. The man screamed and howled out his agony, weakening as his lifeblood sprayed out. *Just like Jonah....* In her mind, the entity whose body she shared laughed and stabbed harder.

The door flew open and a man she assumed to be the butler dashed in. He dragged her arms behind her and hauled her off.

"Let go of me!" she yelled.

He tightened his grip. "Madam. Madam. No."

A younger male and a female servant appeared at the door. The girl blanched and screamed. She clapped her hand to her mouth. The young man cried out, "I'm going for the coppers."

The butler wrestled with Carol, whose strength showed no sign of abating. The woman she inhabited still exerted sufficient control over her own mind and body. She wouldn't stop until that bastard husband of hers was dead. Right now, he had stopped moving.

Her inner voice spoke to the host's mind. *That's enough. You've done what you set out to do. He's gone. He can never hurt you again.*

Gradually her struggles eased. She dropped the letter opener and finally the butler let go. The raging fire died within her and she shook herself and straightened her dress. She smoothed her hair, which the man on the floor had done his best to rip out by the roots. The pain throbbed in her head and at her hip. It seemed barely an inch of her existed that didn't hurt. Self-defense. Surely no police officer would seek to charge her with...murder. Especially not when they saw the extent and nature of her own injuries. If she hadn't done what she did, that man would have killed her. If not today then one day soon. Her host knew it and she knew it.

The butler steered her over to a chair and she sat down. He looked at her, sadly, with fear in his eyes. "Oh, madam, what have you done?"

"What have *I* done?" For the first time. Carol became aware of her – the woman's – voice. It sounded strange, its tone deeper than her own. No trace of an accent, whereas her own voice held echoes of many of the places she had lived over the years. "I defended myself. You must know what I have had to put up with all these years."

"But, madam, look at him."

Carol looked through the woman's eyes and felt her satisfaction. "I am only sorry he went so quickly, unlike me, who has had to suffer for ten years at his brutal hands."

The sound of men talking loudly came from the hall. A few seconds later, a policeman in a Victorian uniform, accompanied by a man in street clothes, sporting a bowler hat, burst in. The uniformed officer took up position by the door as the plainclothes officer knelt by the body and felt for a pulse. He replaced the hand by the dead man's side and stood up.

He addressed her. "I am Detective Inspector Antrobus. The police surgeon has been summoned but it doesn't take a genius to know this man's dead, or to see that he has been brutally murdered. I understand you are the perpetrator of this terrible crime?" His cold blue eyes scanned Carol's face. Maybe he was looking for remorse, or maybe he couldn't believe she could have committed such an act. After all, this woman, whoever she was, was a lady.

"Yes. I did it," she said. "And I would do it again. He has used me most cruelly all the years of our marriage and today he almost killed me. I had to defend myself."

The inspector looked from her down at the body. He knelt down again and peered closer at what he could see of the man's ruined face. The he spotted the letter opener lying on the floor nearby, hopelessly bent out of shape after its hard work. The Detective Inspector folded it carefully in a cloth he removed from his pocket, stood up and handed it to the uniformed officer.

"I am familiar with the deceased, your husband, I believe?"

Carol nodded.

Antrobus got out his notebook and flipped it open. "Lydia Warren Carmody, I am arresting you on suspicion of the murder of Roger Carmody...."

"No! It was self-defense. I demand a lawyer. I demand a physical examination. The injuries he has inflicted upon me, not merely today, but over all these years. The damage he has done is all over my body. This wasn't murder. This was justice."

The inspector ignored her protests and droned on, clearly determined to complete the arrest speech. He nodded to the officer at the door. "Take her away."

"No! This isn't happening. This *cannot* be happening...."

★ ★ ★

Carol shot up in bed, drenched in sweat and trembling. She threw the duvet off her and the chill in the room hit her, drying her clammy skin instantly. She reached for her dressing gown and tied it around herself as her stomach lurched. She raced to the en suite and made it just in time, releasing a torrent of vomit into the toilet bowl. She flushed it and, still retching, leaned her head against the cool tiles of the wall.

It had seemed so real. She could even smell the dead man's blood, the body odor of men for whom antiperspirant had not yet been invented, the beeswax that had been used to polish the heavy, dark furniture. The warmth of the fire and the chill when she moved away from it – all had been as real to her then as this bathroom was to her now.

But they couldn't both be real, could they? *This* was her world. The world of the twenty-first century with its computers, cell phones and social media. Hell, none of those words would have meant anything to the people she had just encountered.

Lydia Warren Carmody. At least she now knew who the poet was. But, she reminded herself, surely she had merely invented someone to fill the void in her knowledge.

Nature abhors a vacuum.

An old science teacher had said that. If a vacuum occurs, natural forces will use any means available to fill it. Maybe that's how her mind had worked. She couldn't find any information on the mysterious poet of dubious quality so she had simply invented someone and turned it into a nightmare.

Her watch read shortly after three a.m. Work beckoned in a few hours and Saturdays were always extra busy. She must put this experience behind her. An unwelcome dream, that's all it had been, fabricated by her increasingly wild imagination. She must get back to sleep.

Carol forced herself to walk to the kitchen, her stomach still uncertain whether it was going to heave again. She poured herself a glass of water and took it back to bed, glad of the warm duvet, fearful of what she would see when she closed her eyes.

* * *

"You look so tired, Carol. Haven't you been sleeping again?" Sarah asked.

It was the lull before the onslaught of weekend shoppers. The store was filling up but no one looked ready to leave yet. Plenty more items to pile into their trolleys before they came her way.

"I can get to sleep all right, most nights. But I wake up at silly times and then can't drift off again."

"Oh, I hate it when that happens. I always get up and make myself a marmalade sandwich. My mum used to swear by them and she was a martyr to insomnia."

"Marmalade sandwich? But what about the sugar?"

Sarah shrugged. "I know. It shouldn't work but somehow it does. Some sort of comfort eating, I suppose."

"I'll try it. I need to do *something*."

"Let me know how you get on."

Carol nodded. A customer began loading items onto her conveyor and Carol picked up a packet of washing powder to scan.

Sarah seemed about to move off. She hesitated. "Fancy a quick drink after work?"

Carol was about to issue her well-rehearsed and often-used excuse, but found herself saying something different instead. "That would be nice. Thank you."

"That's sorted then. You finish at seven tonight, don't you? Same as me. I'll see you outside."

Carol smiled and carried on scanning. Part of her was even looking forward to it. Socializing. She never did that. Then the butterflies and doubts kicked in. What on earth would they find to talk about? She knew nothing about Sarah, but surely they couldn't have much in common. For one thing, the woman was married, with a couple of kids. So why wasn't she with them on a Saturday night?

* * *

"We split up," Sarah said, as she sipped her pint of Carling. "And the kids left home anyway. They couldn't stand all the arguments. Amy was eighteen and Carlene seventeen so they got a flat together. Bit of a traumatic time all round."

"It must have been awful." Carol tried to crush the flashback memories of her own lousy childhood. She concentrated all her effort on listening to the older woman opposite. How old was Sarah anyway? She had thought her to be in her forties but with daughters of that age she could be older.

"It was no picnic but I'm over it now."

She might say that, maybe even convince herself it was true at least part of the time, but Carol knew, deep down, Sarah still hurt. Bet she even cried herself to sleep some nights. Hence the marmalade sandwiches.

The conversation died. Carol knew she should speak. That was the way of things. One person spoke, the other listened, then *they* spoke. Those were the rules of social intercourse. Rules that Carol had never felt comfortable with. She searched her brain and took a long swig of lager to cover the awkward silence. Her fingertips tingled as they always did when she felt ill at ease.

Sarah pointed her empty glass at Carol. "Another drink?"

Relief. "It's my round. I'll get them." Carol nearly leaped out of her seat in her hurry to buy herself a few minutes of thinking time. As she waited at the bar, she struggled to think of what to say next. The weather? No, not that old cliché. Obviously talking about Sarah's children was taboo as was, in fact, anything about her home life.... But she could ask her about any interests she had. Even if Sarah only enjoyed shopping, she could at least tell her about her latest purchases although, in reality, Carol couldn't give a damn. But what if Sarah then felt obliged to ask her about hers. What interests did she have? Reading, occasional trips to the cinema – alone of course – but she could talk about some films she had seen. Oh God.... No wonder she preferred to stay at home. It was far simpler. Except, right now, home wasn't the place it should be. Waverley Court, at least for now, had ceased to be her temporary haven.

Carol had to admit, as the barmaid handed over the brimming glasses of cold beer, that maybe she had made a terrible mistake in taking the place on, but she was financially committed to the full six months. If she left, she would still have to pay the balance of the rent and she couldn't afford to do that and find somewhere else to live.

Sarah thanked her as she placed the glass of Carling in front of her. "I like this place, don't you? Haven't been here for ages though."

Carol looked around at the pleasant, modern décor, clean lines and large photographs of the town in Victorian times that adorned each wall. "I haven't been here before, but I like it. It has a comfortable feel about it."

"So what do you do when you're not serving customers?"

The question she had dreaded had been placed out there. It couldn't be taken back and she would have to address it. Time for another minute-buying swig. She drank. Sarah waited, politely. Carol knew she had to speak or she would risk coming over as rude and unfriendly. *Here goes....*

"Not a great deal, to be honest. I've been busy moving in and getting to know my surroundings." That wasn't too bad. It made perfect sense, and she hadn't been there very long, after all. *Ask me again in four months and I'll still have the same answer.* She would have to handle that if and when it occurred.

"So you don't know anyone round here yet?"

Carol shook her head. "Only you and the others at work."

"May I ask what brought you here? I don't really know anything about your background or where you used to live."

Another question Carol always attempted to avoid. But, here again, she would have to say something in response. "I've lived all over the place. I was fostered as a child." Damn, she hadn't meant to say that. Now there would be more probing questions and she would have to make light of all those miserable years. Maybe if she kept talking, moved the subject on to more recent things....

"When I left school, I decided I wanted to go traveling...." That always sounded better than, *I had to get away from the city I was living in or an evil bastard who raped me was going to come for me. I've been running ever since....*

Sarah's interest grew. She leaned forward. "Where did you go? Abroad?"

"Sadly no. I couldn't afford it, but I lived in a few different places over the next few years. I had a variety of jobs so I learned a lot."

"What did you do?"

"Waitressing, working in various shops and supermarkets. I even sold expensive perfume for a time. That was down in London, in one of the big stores."

"Harrods?"

"Oh no, nothing as grand as that but it *was* in Oxford Street. The store's not there anymore. That's why I left. The wealthy Arab owners pulled out and the place went belly up."

"That's happening a lot. I worry about us sometimes. Profits were down last quarter and there have been some rumors about redundancies. Maybe even store closures."

"But they took me on."

"Yes, but only to cover Jordan's maternity leave. You do know that if she decides to come back full time and there are no other positions, that's it."

Carol nodded. HR had made that abundantly clear. "But they must have realized they couldn't do without someone in her role, so that has to mean they aren't looking to lay anyone off in our branch. At least not yet."

"I hope you're right."

Carol felt her muscles relax. Here she was having an intelligent, social conversation. When was the last time she had done that? Even stranger, she was enjoying chatting to this affable woman who had shown her consideration from her first day on the job.

"Maybe we could do this again sometime, and bring some of the other girls along." Sarah's second suggestion sent Carol's heart plummeting. Having this one-on-one chat was proving much easier than she had anticipated, but adding more people into the mix? She couldn't keep the doubt out of her voice.

"Yes. Maybe," she said.

Sarah looked quizzical. "You're really shy, aren't you? Oh, I'm sorry. I shouldn't have blurted it out like that."

"No, it's okay. You're right. I *am* shy. It's a curse."

"You know, I think deep down most of us are. It's just that we're not as honest as you in admitting it. We cover it up with a show. Bravado or whatever. You've not had it easy, have you? I can tell. It's bound to make you wary."

All that carefully rehearsed reserve, perfected, she thought, over many years, and all for nothing, because Sarah could see straight through to the frightened little girl underneath. Tears pricked Carol's eyes.

Sarah covered her hands with hers. "I'm so sorry to have upset you, Carol. I didn't mean to. Me and my big mouth. I should learn to leave it at home." She smiled.

Carol forced herself to speak, keeping the trembling out of her voice as much as she could. "It's not your fault, Sarah. It's me, I'm afraid." The punctuation. She heard it in what she had said. She could as easily have spoken the words differently and said, *It's me. I'm afraid.* It would have been equally true – if not more so.

They had one more drink, spoke about nothing much, each of them skirting around Carol's earlier distress. She couldn't relax anymore. She felt vulnerable now that Sarah had glimpsed her insecurities. By the time Carol returned home, she couldn't even remember whether they had been discussing the weather or the price of cheese, although she suspected neither.

The apartment felt almost eerily quiet, as if waiting for something or someone. Carol pushed the unwelcome thought aside and changed into her tracksuit bottoms and T-shirt. Saturday night television was hardly enthralling but it provided a voice in the room, one whose origins she didn't have to wonder at. She offered up a silent prayer that nothing unusual would happen that night and settled down to the latest talent show. One hopeful singer after another took to the stage to be selected or rejected seemingly at random. Certainly half the ones the judges picked wouldn't have made it on her vote, whereas artists such as a young girl from South Wales with a voice to easily outmatch Katherine Jenkins was completely overlooked. The poor kid was only eighteen and left the stage bravely attempting to control a quivering lip, and weeping tears that threatened to ruin her mascara and dislodge her false eyelashes.

Carol had become quite absorbed when she heard the crash.

It came from the kitchen.

She jumped up and raced out there. She saw it straightaway.

"What the…."

Through the glass frontage, the exquisite designer tableware had been reduced to a cabinet full of smashed china. Without thinking through the consequences, Carol opened the cupboard and it showered down onto her, the worktops and floor, smashing it still further.

The cupboard was bare except for a few remaining shards, as if opening it had triggered someone into pushing it all out from the inside. How it had even got smashed in the first place remained a complete mystery. A quick check revealed the contents of the other kitchen units were intact.

Moving like an automaton, Carol went to the hall cupboard and took out the long-handled broom and pan. She started to sweep and empty the ruined china into a heavy-duty refuse bag, her heart beating wildly. A cut on her hand bled, staining the white porcelain shards. It must have happened a moment ago, although she hadn't been aware of it. She grabbed a piece of kitchen paper and wrapped it around her palm.

When she had finished clearing up, she secured the bag, tying it tightly with its own handles before placing it next to the front door. She would dispose of it tomorrow. That was the easy part. Explaining the loss to the owners – and being able to afford to replace it – was another thing entirely. Carol pushed the unwelcome thought to the back of her mind. She simply couldn't deal with it now.

Back in the kitchen, she examined the cupboard. It seemed firm, certainly not hanging off its hinges or tilting enough to send an entire dinner service flying, but even if it had been, that wouldn't have explained how the plates, bowls, cups and saucers were smashed *inside* it before she opened the door.

There had to be an explanation but, for the life of her, Carol had no idea what it could be.

An unpleasant smell tickled her nostrils. A mix of some kind of bleach, with ammonia, unwashed bodies and old cabbage. Carol wrinkled her nose.

She opened the sink cupboard and peered inside. The smell was nothing like so bad there. Similarly, the bathroom and en suite checked out fine, with nothing to indicate the origin of the increasingly nauseating stench.

It seemed to be strongest out in the hall.

Carol unlocked the front door and peered out. No one in the communal hallway and no smell either. Whatever it was had begun in her hall and was now rapidly infecting the entire flat.

In her bedroom, she opened the wardrobes, drawers, looked under the bed, searching everywhere. She repeated this in the second bedroom and the living room. Nowhere gave up any clues.

Back in the hall, she forced herself to move to where the stench was most prominent. Right in the middle. Kneeling down, she pressed her nose to the carpet but, by now, the smell had engulfed her and didn't emanate from the floor.

Then it vanished. As fast as it had arrived. Carol heard a rustling sound, like someone walking in a long skirt. A swishing noise, a whisper.

"You're next."

That voice again. Carol sprang to her feet and cried out. "Who are you? What do you want from me?"

A laugh. A distinct, slightly hysterical woman's laugh, coming from far away. Her neighbor perhaps? How she would love to be able to believe that, but she knew wherever it was coming from, it wasn't from this world.

Shadowy, indistinct figures scurried past her on both sides, almost touching her.

Then she felt herself falling into blackness.

* * *

Carol came to on the floor of her hall. Her head throbbed. How long had she been here? A quick look at her watch confirmed it could only have been a minute or so. She struggled to her feet, aware that she must have bumped her knee as she fainted. Her head buzzed as if a swarm of bees had taken up residence.

In the kitchen, she filled her tumbler with water and drank it down as the pain in her head subsided.

She moved into the bedroom and sank onto the bed. The next thing she knew, the morning sun streamed through the window. Panic set in. Carol glanced at her watch. Nine-thirty. Sunday. She didn't have to be at work for another hour. Time to get a shower, coffee, slice of toast and be there in plenty of time.

In the end, she couldn't face the toast and settled for the coffee on its own. Carol felt clean and fresh after her shower, ready to face the day and determined to put the events of the previous night behind her. At least, that was what she told herself.

* * *

"I really enjoyed our chat yesterday evening, Carol," Sarah said as Carol took up her place on checkout number ten.

"Thanks," she replied. "So did I." It *had* been pleasant, hadn't it? For the most part, even if she didn't feel up to repeating the experience yet, especially if others were to be included in the invitation. There was too much going on she didn't understand.

She served her first customer, wishing her stomach hadn't decided to pick then to hit her with a sudden stabbing pain. The same as the ones she had had before. She winced.

"Are you all right?" The customer leaned toward her. "You've gone awfully pale. Shall I call someone?"

"No, no, I'll be fine in a moment, thanks."

The pain shot through her. Much worse this time. She doubled over.

The customer called out. "Someone's in trouble here."

Sarah was there in an instant, putting an arm around her shoulders. "I'm so sorry, would you all please join another queue?"

The customers moved off, muttering to themselves.

Carol hated being the center of so much unwarranted attention but the pain overwhelmed every other consideration. Wave after wave of it. Hot, burning, throbbing. Without warning, bile shot up into her throat, filled her mouth and she vomited. The sour taste made her retch even harder.

"Ambulance please," Sarah called to someone as she helped Carol out of her seat. She could barely focus; everything seemed unreal. Part of her felt as if she had drifted into a different universe, able to see this one but incapable of making any contribution to it other than trying to put one foot in front of another as Sarah half carried her across the shop floor and into the staff area out back.

Someone – Sarah maybe? – brought her a bowl and a box of tissues. Another voice, one she didn't immediately recognize, spoke quietly. "Is she going to be all right? She's gone such an odd color."

Sarah replied, "I don't know. The ambulance should be here soon. It's not as if they have far to come."

"Depends if they're tied up."

"Let's hope not."

Carol sat, hunched over the bowl. It smelled of new plastic. They must have taken it off the shelf.

The nausea had passed as quickly as it had begun, but the pain in her abdomen was still there, reduced to a gnawing throb.

A commotion. Doors opening. A man's voice. "Carol, can you hear me? Can you speak to me?"

"I can hear you." She wished they wouldn't shout. It hurt her head.

A woman spoke now, equally as strident. "Carol, I want you to sit back for me, open your eyes. Yes, that's it. Open your eyes for me."

A bright light nearly blinded her. It flashed briefly into her left eye and then her right. When she could focus properly, two paramedics swam into view. Sarah stood in the background, her face full of concern, gnawing her lip.

The woman spoke as the man took her pulse. "You've been sick and we need to take you to hospital to find out what's going on. Are you in any pain?"

"My stomach."

The paramedic touched the right side of her abdomen and Carol couldn't stifle a cry. A burning sensation swept across her belly.

"Have you ever had your appendix removed, Carol?"

She shook her head and immediately wished she hadn't as nausea swept up through her gut with renewed force. She swallowed rapidly, repeatedly, forcing the sourness back down. "No. I've never had any operations."

I was in a room. There were surgical instruments all around me. They forced me to sit in a chair and tied my wrists and ankles with leather bonds. The doctor held some sort of drill. He came toward me….

"Carol? Are you okay?" The voice of the male paramedic brought her sharply back to the present. She nodded.

To his colleague he spoke quietly, probably hoping Carol couldn't hear him. "Her pulse is racing and her temperature's 100.3."

Carol shivered.

"Are you feeling cold?" the female paramedic asked.

"A bit. Yes."

"Right, we're taking you to hospital now."

"What's wrong with her?" Sarah asked.

The female paramedic answered. "Judging by the symptoms she's presenting, possible appendicitis and it may be at quite an advanced stage. She should be fine, but we do need to get her admitted now before it gets any worse."

The male paramedic had left them and his colleague turned back to Carol. "Is there anyone you'd like us to call? A friend or relative perhaps?"

"No. There's no one."

The paramedic returned with a wheelchair. "Can you get into this chair for me, Carol?" he said.

One on either side of her, they eased her into the chair. The burning sensation increased and, with it, another wave of nausea. She retched. Sarah thrust the bowl onto her lap but it was only dry heaves. Carol realized she hadn't eaten in over twenty-four hours.

A small audience of shoppers and staff saw her leave. Carol closed her eyes, willing the pain to go away. At least the hospital wasn't far. Sirens. They *must* think she was urgent.

Before she could be admitted, she had to go through the rigmarole of a barrage of questions: name, address, date of birth, details of which doctor she was registered with, next of kin.... "I don't have one. I have no known relatives."

"A friend then. Someone we can contact."

"There isn't anyone."

The questions finally ended. The paramedics officially handed her over and left, wishing her all the best. Carol thanked them and then she was being wheeled down for a scan.

From there, she was taken to a ward. She changed into the obligatory hospital apparel, and a nurse joined her, armed with a pair of unflattering blue-green pressure socks.

"You're going to need to wear these for a few days. It's just while you're off your feet. You're having surgery, aren't you?"

Carol's eyes shot open. "Am I?"

The nurse looked embarrassed and stopped in the action of removing the pressure socks from their packet. "Ah, right. I'm sorry, I thought they'd discussed this with you. You're scheduled for an emergency appendectomy. Haven't you signed the paperwork yet?"

"I signed something but there was no mention of an operation. If it will make this pain go away, I'll have it."

"I'm really sorry. It's been a bit manic here today. There was a road crash. Multiple casualties…I'll go and get things sorted out for you right away."

The flustered young nurse left her.

Appendectomy. Surely that wasn't such a bad operation? They could do it with keyhole surgery these days, after all. She'd soon be up and about again. And, at least she would be free of this awful pain. Maybe that was behind the strange things she had been experiencing? What if they were hallucinations brought on by whatever it was that caused appendicitis? The inflammation had sent the wrong signals to her brain.

The comforting thought soothed her as she shivered and sweated. More paperwork. Her signature was required. She managed a shaky effort that didn't look much like anyone's signature, least of all her own.

Kind faces smiled down at her, reassuring nods, a nurse holding her hand, then a slight prick as a cannula was inserted in the back of her left hand. The hum of gentle conversation. Carol closed her eyes.

The soft voice of the anesthetist, muffled slightly by his mask. "You'll start to feel sleepy any second now."

And she did, a feeling of calm and total relaxation enveloping her.

"Pleasant dreams."

* * *

She woke up and knew instantly something was wrong. Very wrong. This couldn't be the same hospital. The smells didn't belong there and when she managed to open her eyes she gasped at the sight of the dingy room, peeling whitewash and an old, waxy-looking linoleum floor. The anesthetic fog in her brain gradually cleared. The smell of ammonia grew ever more pungent. She'd smelled it before. In her apartment when it shouldn't have been there. Now it shouldn't be here. Not in the Royal and Waverley Hospital in the twenty-first century. She tried to sit up, but felt the drag on the stitches she must have been given when they removed her appendix. No keyhole surgery for her, it seemed.

She looked around for a bell she could press to summon a nurse and find out what the hell was going on. She couldn't find one and, given the state of the room and the iron bedstead, there couldn't have been one. Not here. Carol had precious little experience of being in hospital – this was her first time as an inpatient – but she was certain that, however cash-strapped the NHS might be these days, they couldn't possibly have this sort of bed anymore. Today's hospital beds were state of the art, technology-driven affairs, with levers and switches and gadgets. Above her head should have been a fluorescent light of some kind and behind her, a wall of plug sockets, oxygen, and surely, as she had just come out of surgery, there should be staff around. Nurses at least, making sure she came out of it safely.

"Nurse!" she yelled and listened hard for any sound. Plenty to hear but all of it outside the room. Around her she counted eleven empty beds, all made up with pristine white cotton sheets and a blanket identical to her own. "Nurse!" she called again.

The door opened. A woman dressed from head to toe in white and sporting an elaborate cap marched in, a grim expression on her face. "Less of the noise, please, you'll disturb the other patients."

Carol spread her hands expansively to cover the room. "What other patients?"

The nurse ignored her comment. "What's the problem?"

"The problem? I have just had surgery. My appendix has been removed."

"Appendix? Impossible. Such an operation would have killed you."

Carol felt her hackles rise. "Clearly it didn't, or I wouldn't be talking to you now. What's going on here anyway? Why are you dressed like that and what is this place?"

"I don't know what you're talking about. This is the Royal Hospital."

"Oh really? Not the Royal and Waverley then?"

"There's no such place. Waverley Workhouse is next door. Now, Miss Warren—"

"Who?"

"Miss Warren. That's your name."

"No, it isn't. My name's Carol Shaughnessy. You have the wrong person."

"I can assure you we do not. You are Lydia Warren and you have been admitted with severe stomach pains. It appears you have been lacing your corset too tightly and it has caused some internal disruption. Your operation has corrected that and you will be sent home in a few days to rest and recover, but you must learn from this, Miss Warren. Wear your corset a little looser and you should not be troubled again."

Carol listened in disbelief to this tigress of a nurse lecturing her on a garment she had never worn in her life, nor would ever dream of doing so.

"I want to see a doctor," Carol said.

"All in good time. Dr. Franklyn will see you tomorrow. Meanwhile he has left strict instructions that you should rest and sleep. I shall bring you a jug of water but no food today. Tomorrow, a little steamed fish."

Weariness had overtaken her, so she was too tired to protest further. Maybe after some sleep she would wake up and find everything back to normal. Perhaps this was another hallucination.

She lay back against the cool pillows and the nurse left her alone.

Lydia Warren. Where had she heard that name before? Just as she fell asleep she remembered. The poem.

* * *

"Carol…Carol…." The female voice drifted into her sleep.

She opened her eyes.

"You've come to join us then?"

Thank God, a smiling face, a young woman wearing blue scrubs, who called her by her real name.

"You don't know how glad I am to see you. I had such a disturbing dream."

"Anesthetic can do that. Anyway, you're awake now. I'll go and get the registrar."

She left Carol. All around, the bustle and chatter of patients and medical staff. She was in the recovery area, hooked up to a drip. A blood pressure machine stood next to her. Her bed had bars to stop her falling out and, draped over her shoulder, the welcome sight of a buzzer to summon help.

That dream had been so real. She shuddered at the memory and recalled the acrid stench of ammonia. Surely you weren't supposed to be able to smell anything in a dream?

A woman she did not recognize approached her bed. "Hello there, I'm Dr. Sharma. I'm a registrar here. You're looking well. How are you feeling after your operation?"

"Better than before it, I think. A bit sore though."

"You will be for a few days. We had to go in and fetch your appendix out so you have a few stitches. It was certainly ready to go. Another twenty-four or forty-eight hours and it could have been quite serious, but the operation went well and we're confident we caught all possible signs of infection."

She left shortly afterward and the nurse returned. "We'll get you up to the ward as soon as we can get a porter."

Twenty minutes later, she was on her way. In the ward, the porter wheeled her into a space near the door and a nurse helped raise her into a sitting position, adjusting the angle of the bed and fluffing up a number of pillows which she positioned to give her back, neck and head support. Carol's mouth felt dry as desert sand. "Could I have some water please?"

"Yes, of course." The nurse poured some from a jug on the bedside cabinet into a beaker and handed it to Carol. "Sip it gently now or you might find it coming back again."

"I'll be careful."

The nurse stayed with her while she had a few sips before gently removing the beaker from her hand. "I'll leave it here for now. Let what you've had settle and see how you feel then."

Carol shifted in bed and felt the pull on her stitches. "Ouch."

"Don't try and get up yet. Wait until tomorrow, okay?"

She was not about to try that again. "Okay."

The nurse left to attend to another patient, leaving Carol to take in her surroundings. Brilliant early spring sunshine poured through the windows of the bright and airy ward until a nurse adjusted the blinds. Carol wished she hadn't but maybe it was getting in some of the patients' eyes.

A woman sitting in a chair opposite nodded and smiled at her. Carol smiled back, then lowered her eyes. She wasn't in the mood for conversation. That strange dream kept coming back into her mind and, try as she might, she couldn't shake it off.

⋆ ⋆ ⋆

The next morning, two nurses helped her out of bed and she took tentative steps to the bathroom. The stitches pulled a bit, but the relief of not having that awful pain scything through her insides more than compensated for the discomfort.

Breakfast arrived but she didn't have much appetite for porridge and even the orange juice took some getting down. A sudden wave of nausea passed through her and she reached for the papier maché kidney dish someone had helpfully left on the bedside cabinet. She rang for the nurse and one arrived almost immediately.

"It's only to be expected following the kind of surgery you've had," the young nurse said. "You probably won't feel much like eating all day but tomorrow will be better."

A couple of hours later, a volunteer came round with a trolley of newspapers and magazines. Feeling a little less nauseous, Carol chose a tabloid paper and sat in her chair, reading it. She became aware of someone approaching and looked up. The woman from the bed opposite smiled down at her.

"Mind if I join you?"

Carol wanted to tell her she did mind actually but it would have sounded so rude. The woman only wanted to be friendly and she was wearing a scarf that concealed her scalp completely. She wheeled a piece of apparatus from which a bottle dripped clear liquid into a tube, extending down to a cannula in the back of her left hand.

Carol shook her head, pasted a smile on her face. And the woman maneuvered a chair from the next bed. She sat and clasped her hands in her lap.

"So, what are you in for?" she asked.

"They took my appendix out yesterday."

The woman nodded. "I'm in the middle of chemo. Brain tumor. I couldn't keep anything down so I've become severely dehydrated. They're keeping me in for a couple of days."

"Oh, I'm sorry...." What did you say to a stranger with cancer?

"Oh, don't be. I shall be fine. One way or the other."

An awkward pause ensued. Carol wondered if she had committed some terrible social gaffe, but the woman seemed not to be offended.

"I find people either try and wrap me up in cotton wool or pretend I'm invisible. It's the Big C. Unless you've had it, it's the last great taboo. If you talk about it, it's like a death wish. Now I've got it, I find myself making terrible jokes about it with other people in the same situation. Here's me. Terminal and still possessing a sense of humor."

"That must be.... I mean, it probably helps you deal with things."

"You're right. It does. I'm Hester, by the way."

"Carol."

"I know."

How did she know?

"It's on the white board behind your head. You're Carol Shaughnessy."

"Yes." Carol felt tempted to add, *Most of the time*, but decided against it. Those strange experiences had been dreams or hallucinations caused by her diseased appendix. Now they had taken that out, she could go back to being herself again. If only she truly knew who that was.

The woman's face clouded over and for one instant, Carol wondered if she had read her thoughts, but Hester spoke again and her voice sounded pleasant and friendly. "Have you ever been in this hospital before?"

Carol shook her head. "I haven't been in any hospital before. Not that I know of anyway."

Hester leaned forward. "Then you won't know about it."

"You mean its history? I know it used to be the workhouse and asylum."

"Yes, and the rest was the old Royal Hospital. It's supposed to be haunted, by the spirits of some of the thousands of patients who passed through it over more than a century. There is even talk of a demon, a wandering spirit – I have heard it called the One and the Many – who takes over women's bodies and can cause them to travel across time."

"The One and the Many?"

"I know. It does sound a bit odd but it would seem that no one really knows its name, if it even possesses one. The One and the Many reflects its ability to move from one body and soul to another. Legend has it this female entity was cursed to wander the earth for eternity and must find a new host every human lifetime. She's a demon of wrath too. So anytime any of her hosts has thoughts of revenge or anger, her presence in their minds will heighten their rage. This, in turn feeds her. I think it's what they call a symbiotic relationship. Both parties benefit."

Carol wriggled, trying to get more comfortable. The conversation was taking a slightly odd turn and she hadn't a clue about symbiotic relationships anyway. "Has anyone seen anything? Ghostly I mean."

"Oh yes. Plenty. It's a very atmospheric place once you get past the newer parts. There are doors that lead down forgotten and neglected corridors. I'll take you to one if you like."

Carol shivered. "Oh, I don't think—"

"Come on, Carol. It will be fun. More fun than sitting around here all day. Besides they'll be at you to get on your feet and walk about. I'm certainly supposed to."

Hester was clearly not going to take 'no' for an answer. Somewhat reluctantly, Carol placed her half-read newspaper on the bed and stood carefully, supporting her abdomen with one hand and her back with the other as she straightened.

"Ready?"

Hester sounded impatient, almost as if she had an appointment to keep. Carol glossed over it in her mind and followed Hester out of the ward.

At the Nurses' station, Hester spoke to the Charge Nurse. "I'm taking Carol here for a walk. Get her circulation moving."

The male nurse smiled. "That's fine. Not too far though. Remember, the distance you walk is the distance you have to come back."

"We'll behave ourselves, don't worry."

The Charge Nurse nodded and Hester and Carol moved off, down the corridor and out of the double doors.

"Freedom at last." Hester inhaled deeply. "Come on. It's not far." She wheeled her drip and Carol struggled to keep up as she strode down the corridor. At the end she turned left and within moments they had stopped in front of a door. It seemed strangely out of place. Older than the others, dark wood, with a Bakelite handle.

"It's through here." Hester pushed open the door and a rush of cold, fusty air hit them.

Instinctively, Carol covered her nose with her hand.

Hester smiled. "You'll soon get used to that. Come on."

The door swung shut behind them, closing with a slight but audible click. A long corridor with a low roof stretched ahead. The light was provided by flickering wall lamps in glass bowls. To her amazement Carol realized they were gas mantles. *What the hell…?*

She followed Hester, staring at the walls as they moved steadily along. Old whitewash and paint had peeled in curls, some had dropped onto the floor, while the rest clung for dear life. It was impossible to make out any real color, but they could have been a pale buttermilk with a dark green, or maybe black, strip running lengthwise, halfway up the walls.

The floor was filthy, littered not merely with the old paint, but dust and debris, the origins of which were impossible to determine. No one had been down here in years.

"How can this place still be here?" Carol asked. Hester didn't answer.

Carol had been staring so hard at where they were going, she suddenly realized she hadn't seen Hester in a few minutes. Surely she was in front of her. She wasn't. "Hester? Hester, where are you?"

She scanned all around her. There were no doors the woman could have slipped through. A wave of panic swept through Carol. "Hester? Don't play games with me, please. It's not funny."

Her voice echoed off the walls.

A whooshing sound, moving toward her up the corridor. Getting louder by the second. It churned up dust and dirt, swirling it around until it hit Carol with the force of a mini tornado. She coughed and spluttered, her stitches pulling with the effort. The force flung her back against the filthy wall. And stopped.

"Hester?" Carol spluttered. "For God's sake. Where are you?"

Behind her, the wall moved. She had been standing in front of a closed door without realizing it. It opened and she half fell into the room.

"Miss Warren, come in. We've been waiting for you."

CHAPTER FOUR

A male doctor in a white coat held a scalpel. Next to him, a woman dressed in severe black, her expression a hideous parody of a smile as if someone was stretching her lips wide, against her will. Someone pushed Carol farther inside the room. She stood petrified for a second, then started to scream.

Strong arms grabbed her from behind, urging her forward. *Where did they come from?* Carol struggled, ignoring the pain from her protesting wound.

A familiar voice spoke. "You're next, Lydia. The other one simply wouldn't do. This is meant to be."

Carol twisted her head around and saw Hester. No longer in her patient's robe, she was dressed from head to foot in navy blue. This Hester had chestnut hair, parted in the center and tied behind her in a severe bun.

Carol stopped screaming and struggling. "I don't understand. What's happening here?"

The doctor nodded to the orderly who had pinioned her arms behind her. "Put her on the table and let's get to work."

Much to her relief she noticed the doctor no longer brandished the scalpel. Her relief was short-lived. He unhooked a primitive rubber face mask from a gas tank and brought it toward her. She tossed her head from side to side, trying in vain to escape contact with what she knew would be a gas to put her to sleep.

A sweet, sickly smell filled her nostrils. Blackness descended.

Shadows moved, vague snippets of half-heard conversation. The smells of disinfectant, ammonia, other odors she couldn't determine. Unwashed bodies. Armpits too close to her.

No pain though. Definitely no pain….

* * *

"Carol? Carol. Are you awake? Dr. Sharma's here to examine you."

Carol shook herself back to consciousness. She was in her bed at the Royal and Waverley. With no sign of the terrible corridor, or that awful room.

The nurse moved to one side and Carol shot a quick glance across the room. Hester, in her patient's robe and with the scarf once again wrapped around her head, sat opposite, calmly reading a book. She seemed to sense Carol looking at her and, briefly, their eyes met. Carol didn't like the twist of the other woman's lips. She knew. That had been no dream and Hester had been a fundamental part of it.

"Good gracious," the nurse said, picking up Carol's slippers to tidy them away. "These have got dirty. Did you go outside in them?" She held them up. They were covered in muck.

Carol shook her head. "I went for a walk with Hester. She took me through a door and down a really old, dilapidated corridor. The floor was filthy."

The nurse looked bemused. "Where was this? I can't think of anywhere like that in this hospital."

"Not far away. Out of the ward and down the corridor, to the left and the door's just there. It looks really old and…."

The nurse was looking at her as if she had grown two heads. "There's nowhere like that on this floor and I'm pretty sure there's nowhere like it anywhere in this place."

"There must be. We went there. Hester'll tell you."

"Who's Hester?" the nurse asked.

"The lady in that bed opposite." But she was no longer there. "She's probably gone to the bathroom. When she comes back I'll get her to confirm what I've just said. Her slippers must be in the same state as mine. And she was wheeling her drip too."

Dr. Sharma joined them. The nurse – Allie by her name tag – spoke again. She was frowning. "Carol, there's no one in that bed opposite. There's no one called Hester on the ward."

"Problem?" Dr. Sharma looked from Allie to Carol and back again.

"I'm not sure," Carol said. "Apparently I've had some sort of hallucination. I went for a walk with someone who doesn't exist to a place that isn't there and my slippers got filthy in the process."

Dr. Sharma blinked. "Allie? Do you know what's going on?"

The nurse seemed about to speak, but shook her head and lowered her eyes.

"Right," Dr. Sharma said and smiled broadly at Carol. "Let's not worry about that for the time being and have a look at you."

She examined Carol's wound. "Take it easy for a few days when you move around, some of these stitches look as if they've been strained a little. They're holding all right now, but we don't want any of them bursting. Okay, that's fine. If you could put a fresh dressing on please, Allie."

The nurse nodded. Dr. Sharma stood back and peeled off the latex gloves she had put on for the examination. She threw them into the bin.

"I'd like to keep you in for another few days, but then I think we can look at discharging you. Is there anyone else living with you?"

Carol shook her head. "I live on my own in a flat, but it's on the ground floor so I don't have to worry about stairs or anything like that."

"I'd like to keep an eye on you for a while longer until you're able to manage by yourself. Meanwhile, try and keep out of trouble." She touched Carol's hand and winked at her.

Carol forced a smile. Dr. Sharma moved on to her next patient and Allie accompanied her.

Carol stared hard at the empty bed opposite.

Who the hell are you, Hester, and why is it only I can see you?

CHAPTER FIVE

Allie noted down Carol's temperature and wrapped the blood pressure cuff around her left arm.

"There was a Hester Majors in for minor surgery about a month ago but she was discharged well before you arrived, and she wasn't in that bed."

"The woman I'm talking about had a scarf round her head and said she was in because her chemo had made her so sick she needed fluids."

"We've had no patients with those symptoms for a couple of months. Certainly not on this ward anyway."

"Then I don't understand this at all. I must have gone *somewhere.*" Carol suddenly remembered. "The Charge Nurse saw us. Hester spoke to him as we left the ward. He told us not to go too far because we would only have to walk the same distance back again."

"Did you get his name? Oh hang on. You said 'he'. The Charge Nurse today is Sheila Pilkington. The only male Charge Nurse on this ward is Dennis and he's on holiday in Tenerife."

"But I saw a male Charge Nurse."

"You're sure he was a Charge Nurse?"

"He was dressed in maroon scrubs. That's what Charge Nurses wear here, isn't it? I saw a color chart on the wall."

"Yes. Maroon for Charge Nurses."

Allie finished writing up Carol's chart at the same moment the cleaner advanced toward her with a spray bottle of antibacterial cleaner.

"Sorry I can't be more help, Carol," Allie said. She moved away.

"Bet I can though," the cleaner said quietly, smiling broadly and showing perfect teeth that gleamed white against her dark skin. She made sure Allie was out of earshot. "You've seen one of the ghosts that haunt this place and you're not the first to see that particular one. Seen her myself."

"Surely she can't be a ghost? I mean, she was as real as you and I. And then there was the Charge Nurse."

The woman polished Carol's bed table and checked no one else was within earshot. "I can't speak for him. Maybe he's real and maybe he isn't, but the woman you've seen.... Cancer patient? Attached to a drip? Scarf around her head?"

That pretty much summed her up. Carol nodded.

"I'll bet she took you through an old door into an even older corridor with flickering lights and peeling walls."

"How do you know that?"

"Because she took me too, only I caught on right away that there was something unnatural about it, turned tail and ran out of there. Never saw the woman again, even though I had been talking to her right over there." She pointed to the bed opposite. "That very morning. When I got back on the ward and asked where Hester was, no one had heard of her. Just like now. I told my supervisor and she said she'd heard the same story, or different versions of it, from patients and staff going back all the time she had been here. At least one patient said she went down that corridor as herself but seemed to become someone else while she was there. It was as if someone from a time back in history was sharing her body."

"Possession? I thought that was only in books and films." *Although it would explain so much about my life.*

"Oh no. It's real enough. One of my grandmothers came from Haiti and she told me many times of seeing people who had risen from the dead. Zombies. And of people she knew who had become possessed by the spirits of the restless ones. They're real, all right. I just never expected to find them here."

Another, older, woman in a cleaner's uniform beckoned to her from the door. "Got to go. Lucille's on the warpath. Take my advice, don't have anything to do with that woman if she comes back."

"Thanks. I won't."

Carol leaned back on her pillows. First all that at home and now here. What was going on? Could the two things be linked? After all, Waverley Court had been built on land forming part of the hospital and the workhouse. Maybe she was being targeted by the spirits that had once lived here.

Her eyes grew heavy and she drifted off to sleep. The sounds of the ward faded into the background and she dreamed.

★ ★ ★

Once again she looked out of another woman's eyes, but a different one this time, in a different age. It felt like the present. She stood, staring out of a window in an unfamiliar room, gazing over sand dunes toward the sea.

A figure, dressed in a hooded parka, walked slowly across her field of vision. Carol recognized her.

The woman turned, as if she had become aware of being gawped at. Even from this distance, Carol knew her.

She was staring at herself.

Her eyes shot open. No one appeared to notice her startled reaction and, judging by the clock, she had barely been asleep ten minutes, but the bizarre dream had shocked her into wakefulness. She swung her legs out of bed and straightened up. A young woman drifted past the end of her bed. Something about her expression troubled Carol. It didn't seem natural. Maybe she was preoccupied with an upcoming operation. Her attention seemed focused on something straight ahead of her but her head was positioned so that she was looking slightly upward. As if a taller person was walking in front of her and she was following them.

Hester.

Without another thought, Carol slid her dirty slippers onto her feet and wrapped her dressing gown around her. She followed the young woman out of the ward and down the corridor, keeping a slight distance between them and trying to appear as if her attention was diverted elsewhere. Hester must be in front, and probably aware of her presence.

They turned a corner and stopped in front of a wall. There was no door.

Hester and the woman disappeared through it. Carol tried to follow but the wall was solid under her fingers. She stared at it for a few moments. What had she been thinking? Of course she couldn't follow. She wasn't the one Hester had come for. Not this time anyway.

"Are you all right, Carol?" Allie looked concerned.

"Sorry. Yes. I'm fine. A bit confused perhaps but otherwise okay."

"You were staring at that wall."

"You wouldn't believe me if I told you why."

"Try me."

"I saw a patient disappear through it. I think she was following someone. A ghost." Allie's eyebrows shot up. "See? I knew you wouldn't believe me."

"Well, I'd be lying if I said that was the first time I'd heard that. There have been a number of sightings of strange things around here, but you said a patient disappeared through that wall. Do you know her name?"

Carol shook her head. "She's in the bed next to the window, on the same side as me."

"I know who you mean. I'll take you back to the ward and we can see if she's there."

Carol walked alongside Allie, retracing her steps back to the ward.

The bed at the far end was empty. No sign of its occupant.

"Right. I'll see what's happened to her. She's probably in the bathroom."

Carol watched Allie half run out of the ward. She settled herself down with her now daily newspaper and tried to concentrate on the cryptic crossword.

An hour or so later, the patient had still not returned and Allie came to take Carol's temperature and blood pressure.

"Have you found her yet?" Carol nodded toward the empty bed.

Allie shook her head. "No and we've rung her family to see if she's turned up there. She hasn't. Her father's on his way here. Did she say anything to you at all?"

"No, I've never spoken to her. She only came in yesterday I think."

"Yes. She's in for a minor operation. Pleasant girl. Apart from the usual nerves anyone gets before surgery, she seemed fine. I can't understand it. Security have searched the grounds but still no sign."

"I suppose I was the last person to see her before she disappeared."

"Looks like it. If the police get involved, they'll want to talk to you."

"That should be interesting. Do you have any beds in the Psychiatric Ward?"

Allie smiled. "I'm sure it won't come to that."

"We'll see."

"You'll be going home soon. You're doing fine."

"Apart from all the ghosts I'm seeing."

Allie touched her arm. "I'm going off duty soon, so I'll see you tomorrow."

Carol nodded. After Allie had gone, she decided to go for another walk. She took the same route down the corridor and round to the left, pausing where the mysterious door had been. She noted a wall sign a few feet away: 'Gynecology'. No one was in the immediate vicinity so she pressed the wall hard, then tapped it. Nothing to indicate that it wasn't solid concrete or bricks and mortar. Certainly no sight nor sound of a wooden door.

She carried on, along to the lifts, and took one down to the ground floor, where she visited the secondhand book stall which had been set up for the day. Every day a new selection of stalls plied for the trade of patients, staff and visitors.

Carol searched through the paperbacks. She had put a couple of pound coins in her pocket and now chose a book for £1.50 – an Agatha Christie. *The Mirror Crack'd From Side to Side.*

She tucked it in her pocket and returned to her own floor, hesitating once more at the same section of wall. Had she really seen that patient walk straight through it?

She carried on, noting two uniformed police officers – one male and one female – standing at the Nurses' Station. A Charge Nurse Carol had seen on previous evenings nodded toward her.

Clearly, they wanted to speak to her and she knew what it would be about.

"Carol Shaughnessy?" the male officer asked pleasantly.

"Yes," Carol replied.

"Could we have a word, please? It's about Susan Jackson."

"Who?"

"A patient on this ward. She went missing earlier today and we believe you may have been the last person to see her."

She let them steer her to an empty consulting room where she sat and they positioned themselves in chairs opposite. The female officer took out a pad and made notes.

Her colleague addressed Carol. "Can you tell us where you last saw Miss Jackson?"

Here goes. "In the corridor to the left at the end of this one."

"And what was she doing at the time?"

"Walking through a wall."

* * *

"They thought I was lying. It was quite obvious." Carol tried to remember when she had last felt so embarrassed. She couldn't recall.

The cleaner, whose name she now knew as Clarice, paused in her spraying and polishing. "They'll have to believe you when she doesn't show up again, or even if she does. If she comes back she'll tell them the same as you. Don't worry about it. People thought my grandmother was mad. She had the last laugh though."

"How?"

"We buried her in the local cemetery and the very next day, she was back."

Carol stared. The woman was serious.

"I know what you're thinking, but it's true. She came back. Only for a few weeks. We don't see her anymore now. She has passed over but she still manages to communicate from time to time. Little signs. Things only her family will recognize."

Carol wondered if she had come over to the police as unhinged as Clarice did now. Probably. So who was she to judge this woman who was probably the only person in the world right now who believed her?

* * *

"Okay, Carol." Dr. Sharma stripped off the latex gloves and ditched them in the bin as usual. "I think we can send you home tomorrow. I don't think you should return to work yet. A couple more weeks should do it. Any problems, pain or any sign of bleeding or inflammation and you need to call us. The nurse will give you the contact details and we'll give you some sterile dressings for the wound, along with the usual instructions. Your stitches will need to come out around about Wednesday so make an appointment to see the practice nurse at your GP's surgery. They can do that for you. Any questions at all?"

Carol shook her head.

"Good, well if you have any concerns, however small, call us. We're here to help." She smiled.

"Thank you so much."

"My pleasure. Don't do anything strenuous for a week or so. Let everything heal properly before you start weightlifting. No, seriously, don't do vacuuming or anything other than a little light housework. No rearranging furniture."

"I promise."

Dr. Sharma shook her hand and left her.

A sudden, horribly familiar voice in her ear startled her.

"Don't think I've forgotten you. You'll be back," *Hester.*

Carol hardly dared breathe. She glanced down the ward at the bed where, until a few days ago, a young woman called Susan Jackson had lain. Someone else occupied it now. An elderly woman with a hernia. Carol had given up asking Allie whether the missing girl had been found. The nurse clammed up about it and said she knew nothing, but Carol could tell. She had been told to say nothing. Susan Jackson was still missing.

CHAPTER SIX

Carol awoke to her doorbell ringing. She peered at her clock. The muted red digital display registered eight a.m. The bell rang again. She had promised herself she wouldn't answer her door, but that was before her operation. The memory of the awful child's face flashed into her mind, but she pushed it away. For her sanity's sake she had to believe that her inflamed appendix had somehow infected her brain and made her hallucinate. As for what had happened at the hospital, well, clearly there was something wrong with the place, but she had left all that behind now, hadn't she? It was safe to open her door now.

She had not even made it out of her room before the bell rang yet again. She peered at the screen. A tall, middle-aged man she recognized as her neighbor was poised, ready to press the button a fourth time. He did not look happy.

Carol ran her hand through her bed-tousled hair and opened the door.

"About time too," the man's voice boomed out at her.

"I was asleep. I only came out of hospital yesterday."

"Then I would have thought you wouldn't have felt like having rowdy parties until God knows what time on a workday morning."

"I don't understand. I went to bed at ten."

"If that's the case I definitely don't want to know what you were getting up to, but I'm warning you. If there is any repeat of this, I shall be straight on to the managing agents. I know you're on a fixed-term lease and I know the owners would not be at all happy to know their flat is being turned into some kind of… bordello."

"*Bordello?* I haven't the faintest idea what you're talking about. I went to bed early and you've just woken me up with your incessant ringing of my doorbell. Now you're complaining about something I know nothing about that you allege took place here last night. Go away and leave me alone or I'll be the one doing the reporting. For harassment."

Carol slammed the door in the surprised man's face and rammed home the security chain.

Sounds of his continued ranting drifted through the door. She marched down the hall and toward the kitchen. She stopped at the doorway, not believing the sight that greeted her.

Empty wine bottles littered the sink; the owners' exquisite lead crystal wine glasses, that had escaped the earlier assault, lay upturned or smashed. But where had all that drink come from? She couldn't remember buying any, but clearly someone had, and that person had held one hell of a party in her apartment, which, incredibly, she had slept right through.

In the living room, chaos. Red wine had been spilled on the settee. More glasses littered every surface and there were ring marks on each of the side tables. She searched for her phone and eventually found it, stuffed behind a cushion. She intended to call the police, but stopped herself. How would she explain any of this? Her neighbor would tell the same tale he had told her, and Carol could never convince anyone that she was not involved in whatever had been going on here.

She checked the glass outer doors but they were locked securely. In the spare bedroom, the bedclothes were strewn all over the floor, but at least there were no signs of dirty glasses or wine stains. The windows in there were locked as well, so whoever had got in had a key.

The security chain. That had been on when she answered the door to the neighbor. It was a particularly sturdy one. Carol examined it now and found no signs it had been forced.

She dressed hurriedly and began the laborious process of cleaning up. It would take hours and Carol had no clue how to get the stain out of the settee. Definitely a job for a specialist. If she used some strong chemicals that reacted badly to the fabric, the damage could be even worse and there was no way she could afford to replace the expensive furniture.

So much for light housework. This required scrubbing and

sheer hard effort. By the time she had finished, carefully packed up the broken glass and emptied it along with the rubbish into the large bins in the underground garage, she felt exhausted. She tiptoed past her neighbor's flat. Best to keep a low profile and let things die down. If only she could figure out who had done such a thing. And how she could have been oblivious to what was going on when her neighbor had clearly been kept awake by the racket?

Back in the flat, she locked and chained the door, noting once again the impossibility of slipping that chain, key or no key.

A search online turned up a local upholstery cleaning firm who agreed to come out the following day. The woman who took the details sounded hopeful. It happened quite often apparently. But it was still going to be an expense Carol could ill afford, and if this had happened once, it could so easily happen again. Especially as whoever was responsible was clearly going to get away with it.

* * *

She stayed up later that night and it was after midnight before she slipped into bed in her silent flat. No sounds leaked in from outside as Carol closed her eyes and drifted off. When she opened them again, daylight streamed through the windows. She had forgotten to close the curtains and now it was morning. A little after eight.

Feeling refreshed, she got up and padded into the en suite, clicking on the light.

"Oh my God. No!"

The tiled walls were plastered with scrawls. 'You're next' repeated over and over in a variety of different handwriting. Stick men with their heads in nooses, primitively sketched heads with mouths reminiscent of Munch's *The Scream*. Everything drawn in black felt pen. Carol touched it and some came off on her fingers. At least she should be able to get it off.

She caught a glimpse of her frightened face in the mirror – and something darker behind. Something much darker that grew, threatening to absorb her into itself.

Carol cried out and fled the room. She raced into the living room and froze.

The graffiti artist had been busy here too. Scrawling the same drawings over the painted walls of the room.

"*No*. This isn't happening. It can't be happening." Carol burst into tears. The heaving of her sobs hurt her abdomen and pulled at the stitches, but she couldn't stop. She wept until no more tears would come and then she wept some more.

Finally she pulled herself together enough to go and get dressed. Bypassing the en suite in favor of the bathroom, which, mercifully, had been left clean, Carol relished the shock of the cold water splashing her face. With her teeth and hair brushed, she braced herself to return to the en suite armed with a bleach cleaning spray and cloths.

She had just finished scrubbing the walls clean when her doorbell rang and she remembered the upholstery cleaner was due to arrive.

He whistled through his teeth when he saw the graffiti in the living room. "What was it? Burglars?"

"I'm afraid so." Easier this way. He wouldn't have believed her anyway.

He pointed to the stain on the settee. "They do this as well?"

"Yes."

"Bastards. Ought to lock them up and throw away the key."

"If the police can catch them."

"You've got plenty of CCTV around here. They must have been caught somewhere."

"Let's hope so."

The man had a point though. If she could see the footage, or ask the managing agents if someone could check for suspicious movements during the past two nights....

She made coffee for the workman and left him to it while she cleared up her bedroom and checked her papers for the number of the managing agents. She found it and called them. A helpful and sympathetic-sounding woman answered. She said she would get back to Carol but it might be a couple of days. Meanwhile, she advised her to report the suspected break-in to the police. Carol thanked her and ended the call.

"All done," the man called from the living room.

Carol took out the money she needed to pay him from her purse, frowning at the paltry amount it left her with.

"All bright and shiny again." He smiled at her and took the money, handing her a receipt.

The room smelled clean and fresh and the settee was pristine once more.

"It's a shame you don't do walls," she said.

"Oh, a couple of coats of paint will sort that out," he said. "I can give you the number of a good decorator if you like. He's my brother-in-law." He scribbled a name and number onto a slightly battered business card and handed it to her.

Carol took the card. "Thank you so much for doing a brilliant job."

"No problem. I hope they catch the twats that made it necessary. And what's with that 'you're next' crap? That's threatening that is. The police don't take kindly to that sort of thing. Should add a bit onto their sentence with the right judge."

"Thanks again," Carol said, walking him to the door.

After he had gone, she returned to the living room and stared at the ruined walls. Could she do it herself? It wouldn't be the first time she had decorated a room and she didn't do a bad job. But to attempt it now, when she was still so sore from the operation, was asking a bit too much. Maybe she could leave it a week or so. After all, who would see it apart from her? And she couldn't afford to get someone in.

Decision made. But that still left the unanswered question of who was responsible for all this in the first place. Maybe the CCTV would show something up. All she could do was wait and hope nothing else happened.

* * *

Two uneventful days passed and her phone rang. The managing agents had checked the CCTV for the nights in question and found nothing. Residents and visitors had been caught on camera going about their normal business. No one had attempted to force an entry anywhere. No suspicious behavior of any kind. Carol asked if all her windows and the communal entrance were within view of a camera and the managing agent confirmed that they were, along with the two entrances to the underground garage. No one could have gone in or come out without being caught on camera.

Panic started to swell inside her. Everything that had happened at the hospital...and before, here in this apartment. Was she the only one or had any of her neighbors experienced anything like what she was going through? She needed to find out. For once in Carol's life she felt the need to make a friend, or at least an ally. Maybe then she wouldn't feel so alone in battling whatever threatened her. Maybe then she could stop feeling as if she was going mad.

A total of nine apartments were accessible from the communal entrance in this block – three on each floor. Apart from the angry neighbor next door, she knew no one.

Better change that then.

Before she could lose her resolve, Carol left her apartment, keys in hand, and crossed the hall. She rang the bell and waited. Presently she heard the sound of a chain being removed. The door opened and an elderly woman with white hair frowned up at her.

"Hello, I'm Carol. I live next door."

"Oh it's you. Come to apologize, have you?"

"I'm sorry, I don't understand. What am I supposed to have done?"

"You know perfectly well. All that ruckus a couple of nights ago. Kept me awake all night. Disgraceful."

"I'm so sorry you were disturbed but I can assure you I had nothing to do with it."

"You were there. Mr. Faraday at number one told me he'd taken it up with you. He said your attitude left a lot to be desired. We don't allow that sort of thing at Waverley Court. It lowers the tone."

"I can only apologize. I'm at a loss to explain any of it—" But Carol was talking to a closed door. She would find no ally there.

She ignored the lift, mounted the staircase to the next floor, and rang the first doorbell she came to. The sound echoed from within. Another door opened and a young woman around Carol's age peered out.

"No one lives there at the moment," she said, pleasantly enough. Could this be a neighbor she hadn't managed to upset yet? "I'm all alone on this floor. Both the other flats are up for sale and the owners have already gone. Or maybe you've come to view one of them?"

Carol shook her head. "I'm living downstairs at number three. I wondered if I could have a word with you if that's all right?"

The woman opened her door wider. "Come in. I was going shopping but that can wait. I'll put the kettle on."

Carol followed her along a hall similar to her own and into a bright, sunny living room.

"I'm Joanna, by the way." The woman extended her hand, revealing neat, expensively manicured nails.

Carol shook her hand. "I'm Carol."

"Coffee all right for you, or would you prefer tea?"

"Coffee's great, thanks."

Joanna smiled and left her. Carol wandered over to the tall window and peered out. A balcony with a small bistro table and two wrought-iron chairs afforded a view over to the hospital where she could just make out patients, staff and visitors going in and out, a constant stream of people. Ambulances would come in on the far side of the building hidden from her current view.

She turned back to examine the room. A burgundy leather three-piece suite, chrome and glass coffee table and an enormous, wall-mounted television took up most of the available space. A light oak fire surround framed a modern gray slate fireplace, housing an attractive and realistic-looking flame-effect fire. A rattle of china and a delicious aroma of fresh ground coffee heralded Joanna's appearance.

"There's sugar and milk if you prefer." Joanna depressed the plunger on the cafétière and poured two steaming mugs full. Carol accepted one and added two sugars and a splash of milk.

Joanna leaned back on the settee opposite Carol, who had chosen one of the two deep, comfy chairs.

"So," Joanna said. "You're living in the Hathaways' flat?"

"Am I? I didn't know their names. No mail has arrived for anyone and the agent never said."

"I get their mail. Adele Hathaway is a good friend of mine. We Skype every few days. They're loving Dubai. I think if Adele had her way they'd probably stay there, but Christian's contract is strictly six months. He's a project engineer, working with a civil engineering company out there. Very high-powered stuff apparently."

"It must be interesting work though."

"I expect so. Certainly keeps Adele in Jimmy Choos." She laughed lightly and sipped her coffee. "How are you finding their flat?"

"It's lovely, but…." Where to begin?

"Problems?"

Carol nodded. "That's why I'm here."

"Go on. Tell me."

Joanna was clearly unfazed and unsurprised. Carol swallowed and began, "I see things sometimes and, worse than that…." She stopped. How could she tell the owners' friend about the damage to their apartment? She couldn't tell her about the graffiti, the red wine stains or the broken crockery, and certainly not about upsetting the neighbors.

"Go on," Joanna said. "Worse than that, what?"

Carol settled for, "Noises. Whispering, that sort of thing."

"Sounds about right. Adele told me similar stories. She hates that flat but Christian won't sell. He loves it. You know about the history of this place don't you?"

"I know where we are used to be the old hospital and there was a workhouse, asylum and cemetery."

"That's right. We're probably only a few feet away from tons of buried corpses. But it's the layout of this place that's so significant. If you believe in the supernatural that is. And I do."

The way she said it almost challenged Carol to disagree with her. She didn't. She felt a sense of relief. Here, at last, was someone who believed her.

Apparently satisfied she wasn't going to get any argument from her, Joanna continued. "Back in the day when this was the old Royal Hospital, the ground floor, where you are, was actually below ground level. If you go outside and look carefully, you can see it still is a few inches lower, but because of the way they've dug the grounds and landscaped, it blends in. Where your flat is used to be the morgue and apparently, a tunnel ran from there, right under Waverley Court and up to where the Royal and Waverley is today. I've heard it may still be there."

"A tunnel? Whatever for?"

"To transport the bodies from the hospital, workhouse and asylum to the morgue."

"Good grief. That sounds a bit sinister."

"It saved a lot of panic whenever there was an outbreak of fever, and there were plenty of those, especially in the earlier days of the workhouse. Sanitation wasn't great and hygiene was primitive at least."

"How do you know all this?"

"I've done my homework. It helps that I'm an archivist at the university and I've got access to a load of records not normally on public display. It's fascinating stuff. Hang on, I've copied some pictures. I'll get them."

This was the break Carol had hoped for. Joanna could help her sort out fact from fantasy.

Presently she returned, with a twin-lock file under her arm. She laid it out on the coffee table and Carol leaned forward as she flicked over the pages.

"Here it is." Joanna tapped a copy of a grainy photograph. It showed a corridor, fairly dim but with distinctive wall lights.

Carol drew in her breath sharply. In the foreground, slightly off to the left, stood a familiar woman dressed from head to toe in a dark dress, her hair parted in the center and drawn back severely off her face. She stood next to two other people Carol recognized – a man in a white coat and another female whose hair was coiled up in a bun and whose pale, piercing eyes stared out at her.

"What is it?" Joanna asked.

"I know that place. I could swear I've been there, or else

dreamed about it. And I'm certain I've encountered these people. I know two of their names. The woman on the left is called Hester, or at least she was when I came across her in hospital, and the man is Dr. Franklyn...I've seen the other woman but I don't know her name. Look, I know I sound crazy but I'm *sure* I've met them in their own time, and it was a nightmare. Hester seems to be able to.... I've seen her in the present day as well."

"I'm the last person to disbelieve you. By the way, where they're standing is alleged to have been the underground tunnel I told you about."

"Were there rooms off this tunnel? Rooms where people might have been kept for some purpose or another."

"I don't know. I suppose it's possible but all I know about is what I've told you, that it was a means of getting bodies from the workhouse to the morgue."

Carol stared down at the cold eyes of the woman she was sure was Hester. They had told her in hospital that the modern-day Hester she had met didn't exist, but here she was, in her alternate persona, captured on an old photograph. What the hell was going on? "Is there any way of finding out who she was for certain? When I was there, they called me Miss Warren. Lydia Warren. And I have a poem written by someone with that name. I think she murdered her husband – Roger Carmody."

Joanna's eyes grew wider at the mention of the name. "That's really interesting. That murder was hushed up at the time. The judge ordered all records of it to be sealed for a hundred years. It's been well over that now but you'll still find no mention of it on the internet. I only came across it by accident. Someone had been a bit careless at the time and a junior newspaper reporter's scribbled notes from the trial survive."

"Do you have them?"

"No, but I know where they are."

"It felt so real." Carol's skin prickled as she relived the experience. "It was as if I was her. As if she had inhabited my body, or I hers. I'm really not sure which. Her husband had beaten her badly and I could feel her pain. Every inch of my body was on fire or throbbing, aching. I felt his blows. I reached for the letter opener and stabbed him. Again and again. I couldn't stop. I mean, Lydia…Lydia couldn't stop. And then he was dead and the police came. Antrobus. That was his name. Detective Inspector Antrobus. He charged Lydia with murder."

Joanna had paled. "There's no way you could have known any of that unless you had either read the notes I've seen or…." She inhaled deeply. "Or you had been there. I know you couldn't possibly have seen the notes, so…."

"My God. It *was* real."

Joanna whistled. "Oh, I think you've known that all along, haven't you? It's just a lot to process. This is fascinating. You know, Adele heard voices, indistinct whispers and she would smell something in the flat from time to time. Ammonia…and worse."

Carol nodded. "Boiled cabbage and body odor."

"You too? Adele said that was when she started to want to get away from the flat. Christian told her she was imagining stuff. She should get out more. Get a part-time job or something, so she volunteered at the local hospice charity shop. She told me it helped but whenever she came home, it would all start over again. Never when Christian was there though."

"Someone keeps telling me I'm next. But I don't know what they mean. Next for what? Did Adele hear that?"

"Not that I know of. She could never make out anything that was being said. She found it so frustrating and said if she could have known what was behind it all she could have met it head on. As it was, she had nothing to go on, other than what I've told you. It was her experience that spiked my curiosity to research this place more thoroughly."

"Have you experienced anything?"

Joanna shook her head. "Maybe living up here I'm a bit too far away from the vibes. Your two ground-floor neighbors haven't mentioned anything, but then we don't speak much. I meet them occasionally when I'm putting out the rubbish, and we exchange what polite people call pleasantries, but that's about it. I couldn't even tell you their names. He's golf mad. You'll see him coming in and out with a bag of expensive clubs, and she's a stalwart of the local Methodist Church. Doesn't approve of drinking, gambling, smoking or anything remotely resembling fun. That's what Adele said anyway. I don't even think *she* knew her name. She always called her Mrs. Number Two. Quite funny if you think about it."

Carol smiled. "I'll remember that. She's quite fierce." She hesitated but decided to ask anyway. "Did you hear any noise coming from my flat a couple of nights ago?"

"Can't say I remember anything. Mind you, the floors are quite thick and solid so not much wafts up or down. Why?"

Carol told her about the complaints but again stopped short of mentioning the damage.

Joanna smiled. "Oh, you've definitely been targeted by whatever is still here."

"But what do I do about it? I have another four and a half months on my tenancy and there's no way I can afford to break it."

"You're all right when you're not here? I mean this – whatever it is – doesn't follow you?"

"I'm not sure. I've always seen things. Shadows, shapes, out of the corner of my eye. All my life that's happened. Once I almost saw her face. Oh yes, I'm certain it's a female. Much older than me. At least that's the impression I get. I've never properly seen her. She's followed me but never threatened me. At least, I don't think so. But now I get confused as to who's whispering to me. Is it something in this building? Or is it my familiar? That's what I call her. But now I think about it, I haven't been aware of her much since I moved here. Stuff happened when I was in hospital too, but I'm as sure as I can be that she wasn't responsible for any of it. Maybe she's moved on."

"Tell me about what happened in hospital."

Carol told her everything, including Susan Jackson's mysterious disappearance. Joanna listened intently, saying nothing until she had finished.

Joanna picked up the photo again. "Okay, this all seems to tie in. As far as this place is concerned, from this photo, I'd say it's pretty certain the rumors of this tunnel are correct. From what you've told me, I'm guessing one of the original entrances is where you went with that woman, Hester, and I'm guessing another is near your flat, or maybe even in it." Joanna stood. "Come on."

"Where are we going?"

"Downstairs to your flat."

"But—"

Joanna was at the door, keys in hand. There was no going back now.

* * *

"Bloody hell." Joanna stared at the graffiti-covered walls of the living room.

"It'll be okay. I'm going to redecorate it in a few days. Please don't tell Adele."

Joanna didn't seem to hear her. "This is serious stuff. Is there any more of this?"

"There was some on the tiles in the en suite but I was able to clean it off. I think they must have used a Sharpie pen or something similar."

"Have you had any other experiences?"

"In the kitchen. And my bedroom. I've seen shadows and heard whispers in there. The thermostat in the bathroom was changed and the shower came on, but that's only happened once. The night the alleged party took place, the bedclothes were turned upside down but nothing else has happened in the second bedroom. The smells seem to come from the hall."

"They really have come after you, haven't they?" Her voice was gentler this time as if she had remembered that, for Carol, this whole experience must be terrifying and not merely an interesting bit of supernatural activity.

Carol avoided her gaze. Tears pricked her eyes. She wished Joanna wasn't being so nice to her. She wasn't used to it and it made her feel vulnerable.

Joanna came over to her. "Don't worry, Carol. We'll get to the bottom of this. I promise."

"If only it were that simple."

"It's probably an unquiet spirit searching for release."

"How do you know about such things?"

"I did my dissertation on the occult and supernatural, focusing on the traces of past lives that can leave an imprint on a building or location. Fascinating stuff. It's one of the reasons I came to live here. I knew it was going to be an interesting experience. All the suffering, not only from the medical patients, but those in the asylum and the workhouse. If anything is going to leave a residue, those are the sorts of places it's going to happen."

Carol wished she could view it that way, but it was a bit difficult when your life and sanity were being threatened.

"Let's start with your bedroom."

A figure skittered out of sight. Carol gripped Joanna's arm. "Did you see that?"

"What?"

"A shadow…a figure. It was only there for a split second. I saw it out of the corner of my eye. Not the same as…. Not my familiar."

Joanna moved directly in front of her and lightly clasped both Carol's arms. "I'll say this again. I'm not going to disbelieve you. If you say you saw something, then as far as I'm concerned, you did. Now, what exactly did you see?"

"All I know is, this one is menacing. There's so much hatred in it and it's fighting to get into my body. Not only to share it, but to take it over and control every thought and every action. But more than that…."

"What?"

Carol bit her lip. She was finally going to voice her fear to another person. "It wants my soul, Joanna. And not just mine either."

Joanna blinked and dropped her hands.

"You think I'm crazy too, don't you?" Carol asked.

"No. Far from it. Everything you've said adds up. You're psychic, that's for sure. Spirits find it easy to connect with you. Sometimes that's a good thing, but other times, like now…. Well, let's just say the bad ones are good at grabbing opportunities."

"And you think that's what's happening here?"

Joanna nodded. "What do you feel right now?"

How to describe the sudden change in the air around her. "The atmosphere in here. It's as if there's a fog even though I know there isn't."

"I'm relying on you to tell me if anything changes. I can't feel anything. I don't have your powers."

"Powers? I've never thought of it like that."

"You'd better start because you undoubtedly have them. Let's begin with the wardrobes." Joanna opened the first door of the fitted units that ran floor to ceiling all along one wall.

Carol opened the one at the far end. "What am I looking for?"

"I'll be honest, I don't really know but I think it might be better if we worked together."

Carol closed the door and joined Joanna, who had engaged in removing her clothes from the rails, laying them carefully on the bed. Carol helped her.

"I think," Joanna said. "We need to look for anything that doesn't quite fit. The rear wall, for example. Is there part of it that's hollow? That sort of thing. Any anomaly, however small, that could indicate that something has been covered over at some stage. It might conceal an old entrance. Something that a spirit from the building's history could use to get through."

Joanna climbed in the now-empty wardrobe. She knocked along the wall. Only the sound of solid masonry. She peered down at the floor and stamped her feet. Nothing.

"I'll get out now and you get in. See what you feel. Tell me if anything changes."

They swapped places. Carol did exactly as Joanna had done, with the same lack of result. She peered up at the top of the wardrobe. Nothing unusual. "But the entrance wouldn't still be here, would it? They wouldn't just cover it over. They demolished the old building, didn't they? Twice, I believe. Once, after the bombing and then again later. All of this is relatively new."

"So is the hospital, but you went through into the tunnel there, didn't you?"

"But when I went back the second time, the wall was solid. For me at any rate."

"I know it's a long shot, but let's at least give it a good go. Let's try the next one."

That was easier. The wardrobes, apart from the first one, were empty except for a few pairs of well-worn shoes. Knowing how different these must be from Joanna's smart belongings, Carol felt a wave of shame and embarrassment, but Joanna gave no indication of surprise at Carol's evident relative poverty.

They repeated the tapping, knocking and stamping but nothing happened.

"Let's check the rest of the room." Joanna led the way.

Still nothing.

"Okay, now the hall." She crossed the threshold.

As soon as Carol put one foot out of the bedroom, her nerve endings fizzed. She gritted her teeth and hugged herself.

"What is it?" Joanna asked. "What are you feeling? Can you see anything?"

Her voice faded into the distance.

* * *

Carol looked out of Lydia's eyes at the assembled hushed audience, but this was no theater. A courtroom. The bewigged judge was reading a slip of paper. Sitting behind desks, a number of well-dressed and important-looking men listened, legal papers and books piled in front of them. Carol's hands gripped the wooden rail of the dock. The judge set the paper down. He reached forward and picked up a piece of black material, which he set carefully on top of his head. Members of the all-male jury whispered to each other, their voices mingling and drifting toward her like leaves tossed in the wind.

The judge stared directly at her. She felt his eyes boring into her. The court fell silent.

"Prisoner at the bar."

All heads turned toward her. Carol felt a sickening palpitation.

"You have been found guilty of the crime of murder. The sentence of this court is that you will be taken from here to the place from whence you came and there be kept in close confinement until a date yet to be determined, and upon that day that you be taken to the place of execution and there hanged by the neck until you are dead. And may God have mercy upon your soul."

Each word stabbed her soul. Carol's knees buckled and the crowd gasped. Two female prison warders manhandled her down the steps and straight down into the bowels of the building.

A murderer. They had found her guilty. No mitigating circumstances. No self-defense. In their eyes she was a cold-blooded killer. Or Lydia was. She must remember, *she* was Carol Shaughnessy. She closed her eyes and prayed. *Take me out of this body. Take me home.*

A mist descended in front of her eyes. The sound of horses' hooves, the lurch of the prison carriage faded away and when her sight returned, time had passed.

She stood on a small wooden platform. Somewhere a bell tolled and next to her a priest was reciting the 23rd Psalm. A stocky man placed a noose around her neck. The rough fibers of the crude but sturdy rope stung like an army of red ants as it cut into her throat, and warm blood trickled down her neck, splashing her dress, even dripping onto the floor beneath her shaking legs.

She could smell the stench of death from the black hood they put over her head, hear her own shallow, feverish breathing as she waited for the trapdoor to open. Waited for death to claim her, when finally her legs would stop quivering and her neck would be broken or she would be strangled from a short drop.

The woman whose body she occupied spoke in her mind. *I am Lydia Warren Carmody. I am innocent of the crime they say I committed, but life means nothing to me anymore. Death, come to me…come now….*

A sudden glimpse of a man, broken, bleeding. Lying on the floor. Dead. A man who wasn't Roger Carmody.

Jonah….

A scurrying. A door banged and a male voice boomed out, echoing off the walls. "The woman has been spared. Take her down and return her to her cell."

The words reached Carol through the hangman's hood. Someone whipped it off her face and she blinked at the sudden bright light. The same person relaxed the noose around her neck and dragged it off and Carol collapsed into the arms of a wardress who half-carried her out of the death room and into a side room.

"Someone will come for you," the rough woman said. "They're taking you to the loony bin. That'll be your home for the rest of your life."

Carol overbalanced and fell to the floor. The door slammed and the iron key clanked in the lock.

Using the one battered chair for support, Carol struggled to her feet and sat down at the poor excuse for a table. She put her head in her hands and wept. How had it come to this? The Lydia within her had killed her husband or he would have killed her, but a jury had found her guilty of murder and a judge had wanted her to hang. She almost had. She touched her stinging neck and her hand came back red with her blood.

Someone had intervened mere seconds before they would have executed her. Which member of her family would have done that? They had all disowned her. So many memories filled her brain. Faces, people, events. All her memories, yet all unfamiliar to the part of her that was still Carol Shaughnessy.

A distant, half-overheard conversation between two older men swam into her brain. The language was strange, as if they were talking in some kind of code.

"I see you are a traveling man, Brother."

"As are you, Brother."

"Then naturally it is incumbent upon me to take care of that for which you solicit."

"I pay homage to your judgment."

"The question of your daughter's guilt in this affair has been determined but I have reflected upon your plea and am prepared to show mercy. Furthermore, I will vouchsafe that no records of her trial shall be released. None shall be shewed for one hundred years or more. And may the great Architect of the Universe protect us all."

"So mote it be…."

The voices faded.

A sudden knife of pain seared through Carol's stomach. She bent over. Another stab of pain made her cry out. She doubled up, slid off the chair and passed out.

* * *

Carol opened her eyes. Somehow she was back in the dingy old corridor, with no recollection of how she got there. The old wall lamps flickered their gas flames. Murmurings of conversation wafted past her, before becoming more distinct. Shadows writhed in the gloom, and took form. Women dressed in drab, ankle-length dresses, patched and rusty with age. Body odor, ammonia and other smells Carol was unfamiliar with assailed her, while the now all too familiar lingering stench of boiled cabbage reminded her how much she hated the stuff. One of the foster mothers had forced her to eat it when she was seven years old. The memory flooded back. But something else overtook it.

"You will come with me. You are to be examined." Hester, in her Victorian guise, had appeared from nowhere, her eyes boring into Carol's with no trace of humanity in them. She grabbed her arm so firmly, her nails dug into Carol's flesh, half dragging her down the corridor. The other women, milling around, took no notice of her. Maybe they couldn't even see her.

Hester pushed her into a side room and closed the door behind them. Dr. Franklyn stood waiting. Next to him stood a rusted iron bed.

"Now that your stomach malady has been cured, we must address the real cause of your dementia. Lie down," he ordered, his voice emotionless.

"My name is Carol.... Carol...." But she couldn't remember her surname. It had been there, but in a second, had drifted off somewhere into the darkness of her mind where a black curtain descended, keeping her from memories she knew she must have. The curtain rolled forward and expanded, robbing her of more and more until she could protest no more. She no longer had any idea what she was protesting about.

The doctor's face loomed closer. She tried to move, but her wrists were tethered – tried to kick out, but so were her ankles. Tried to scream, but they forced a leather gag into her mouth.

"Hold her steady."

Hands pushed down on her shoulders. Someone she couldn't see behind her held her head.

The sound of a drill.

Coming closer.

No. They couldn't.

Excruciating pain in her head. The sound of bone crunching….

CHAPTER SEVEN

"Carol. *Carol!*"

She opened her eyes and found herself lying on the floor of her hall. She sat up and a fierce headache pounded, sending white hot shards of pain through her brain.

Joanna helped her stand and steered her into the living room, where she sank down gratefully onto the settee.

"I thought you were having a fit. I was about to call an ambulance but then you came out of it. What happened?"

For a moment, Carol could remember nothing, and then it gradually came back to her. She told Joanna as best she could, but her words seemed jumbled, garbled. "I'm not making any sense."

"Oh you are, don't worry. And it's all sounding a little familiar. Firstly, that odd, archaic conversation you heard. I believe that gives us the answer as to why the records of Lydia Warren's trial were kept secret for so long. Those words and some of the phrases? They're Masonic. I reckon you heard the judge and Lydia's father speaking and both were Freemasons. The judge decided to show leniency to help a fellow brother out. I'll bet he made sure that jury were contacted individually and warned to keep their mouths shut too. It was a different age then. People were more deferential. Any scandal that had crept out would soon die down. It's not like today when everything you do stays online to haunt you forever. With no official records to refer to, it would be yesterday's forgotten gossip in no time. The newspaper barons were all Masonic brethren so they could be relied upon to quash any reporting. Just that one junior reporter who couldn't resist keeping his notebook."

"But what about anyone else there? Members of the public?"

"Did you see anyone there apart from the judge, jury, lawyers and court officials?"

Carol went over every detail in her brain. The courtroom hadn't been full. Everyone there seemed to have an official role to play. She shook her head.

"There you go. The judge excluded members of the public from the hearing, knowing her father was a fellow Mason.

"As for the rest of it, when I was doing my research, I came across an account of a woman in Wales – Rhian somebody. She found herself somewhere she couldn't possibly be, where everyone she encountered recognized her as another person entirely. In her case, the time frame was the present day, but it was as if she had somehow slipped into a parallel universe. It reads like the stuff of science fiction, but it really happened. To cut a long story to the quick, the incidents stopped when she found out that her alter ego actually existed and was having similar experiences. Only in *her* case, she was finding people recognized her as Rhian. They had somehow managed to swap identities. They had never met and the other woman lived in Chicago. They were no relation to each other and this was in the 1980s so they couldn't have even met on social media because there wasn't any."

"But you say they were in the same time frame. My experiences aren't. What happens to me is happening in the nineteenth century. The real Lydia Warren Carmody, whoever she was, must be long dead by now. But what happened out in the hall? What did I do?"

"One minute you were following me, the next you let out a cry and fainted. You tossed and turned a bit, then went quiet, and I was about to phone for an ambulance when you came round."

"How long was I out for?"

"Not long. Maybe a minute?"

"Time isn't the same then because I was there longer than that."

"Time isn't linear."

"Sorry?"

Joanna shook herself. "It's a theory I heard. There are people who believe that time isn't as straightforward as we think. It doesn't relentlessly move forward, ticking away the seconds hour after hour, year after year. It can be bent, twisted, coiled round even."

"That sounds weird."

"I agree. But in your case, it would be a possible answer to at least part of what you are going through during these episodes."

"But I become her and she doesn't become me, because you were with me and she didn't manifest herself."

"That's true." Joanna frowned.

"What is it?"

"Oh nothing. It's nothing. I think we can safely say we have found the hotspot in your apartment though."

"But there isn't a doorway."

"Isn't there?"

"I didn't go anywhere. I stayed here. Physically at least. You were here with me all the time. In the hospital, I actually went through the door in the wall. So did Hester…and Susan Jackson."

"There was no one else with you at the time so you can't actually be certain you did go through an entrance, although, admittedly, it does seem likely simply because when you 'returned' you weren't in the same place as when you crossed over, if I can use that term. Whatever the truth of that, we do know that when you followed Hester and Susan Jackson you couldn't see or find the door in the wall through which they disappeared, and I believe it's because you weren't meant to. It doesn't mean it wasn't there, only that its existence was being withheld from you by someone or something." Joanna looked thoughtful for a moment. "It might help if we knew where Lydia Warren Carmody died. And even where she's buried."

"The Warrens seem to have been a well-respected family," Carol said. "Her father was an alderman and doctor. He laid the foundation stone here. Wouldn't they have had a burial plot somewhere?"

"I'll see what I can find out. The trouble is so many cemeteries have been remodeled and gravestones removed, including the graveyard here of course. We can only hope they had a mausoleum or that at least some family members survive who would have ensured their ancestors continued to rest in peace where they were originally laid."

Joanna went shortly after, leaving Carol to her thoughts and fears. It took her two hours to pluck up the courage to cross the hall into her bedroom, and then only to remove all her things and transfer into the spare room. As possibly the least 'active' room in the flat, maybe she would be safer here.

* * *

She lay in the darkness, her head cradled by the soft pillows in bed in her new room. Peace. Quiet. Tranquil silence. She drifted....

Outside, something scratched at the window. Insistent, persistent, like a cat's claws.

She shot awake and snapped on the bedside lamp. She gave a start at the figure in the mirrored doors of the fitted wardrobes.

Stupid. Jumping at my own reflection.

Carol pushed the duvet aside and lowered her feet to the carpeted floor. She padded to the window and gingerly tugged the curtain aside a few inches.

A white face stared at her. Ghostly yet solid. Hair in an outdated bun. Hester.

Carol cried out and jumped back, letting the curtain fall. Through it she saw a shape move. It stopped. Disappeared. Carol panted, every nerve on edge, scalp prickling with fear. But she *had* to know.

She stepped forward, put out her hand and tweaked the curtain. Nothing there. She opened it wider and looked out on the deserted walkway and the curve of the drive. Nothing stirred.

But she *had* been there. The woman she knew as Hester, in her Victorian guise. She had made no attempt to blend into the twenty-first century the way she had in the Royal and Waverley.

* * *

"You're not going to believe what I've found out." Joanna threw her handbag down on the settee in Carol's living room and sat down.

"I hope it's something good, or at least something that answers all these interminable questions."

"Oh, I think you'll be clearer when I've finished. First of all, remember the photograph I showed you of the three people from the asylum? You knew two of their names. Now meet the third."

Joanna rummaged in her bag and produced a small sheaf of papers. Flicking them over, she showed one to Carol.

It was a copy of a photograph. Two familiar figures stood side by side. "Read the caption underneath."

"'Dr. Oliver Franklyn and Miss Arabella Marsden. Pioneers in the diagnosis of disorders of the brain, praised for their work in treating patients at Waverley Asylum.' Where did you find this?"

"Well hidden in the archives at the university. And there's more. Apparently these two had carte blanche to experiment on the inmates, all in the name of science. There's a vague and – unfortunately – partial, report of them practicing the art of trepanning."

"What's that?"

"It's where a special type of drill is used to remove a small, circular piece of bone from the skull. Back in history, it was believed this could let out evil humors, but it does have some genuine applications such as when pressure has built up on the brain. As far as Franklyn and Marsden were concerned though, it was for one purpose only and that was to satisfy their own sadistic pleasures. They performed their operations without anesthetic."

"They did it to me," Carol said quietly.

"Then my hunch was right. You *are* the one. The report I found must be about you. It has to be. It states that they performed an operation on a woman who insisted she didn't belong there and that she had come from some time in the future. They deemed her to be hysterical. Typical Victorian assumption, or, in their case, a convenient excuse. Strange how few 'hysterical' men there were compared to the shedloads of women diagnosed with that disorder. That's all there is, I'm afraid. It's not even dated. I searched everywhere but the rest of the report appears to have been lost. I suppose I was lucky to find what I did."

"So, if this is right, then I really do slip backward and forward in time. I've lived in more than one time frame."

"The theory could be right then. Time isn't linear. The past, present and future all exist at the same time. Wow, and I thought that only happened in *Star Trek.*"

"I don't suppose you've been able to find out where Lydia Warren Carmody is buried yet?"

Joanna shook her head. "Not a trace. Odd really in one way because the Warrens were, as you said, a well-respected family, but apart from birth and marriage details for Grover Warren, there's only what I discovered a few days ago. Of course, records get lost and I may be looking in entirely the wrong place. Or, yet again, maybe the Masonic influence is at work. "

"They told me…I mean Lydia…she would be staying in the asylum for the rest of her life."

"I checked the asylum records but they're sketchy. There was a major fire there early in 1890 and all the records up until then were destroyed. I did check the list of patients who were transferred to other asylums when that was temporarily evacuated and her name wasn't among them, but as we don't know for certain when she was sent there, that really proves nothing."

"So we don't know when Roger Carmody died then?"

"Oh yes, we know that. He died in 1889."

"And the trial would have been held soon after?"

"Probably within a few weeks or months. To them it would have seemed an open-and-shut case, so the defense counsel probably wouldn't have had much to say."

Carol moistened her lips. "If she wasn't on the list, she must have only been in the asylum for a short time." She wished Joanna wouldn't look at her that way. As if there was something else she wanted to say but didn't know how to approach it. "Please tell me. I know there's more. Whatever it is, I need to know."

Joanna looked upward and took a deep breath. "I found two hospital records. One dates from 1890 and it lists the admission of Lydia Warren Carmody, whose address is listed as the local asylum. She gave birth to a baby girl and was discharged back to the asylum a few days later. The fate of the child is not recorded. The other record is later and is from 1891. I found it quite by chance but it lists the admission of a patient who was kept under close watch following a failed suicide attempt. There are a few notes and a photograph." She rifled through her papers and picked up the ones she was looking for, making sure Carol couldn't see them. "The notes are rather brief but they state that the patient had made an unsuccessful attempt to sever arteries in her wrists. She had been found by her landlady, resuscitated and brought to the hospital, where she complained of voices in her head, other entities possessing her body and of finding herself in the past and future. When her injuries were sufficiently healed, she was committed to the asylum. Obviously there's no record of her arriving there, but we have to assume she did. I want you to prepare yourself."

"What do you mean? This is good news, isn't it? It proves I'm not mad and that someone else has had similar experiences."

"It certainly proves something all right. But not what you might think. The patient's name was Carol Shaughnessy and this is her photograph."

Carol stared in disbelief at the faded sepia image. The familiar features stared back at her and inside her a distant memory stirred. "My God. It's all true then. Every last bit of it."

* * *

The shadows lengthened and Carol switched on the lights and drew the curtains tightly closed in her bedroom and living room. The bathroom and kitchen had no windows and she hadn't set foot in the other bedroom or en suite since she had changed rooms. Trying to process what Joanna had revealed to her today had taxed every ounce of mental and physical strength. Joanna had let her keep the papers, and time and again she went back to the photograph. She also noted that the doctor's signature committing her to the asylum was Oliver Franklyn. And that date, 1891. According to the attribution on the poem, the same year Lydia Warren Carmody died.

The graffiti on the living room wall still taunted her. As soon as her stitches were out and she had healed sufficiently to be able to stretch without pain, she would redecorate. But, for now, the only thing she could do was try and ignore it as best she could. Not easy when every wall was covered in scrawls.

She poured herself a glass of red wine, carried the bottle into the living room, and placed it and her glass on coasters on a small table within reach.

For once there was a decent film on television and she settled down to watch *The Shape of Water.*

Absorbed in the touching story, she topped up her glass and sipped from it, but not for long.

A massive curl of writhing shadows began in the far corner of the room. It brought a torrent of wind, knocking over the half-full bottle, which spilled its contents, like blood, saturating the carpet. The force of the wind smashed the bottle against the wall, shattering it.

Carol cowered on the settee, unable to flee. Something knocked the glass out of her hand, staining the newly cleaned fabric.

Across the room, a shadow separated from the main one and settled into the shape of a young girl. She looked at Carol through dark eyes, set in a bloodless white face. Carol cried out.

The girl from the window.

The child grimaced, showing rotten teeth. A flick of her hand and the iPod sprang into life on its deck, pelting out Guns N' Roses' 'Sweet Child O' Mine' at full volume.

Someone hammered on the door. The volume rose even higher on the iPod; Axl Rose screamed out the lyrics.

The child threw back her head and laughed. The larger shadow settled itself into the form of Arabella Marsden.

"You…." Carol's mouth ran dry and no more words would come out.

The noise was so loud from the iPod, Carol was sure her eardrums would burst. The hammering on the door grew louder. Someone was banging on the outer glass doors as well, but she couldn't move. She was paralyzed and Arabella had to be responsible.

Arabella raised her hand, fingers pointing toward Carol, her expression a snarl. "You have no place here in this time or any other. You do not belong." Her words came to Carol through her mind rather than her tortured ears.

Carol found her voice at last, screaming over the music, "You're the one who doesn't belong here. Get back to your own time and leave me alone!"

Arabella flicked her fingers and Carol was flung off the settee and crashed into the wall. A mist descended and she passed into oblivion.

CHAPTER EIGHT

Carol opened her eyes. A nurse and a doctor stood over her. She was back in hospital, mercifully in her own time.

"You're awake. Excellent," the doctor said, smiling at her. "I have to tell you that you hit your head quite badly and this caused some swelling on the brain, so we put you in a medically induced coma for a week while your body healed itself. We've brought you out of this today, but you'll need to stay in hospital for a while so we can carry out some tests and make sure everything's okay before we send you home."

Carol listened to the doctor, heard his words, but they made no sense. She surveyed the room, four beds, one of which was hers, all of which were occupied. A lingering smell of food made her stomach clutch. "I don't remember…."

"You were found on the floor of your apartment. It seems you may have had a little too much wine and passed out after hitting your head hard against a wall. There was quite a mess, I understand."

Arabella Marsden. And that child. Now she remembered. "I have to get back—"

"I don't think so. You're far too weak and you need to rest. Someone else is taking care of things at home. A neighbor. Joanna Lawrenson, I believe."

"Joanna. Yes." Carol tapped into a vague memory that should be much clearer. "I don't remember what happened."

"Alcohol can have that effect."

"But I don't drink much."

"The bottle was smashed so it's impossible to know for sure how much you had drunk, but more than one glass at least. How's your head? You took quite a bashing when you hit that wall."

"I was thrown."

The doctor looked perplexed. "You were on your own when they found you."

"I was thrown. I remember that much."

The doctor shook his head and made a rapid note before replacing the pen in his pocket. "Rest now and we'll see how you are tomorrow."

"Arabella Marsden."

"Who?"

"Arabella Marsden. That's the name of the woman who threw me against the wall."

"Sorry, that name doesn't mean a thing to me. All I know is the paramedics said you were alone. Officers from the Fire Brigade had to break in, but don't worry about your apartment. Your neighbor's arranged for it to be made secure. Now sleep and everything will seem much clearer tomorrow."

Carol closed her eyes. She hoped so because, right now, nothing made any sense at all. She tried to remember incidents from her recent past but her thoughts were dominated by Arabella Marsden and the hideous doctor, hell-bent on destroying her mind and sanity.

The present seemed far away, lost in a dream.

My name is Carol Shaughnessy and I live at Waverley.... Waverley Asylum. No. Waverley....

It wouldn't come to her. However hard she concentrated, she couldn't remember her address.

I went to school at....

Another blank.

I work at....

Maybe the aftereffects of the coma, or the swelling that had forced them to induce one in the first place. That had to be it.

Joanna Lawrenson.... Neighbor....

The name seemed familiar but it conjured up no image.

My name is Carol.... Carol....

She couldn't remember her surname. Or how old she was. Where she had grown up. The name of anyone she knew at any time in her life. All drew a blank.

It was as if she had never existed before this time.

* * *

It grew worse over the next few days. They transferred her to a Psychiatric Ward, where the days blended into each other and she spent her time staring out of the window, or engaged in endless childish board games.

She attended group therapy but participated little. How could she when she didn't know who she was anymore? All she knew was what they told her, but at least she wasn't violent. "No danger to herself or others," she had overheard a doctor saying. She had felt something pass out of her and she was glad to be rid of it.

Three weeks later, they discharged her. She would continue her treatment 'in the community' as they put it. By now, she had learned her name, date of birth, address and work place. She could recite them by rote. Not that they meant much to her. The occasional flash of recognition, the odd trace of a memory perhaps.

Carol returned to Waverley Court with Joanna, who came to collect her. She still could remember precious little of any former friendship but acted as if she could. She found it easier that way. Carol remembered to thank Joanna for having the windows repaired and also for getting decorators in to cover up the graffiti. *What graffiti?* The settee too had been cleaned and no one would ever have guessed the place had been in the shambles that Joanna had told her about.

Joanna had also smoothed over the neighbors at numbers one and two by telling them Carol had experienced a seizure, fallen against the iPod and somehow switched it on at full volume. When they heard about that, they were almost sympathetic, or so she told Carol.

Her first night back, Carol got ready for bed early, at around ten. A headache nagged at her temples so she opened the bathroom cabinet and took out a packet of paracetamol. She was about to close it when she saw something that made her gasp. She picked it up and twisted it in her fingers. A black Sharpie pen. Instantly, her brain triggered off a series of flashbacks.

The Sharpie in her hand. Writing on the bathroom wall, scrawling over the walls in the living room. Taking a hammer to the china in the kitchen cupboards and closing the cabinet on the devastation within. Drinking red wine, deliberately pouring it over the furnishings. Turning up the iPod. Music blaring out. A fierce, white-hot rage burning inside her. Anger against the people that could afford to live in this place. Uncontrollable jealousy that they had so much and she had so little.

Farther back her mind drifted, farther still, to a filthy basement. She wielded a hammer, bringing it down on a man who had hurt her so many times. *Jonah.* Unseen hands had helped to tether him and she ignored his pleas for mercy. She would show him none. The voice wouldn't let her. Blow after blow, the sickening crunch of bones, his cries weakening and then silent. Still she hit him, with a force far more than her own. He lay there, dead, at the bottom of a derelict building she didn't recognize.

All her anger and thirst for revenge had been kept hidden from her conscious mind, fueled by a devil that seethed within her, urging her, feeding on bursts of negative energy, searching for more but finding nothing.

Carol stared at the Sharpie, quietly returned it to the cabinet and shut the door.

Almost as soon as her head hit the pillow, she found herself back in that awful place again. She came to in the chair they had put her in, her wrists and ankles restrained.

A rough cotton shift, stained with blood, chafed her skin. Her head pounded and felt as if a weight had been pressed down on it.

Dr. Franklyn's face loomed in front of her. No sign of Arabella Marsden or Hester this time. Carol remained there long enough to see he held a bloody drill in his hand. Some sort of matter clung to it. Something that gleamed white. A sickening lurch thrust her back into the present – to a world that felt more unfamiliar to her than the one she had slipped into. She sat bolt upright, her skin crawling as if a thousand insects had taken up residence, determined to explore every inch of her body. Her raw, dry throat stung and she became aware of the staleness of her breath. The sudden chill of the room enveloped her in an icy blanket and she grabbed her dressing gown, wrapping it tightly around her. The stench hit her in the hall. She retched at the mixture of ammonia and stale sweat. It didn't belong in this sweet-smelling apartment and, at that moment, she didn't feel she did either.

Disoriented, she stumbled on icy feet to the kitchen. It seemed unfamiliar. She was seeing it through someone else's eyes. Someone not used to stainless-steel sinks and modern kitchen units. Someone who, nevertheless, felt grateful to be free and safe from whatever lay inside the walls of Waverley Asylum.

She was still in the dream. Part of her anyway. Living the nightmare of being Lydia Warren Carmody.

Who am I? Lydia? Or Carol? Or…?

She sank slowly down onto the cold, tiled floor. Darkness wrapped around her, warming her after the frosty cold of the apartment. She gave herself up to it, grateful of its cocoon.

Deeper…deeper…her mind led her down swirling corridors, past lines of women all dressed the same in their long brown dresses, all staring at her through empty, hopeless eyes.

They vanished and she was alone in a room with only one small, barred window, too high for her to see out of, its only function to provide meager light.

Gray slivers of it crept in, creating faint checkered patterns on the dirty stone floor.

The walls had been whitewashed, but so long ago most of it had peeled away. She knew the heavy wooden door would be locked from the outside, but she checked anyway, moving on unsteady feet and trembling legs. Her head throbbed with agonizing force and she put her hand to it, finding rough bandages.

The drill. They had used a drill on her head. Penetrated her brain. Her left hand felt weak. When she lifted her arm, she had poor control and no strength. The left side of her face felt numb, as if the nerves had been damaged. Her vision in her left eye seemed oddly blurred, as if the lid was stuck half open, half closed, and her unsteady gait resulted from dragging her left leg.

They have crippled me.

Memories returned in short blasts. Disjointed and out of order. Were they even *her* memories?

The door unlocked and Arabella Marsden entered.

Carol tried to make her mouth work, but her control was limited to the right side only. "What…do…you…want…from… me?"

"You are no longer of any use to us. You weren't suitable. Too damaged. Here." She tapped her head.

"I…don't…understand. Suitable?" The strain of trying to speak proved too much. A trickle of saliva traveled down her chin.

"The spirit that lives inside you lived inside me for a time. An ancient soul, restless and full of wrath. She is known as the One and the Many. Her handmaiden, Hester, brought you to us and she entered you, but—"

She was interrupted by the doctor who entered, his white coat stained with blood flecks. Hers?

"Everything is ready," he said, dispassionately. "Bring her."

An orderly wheeled in a creaking wooden chair and roughly positioned Carol onto it. He wheeled her past a silent line of women. He opened a door and inside were two beds – one surrounded by instruments, rubber tubes, strange and unfamiliar machines. The other bed was occupied.

The orderly unceremoniously hauled Carol out of the wheelchair and she fell to the floor. The woman in the other bed rushed to her aid.

"I…know…you," Carol said, her mind fumbling for a name.

"Nessa," the woman said. "I'm Nessa. We've met before."

PART TWO
…SHADOWS BREATHE

CHAPTER NINE

Vanessa…Vanessa….

The voice echoed from far away. I couldn't reach it. I knew I had to somehow, but I couldn't. My feet moved like lead weights, barely supporting my body. My nightdress brushed my ankles and darkness shrouded me except for a faint glimmer of light dead ahead.

I expended every effort of my clouded brain to force my feet to move forward. One step…two…no. The next step wouldn't come. But it *had* to.

Vanessa….

The voice seemed ever farther away. I had no idea how. Slow I might be, but I was moving forward. A little. Tiny faltering steps, but forward.

The light grew dimmer. Somehow, against all reason, it was moving away from me.

Don't leave me.

It flickered once. Twice.

Out.

My screams echoed off walls, reverberating round and round. I must be in a tunnel. An echo chamber. I reached out my hands and touched something cold, solid, slippery. I ran my fingers up and down. Not one ridge. Maybe steel. Not wood. Satin smooth. Stone? I was too confused to make sense of it.

No other sound reached my ears. The voice had gone. Only my breathing and my tortuous efforts to move forward remained.

Or was I going backward? Maybe the light hadn't moved away from me. *I* had moved away from *it*. Where was this place anyway? Why couldn't I remember coming here? So many questions and all the while my body didn't seem to belong to me anymore.

It had let me down. Betrayed me. Ever since....

No, I wouldn't think about that now. Concentrate. I must get out of here.

One step...two...*for God's sake, move.*

Left hand sliding along the wall an inch at a time.

Then

Clamor.

Voices. All speaking at once. Cutlery clattering. Or maybe instruments. Not musical. Medical. That made sense, although for the life of me I hadn't a clue why.

The light blinked on. Closing in on me.

"Vanessa...Vanessa. Can you hear me?"

The voice. A woman. Unfamiliar. The name. My name.

The wall slipped away. I felt nothing with my left hand. I raised my right, stretched it around me in a wide arc. Nothing. Then....

"Time to wake up now, Vanessa."

The tunnel vanished. I struggled to open my eyes. A nurse smiled down at me.

I tried to speak but my throat closed up. Stinging pain like the worst sore throat I could remember.

"Don't try to speak yet unless you feel comfortable. You had a breathing tube in so you'll be a bit sore for a day or two. I'll get the doctor to come and see you."

She patted my hand. Exhaustion overwhelmed me as my memory returned. Hospital. The Royal and Waverley, with a reputation as one of the best cancer treatment facilities in the country. I had had an operation. Oh God, yes. The operation.

A smiling young man appeared in my field of vision.

"Good to see you awake, Vanessa. How are you feeling?"

I tried to answer him, my voice no more than a frog-like croak.

"That good, huh?" He grinned. "You're one of Miss Gavras's patients, aren't you? She's tied up with someone else right now but she'll be along to see you as soon as she can."

"How…did…it…go?" I managed and didn't like the split-second shadow that passed over his face.

"Miss Gavras will explain everything when she sees you. Try and get some rest. There's still anesthetic washing around your body."

Yet another wave of fear grabbed my nerves and sent acid shooting up into my throat. More bad news. Well, that was nothing new. I had experienced this countless times in the past year or so. That was the trouble with my condition. It was unusual and didn't behave within usual parameters.

Enough anesthetic remained inside me to send me back off to sleep. Mercifully, dream-free this time.

I awoke to someone gently shaking my arm and opened my eyes to see the serious, compassionate face of my consultant oncologist, Maryam Gavras.

"How did it go?" I asked, my voice a little stronger than earlier, but my throat still burning. The accompanying nurse handed me a beaker of water with ice floating in it. I drank and it soothed the rawness.

"Not too much all in one go," the nurse said, gently taking the beaker off me and placing it on the bedside cupboard.

I didn't like the half-frown on her face. When she took my hand, I knew bad news was imminent.

A younger nurse, bearing the logo of the local university on her pale blue and white striped uniform, brought two chairs and left, after closing the curtains around my bed. They only did that for examinations and imparting bad news. The other patients – no more than five of them if the bay was full – would probably guess something was up. I heard the clatter of knives and forks. By the smell of it, cottage pie was on the menu today. My stomach clenched. I wouldn't be eating any of it.

Maryam and the nurse sat on either side of me.

"I found something I wasn't happy with," Maryam began. I swallowed, ignoring the gravel and broken glass in my throat. "I stopped the operation I was due to perform and we switched our attention to your vagina. So I haven't performed the scheduled vulvectomy today."

That should have been good news, but I knew worse was coming.

"I have performed a mapping biopsy of your vagina and sent the tissue off for analysis. I wish I could give you better news, Nessa, but I'm afraid we are going to have to schedule you for a much bigger operation. We need to perform a vaginectomy, full hysterectomy and vulvectomy and you will need vulval reconstruction. I am proposing to bring someone in from Moreton Grange to do that because they're the best. You will have the most experienced and talented people working for you, Nessa. I can promise you that."

I knew of Moreton Grange. It specialized in plastic surgery and had a burns unit, along with a reputation as world class. Yes, with the team here and someone from Moreton Grange, I would have the best.

But with the operation, I would lose so much. No vagina. No more sex. Ever.

I struggled to concentrate. "I have to have a full hysterectomy, so that's ovaries, cervix…the lot?"

Maryam nodded. "To be honest, the hysterectomy is nothing to worry about in terms of your recovery. We should be able to perform that through a laparoscopy – keyhole surgery. It's the vaginectomy and, of course, the vulvectomy, that will need time to heal, but we'll be with you every step of the way." She squeezed my hand.

I nodded, trying to hoist myself up in bed, feeling the multiple stabbings of needle-like pain emanating from my much-biopsied vagina. Irrational thoughts went through my head. *At least that won't hurt much longer. It'll be out soon. In the meantime my body will go through the motions and wasted effort of attempting to heal it. Save your energy for when I really need you.*

"Please will you do me a favor?"

"Of course," Maryam said softly.

"Paul will be in…." I glanced at the wall clock. "He'll be here any second to see me. Please could you tell him what you told me? I may get it wrong. It's a lot to take in."

Maryam smiled. "Of course I will. And, yes, it is a lot to take in. I'll make sure he understands the implications and extent of your condition and the surgery we need to do to cure you."

Cure me? "So I will get through this?"

"Oh yes. We'll know more when we get the results back, but I believe we have caught this early enough so that with appropriate – if radical – surgery, and possible radiotherapy afterward, there is every chance you will be fine. I won't deny you are in for a few uncomfortable months, but, as I said, we will be here for you every step of the way."

"Thank you," I said and a tiny part of me felt reassured. Only a tiny part. But it was a start.

* * *

Paul's ashen face told me Maryam had headed him off and spoken to him.

"You know?" I asked.

He nodded, tears filling his eyes. He sat on the chair recently vacated by Maryam. "We're going to get through this,' he said.

"I know," I said.

He kissed me on the forehead and then on both cheeks.

"You know my vagina has to go," I said.

He nodded. "It hasn't been doing much for you recently anyway, has it?" His attempt at levity almost worked. Not quite.

"It's been so painful. Every time we tried…. And the bleeding. It was only a few spots and I thought it was the menopause. What do they call it? Vaginal atrophy. The first consultant I saw agreed with me."

"Until he thought it was something else as well."

"Lichen sclerosus. The symptoms fitted the bill. I know. I looked them up."

"But it wasn't that, was it? Weeks and months have been wasted on the wrong diagnosis."

"Don't get angry, Paul. It won't do us any good."

The look on his face wrenched my gut.

"I know. I'm sorry. I just want to do something. I feel so… powerless, I suppose."

"Me too."

"Your voice sounds awful. Water?"

I nodded. "I have to sip. It was the breathing tube. It dried my throat out well and truly."

"Poor kid."

"Hardly a kid at fifty-seven."

"You've aged well."

"At least I shall be able to say that there's less of me than when you married me – as long as I don't specify in which way."

Paul leaned over me, kissing my head. I smelled his aftershave. That familiar warm scent of Armani. Tears welled up in my eyes and I willed them not to spill over. I would not cry. I would not give cancer the satisfaction of crying over it. I would not be a cancer *sufferer*. I would be a cancer *survivor*.

A tall, slim woman approached us, a friendly smile lighting up her pixie-like face.

"I didn't want to interrupt but I did want to introduce myself. You saw my colleague when you came in for your pre-op and she told you she was standing in for me because I was away on holiday? I'm Sandra, your Macmillan Specialist nurse. I'm here to help you through the next few weeks and months, both in hospital and when you go home after your treatment. You know you've got a great team of oncologists and clinical nurse specialists here in the hospital, looking after your medical needs, but I'm here to help with the other stuff; when you need someone to talk to, or if you need any financial or other practical advice."

"Lovely to meet you, Sandra. This is Paul, my husband."

He extended his hand and she shook it. "Pleased to meet you, Sandra."

"May I sit for a moment?"

"Of course." I indicated the vacant chair and she sat down.

"Maryam has brought me up to speed. I'm so sorry it wasn't better news."

"We're trying to come to terms with it," I said.

"And that's why you've got me. I'm your support service. Your wingman if you like. You can contact me at the office and I'll be popping in while you're here. When you go home, if it's all right with you, I'll ring you the day after you're discharged and then keep in touch a couple of times a week until you come back in for the operation. But if you need to talk to me in the meantime, don't wait until our next scheduled call, just ring the office and they'll get a message to me. Whatever you do, don't sit at home brooding and worrying. You can ask me anything. I'm here for you."

"Thank you."

* * *

Tiredness finally overwhelmed me again. Sandra left and when my eyes wouldn't stay open any longer, Paul slipped away, promising to return the following day to take me home.

I managed a couple of spoons of ice cream, which soothed my burning throat a little, but I couldn't face anything more substantial, even though they told me I could eat. My stomach had tied itself in knots and my brain ached with the crashing thoughts slamming through it.

Sleep came hard that night. The bay was mercifully quiet, my neighbors preferring to keep to themselves, for which I was grateful. I didn't feel like making any small talk. I discovered I had four fellow patients and gathered a couple of them at least were wrapped up in their own personal misery. The occasional muffled sob being a dead giveaway.

Finally, I drifted off, but not into a peaceful dream world. I was back in the tunnel.

A ghostly light, misty and silvery gray, swirled around me. In the distance, indistinct voices murmured – chanting, like plainsong but more fractured. I touched the wall to my left, smooth as I remembered it and cold to the touch. It gave off a dull sheen. I concentrated, willing my right foot to take a step forward. It obeyed. Now my left. It too moved a few inches, but the effort drained me of my already depleted energy. Needles of pain stabbed at me from inside my diseased vagina.

A shadow moved in front of me, partially blocking out the light. A figure, in silhouette, backlit. I couldn't make out any features, but I knew she was female even though she appeared to have shaved her head for some reason. She seemed familiar, as if I'd met her somewhere before. She stood silently, watching me, but I couldn't see her face.

"Who are you?" I asked. She didn't move. Statue-like, she continued to stand as the light behind her expanded and contracted.

It's breathing.

But I couldn't tell if *she* was or not.

"Please tell me who you are."

Nothing. Still the light faded in and out. In and out. In and out.

I took another shaky step forward, leaning against the icy wall for support, feeling again the shards of pain. I imagined my skin cells already multiplying in an ultimately futile attempt to heal my wounds.

Without warning, the figure turned to one side and winked out. One second there, the next...gone.

The light settled back to its swirling fog-like transience. I resumed my struggle forward. I had to get out of this tunnel. I looked up but only blackness greeted me. To my right, a few feet away, another wall – the mirror image of the one I now clung to – soared upward.

The chanting voices stilled. Inch by agonizing inch I drew closer to the source of the light. Surely the end of the tunnel.

The light snapped off as if someone had thrown a switch. I held my breath.

Then I felt it.

Feathery. Hardly there at all. But it stroked my arm, raising goosebumps. It moved up to my neck and caressed it, before moving onto my face. I closed my eyes. The sensation of being touched in such a tender and sensuous way contrasted so sharply with the terror of being trapped alone in the dark.

But not alone. Something – or someone – had joined me.

"Who are you? Please tell me."

A ghost of a breath on my cheek. The faintest hint of a kiss.

And it was gone.

I opened my eyes. The light had come on. Brighter than before. Or...somehow I had moved much closer to the source. It grew so bright I shielded my eyes from it, letting go of the wall in the process. Taking care to avoid the worst of the glare, I looked around me. I stood on a floor I recognized from the hospital. The shiny walls had been replaced with those of a corridor, like the one on my ward. Above me, fluorescent lights. One a little farther down flicked red slightly then steadied itself. The corridor was deserted.

And then it wasn't. Two nurses thrust open double doors at one end. I stood stock-still, not knowing if I was dreaming or this was reality, and if it was, how had I arrived here? I should be in bed, asleep.

Then I realized that was exactly what one of the nurses was saying to me.

She took my arm. "Let's get you back to your bay now. It's very late."

"What time is it?" I croaked.

"About four. It will be breakfast time in three hours. You'll be shattered. What were you doing out here? Going to the bathroom?"

I hadn't been aware of it but my bladder now gave a lurch. "Yes. Yes, I need to go to the bathroom."

The nurses exchanged looks. One of them moved away. The other took my arm. "Come along then, I'll walk with you."

Walking still presented some difficulties. I felt about ninety years old, shuffling along.

"Don't worry," the nurse said. "You're bound to be a bit shaky after the anesthetic. You'll be up and about again in no time."

I sat down on the toilet and waited, bracing myself. Sure enough, as I started to pee, a feeling of being shredded by broken glass hit me. When I finished and patted myself dry with toilet paper, I noticed spots of bright red blood. I mentioned it to the nurse as I emerged from the bathroom.

"Don't worry. That's perfectly normal. There are so many blood vessels down there. If it gets any heavier, let us know, but what you've described is only to be expected. It'll pass within a few hours."

One tiny relief in my increasingly baffling world. "Is it normal to have vivid nightmares? I mean ones that are so real you can feel the cold and texture of a surface and of the floor you're standing on, and then you wake up and you're actually there?"

She looked at me curiously. "Is that what happened when we found you in the corridor?"

I nodded.

"I have had patients complain about having nightmares after their operations and others who have described beautiful dreams. What was yours about?"

I described the tunnel, the strange light. "And I saw a figure, silhouetted against the light. I couldn't make her out. She never spoke but I do remember she had a shaved head and for some reason she seemed familiar."

The nurse's face grew paler as I described the apparition, if indeed that was what it was. "Are you all right?" I asked her.

"Yes, it's weird, that's all. A colleague of mine on another ward told me that a patient a few weeks ago described exactly the same dream as you've done, right down to the woman you saw."

A chill swept through me. "How extraordinary. Is she still in the hospital?"

The nurse shook her head. "Now, come on, you must get some sleep." I wanted to ask her more, but we had entered my bay and the other patients seemed to be sleeping. I didn't want to disturb them.

She pulled the sheet and blanket over me and left. The next thing I remembered was waking up to the rattle of teacups and the clanging of a metal trolley.

* * *

All thoughts of nightmares and strange figures deserted me as I concentrated on getting ready to go back home. Paul would be along at two o'clock when we hoped I would be discharged.

Maryam came in on her rounds late morning. This time she was smiling. "You have a lot more color in your cheeks today. How are you feeling?"

"Oh, I'm okay." I hoped I sounded cheerier than I felt. It seemed to work.

"Good. I'll see you in my clinic on Wednesday. They'll give you an appointment card when we discharge you later. Try not to worry too much and keep off the internet. You'll only see bad stuff there. Everyone's cancer experience is different and it's important to remember that."

"I'll try. I'm certainly not going to do any more internet research. I frightened the life out of myself when I looked up lichen sclerosus."

Maryam's grin lit up her face. "I'm sure you did."

* * *

Back home, I carried on pretty much as usual. Once I had become ill I had opted to apply for early retirement from the university where I lectured in Modern History. I still hadn't heard if my application would be successful and, meanwhile, remained signed off sick. Without my work, a void had opened up in my life. I brooded and couldn't settle. My active mind had to focus on something and, in the absence of my job, concentrated itself on my cancer to the point where all I wanted to do was scream my head off. I hadn't realized how much of myself had been defined by my career up until then.

Searching for something to fill my time became a priority. If I didn't have another interest to concentrate on, the horrors of what lay ahead swept in like a tsunami, threatening to overwhelm me. I couldn't allow that to happen. Paul was doing his best to keep it all together and I had to do my part.

For the first week I cleaned the apartment, polishing surfaces, scrubbing the kitchen, emptying all the cupboards and washing down everything within an inch of its existence. I cooked Paul a meal from scratch every evening and explained away my own poor appetite by saying I had eaten at lunchtime and wasn't hungry. I don't think he believed me.

Still I cleaned. I took down curtains, washed, ironed and put them back up, wincing as the forbidden stretching threatened the stitches, which were surely by now already dissolving. Thankfully no more blood appeared. I hadn't done myself any more harm than had already taken root inside me.

Considering the turmoil in my mind, I slept remarkably well. No nightmares or strange apparitions to bother me. Probably all that physical activity was wearing me out each day.

When the last curtain was washed and put back up, all that remained was the day-to-day housework stuff. Not enough to occupy me. I turned to our heaving bookshelves. Forty or more books that I hadn't yet read. I started by devouring Bill Clinton's weighty autobiography in a day, followed by a mixed diet of historical fiction, horror – where I rediscovered my love of Ramsey Campbell's work – biography, Barbara Erskine, Martin Millar and a collection of cozy crime novels I had picked up at a charity book sale five years earlier. I had always been a fast reader and the forty books dwindled all too quickly. They provided me with much-needed escapism and entertainment but, after a further ten days, I was down to the last few and in no mood for light, frothy romances I couldn't even remember buying.

The days moved swiftly on. My visit to Maryam produced an appointment for the operation. The next day that was brought forward. Clearly I was being treated as a priority case. Good in one way, but in another, this added to my teetering list of worries. If I was so much of a priority they had brought the operation forward, that must mean they were seriously concerned about my deteriorating condition.

And I knew I was deteriorating. Despite the soothing lotion I applied twice a day, the angry red rash had spread so that it covered almost every morsel of skin on my vulva. At first it had itched, then it had stung and now it burned, and I found I needed to change my dampened panties up to four times a day. At home, I sat with legs wide apart, and my days of wearing jeans were over, the friction being too great. I constantly fidgeted, trying to get comfortable, to gain some relief from the relentless discomfort. Showering helped, for a few minutes. Directing the shower head onto the rash brought some margin of relief.

Paul laughed at my accompanying gasps of, "Oooooh…aaaah."

He stood at the partially open bathroom door. "Are you having fun in there?"

I threw a sponge at him and missed. His laugh became a guffaw. It lightened the tension.

We had never had children. It simply did not happen and we were both so wrapped up in our careers anyway. Right now, I was glad. I had no idea whether what I had could be genetic. If it was and I had passed it on to my progeny.... It didn't bear thinking about. Thankfully, that was one worry I didn't have.

One morning, two days before I was due to go into hospital, I stood staring out of the bedroom window, over the sand dunes to the Irish Sea. A dramatic sky, laden with rain clouds, and a few people out walking their dogs. A container ship bound for the docks nearby sailed steadily past. What lay in those containers? Furniture made in China perhaps. Machine parts, tractors, cars. The ship sailed out of my line of sight. An excited dog – a Golden Labrador, I think – leaped up at his master. Or maybe his mistress. Hard to tell with the hoodie and jeans.

Normal life.

Life that, up until a year or so ago, I had lived. Before the first signs that something was wrong and the ensuing medical appointments and failed treatments. Before someone mentioned the dreaded word.

Cancer.

When we first moved here, I used to enjoy walking along the promenade, leaning over the railings and tasting the salt in the air, feeling the wind through my hair. Somewhere along the line I had lost the habit. Now I would rediscover it. Who cared if it might pour down any moment? I had no idea when I would be able to walk any distance again.

I grabbed my coat, thrust my feet into my trainers and pocketed my keys. Five minutes later, I was strolling along, hearing the waves break on the shore. I deliberately walked against the wind so I could feel its icy coldness slapping my face, the November wind chilling my cheeks and freezing my lips. Salt crusted my mouth and I crunched grains of sand. As I ventured farther from home, the wind picked up to almost a gale, whistling and whipping up more sand. On the beach, people with their dogs scurried, eager to escape the oncoming storm.

"Bring it on," I yelled, my voice shipped away by the wind.

I clung onto the railings as the gale buffeted my body and threatened to knock me over. My eyes teared up and mingled with raindrops which quickly gathered momentum. That's when I knew I should go home.

"Fuck that!" I cried. Too soon I would have to do what I was told by doctors, nurses, all and sundry. If this was to be my last day of freedom in God alone knew how long, then let it be like this. Alone. Me and the elements. The raw wind and the majestic sea.

An urge to scream hit me and this time I gave in to it, screaming loud, long, hard, all my anger, frustration, pain. The injustice of cancer. *Why me?* Fear I had suppressed for months shot up to the surface and I screamed it out. The harsh wind grabbed it all, greedily wrenching it out of me, tossing it out over the sea, into oblivion, cleansing me, a sense so addictive I didn't want it to end, or to go back home to reality, to Paul's sadness and fears. To my own. A part of me wanted to ride on that wind. That old Doors song came into my mind. Jim Morrison's husky baritone…. 'Riders on the Storm…'

"You should go home now."

The unfamiliar voice, right behind me, came unexpectedly. I jumped and spun round to face a stranger, muffled in a warm parka, the fur-trimmed hood half-covering her face, yet for some unaccountable reason I felt I knew her.

"I'm sorry, have we met before?"

The woman didn't answer. Without another word, she moved on. I wiped my rain-misted eyes and saw her fade into the distance. Yet floating back from her, I could have sworn came the words, "You're next."

* * *

The night before the operation arrived all too quickly. A chilly one, clear skies and a bright full moon cast a ghostly, silvery-white glow across the water. I hugged myself as I stood at the window. In the bedroom, Paul slept on, gently snoring. My thoughts jumbled together like tangled octopus tentacles. Between my legs, the rash burned like some raging monster, my body battling against itself – an unholy war waged for control of my most intimate parts. I attempted to reassure myself it would all be over soon. One way or the other.

Getting comfortable had long been a thing of the past. If I sat for more than a few minutes I had to shift position. Lying in bed, if I didn't fall asleep immediately, the old familiar feeling of needing to empty my bladder persisted. I knew nothing but a trickle would emerge and every drop would sting and ratchet up the pain. Even here, standing up, what I had at first taken for chronic cystitis gave me no peace and sent me off to the bathroom on a fruitless mission. I sat down, gritted my teeth, clung onto the sink and let the few drops disperse. I swear someone took razor blades to my vulva.

Tomorrow someone actually would – or at any event a scalpel.

I checked my watch. Just after eleven. I wouldn't be able to drink anything after midnight. I wandered into the kitchen and made a cup of tea. What would I feel like tomorrow? After they had taken away most of what made me female? Strangely that part of it didn't upset me nearly as much as I would have imagined. By now, in so much discomfort and actual pain, I wanted all those diseased, and potentially diseased, parts out of me.

I sat carefully on the sofa, trying as far as possible not to set up a fresh wave of burning. As usual, it didn't work. I sipped my tea and contemplated switching on television. If I kept the volume low I wouldn't disturb Paul. I flipped through the TV guide. Nothing took my fancy. These days, I had the concentration of an agitated gnat anyway.

I finished my tea. Now what?

Solitaire, or Patience as we used to call it when I was a child. I must have been around five or six when I learned how to play the game. My parents had thought it a fun way to help me with numeracy. I asked my mother why it was called Patience.

"Because you need the patience of a saint to keep going until you get out," she said, laughing. I never did find out the true origin. Now there are so many variations of Solitaire, but I always fell back on the original version. I fished out a much-used pack of cards from a drawer in the sideboard.

I sat at the glass dining table in the window, with the curtains drawn back so a little of the moonlight could filter in, casting its spectral glow.

Game after game I played as the hours ticked by, until a faint pale-yellow glow in the sky told me morning was approaching.

A noise from the bedroom. Paul was stirring. I put my cards away and he appeared at the doorway, dressing gown on, feet bare, yawning and in need of a shave.

"You're up early."

"I couldn't sleep." He needn't know I had been up all night. "Anyway, I'll be doing plenty of that later." I forced a smile on my face and Paul returned the gesture.

He turned quickly and headed for the kitchen. "Are you still allowed water?"

"Not until I come round."

Half an hour later, we were on the road, headed for the Royal and Waverley. We spoke little; our thoughts preoccupied with the unknown that lay ahead.

The next few hours passed in a blur. We were shown into the same ward I had occupied previously and to the same bed. A pleasantly smiling nurse called Joyce drew the curtains around us and I undressed and put on the hospital gown she gave me. Then I climbed into bed, onto a surprisingly comfortable mattress.

"I'm sure this is thicker than the last one," I said.

"You're the star turn," Paul said. "Remember Maryam said most of the doctors and nursing staff had never seen an operation like yours before. Three surgeons no less."

"The viewing gallery, or whatever it's called, is going to be packed. I wonder if they have an interval and serve ice creams."

Paul squeezed my hand. "You never know, but when you come around, I'll be here."

Bloods were taken. "My arm's like a pin cushion these days," I joked. Blood pressure. Temperature. All were taken and duly noted. Apparently I was within normal parameters. At my pre-op appointment they had checked all this, plus weight, body mass index, swabs to check for MRSA, lifestyle questions. Okay, I fudged a bit on the alcohol side. Hell, I had to have one vice, didn't I? I quit smoking twenty or more years ago, never did illegal drugs, and sex? Not me, guv. Not anymore.

Joyce inserted a cannula in the back of my left hand. "This way you'll stop being a pin cushion." I smiled. She left us alone for a few minutes before reappearing, accompanied by a tall, slim woman with a cheerful smile and a clipboard.

"Vanessa. This is Anita and she is your anesthetist."

"Please call me Nessa. I keep thinking I'm back at school and in trouble again."

Joyce grinned, nodded and left. Anita sat on a chair next to me, opposite Paul. I introduced him.

"I just need to go through a simple checklist and then I'll leave you in peace," she said and proceeded to ask me a series of questions. Then concluded with, "I'll be monitoring you all the way. All you need to do is have a nice sleep and dream of somewhere lovely."

"I'll do my best," I said and my brain went into autopilot while it searched around for some suitable location. I could dream I was on a vacation, visiting fabulous sites with Paul. Egypt maybe. Or Paris…. Anywhere as long as it wasn't that bloody tunnel.

After Anita had left us, Maryam arrived. She was her usual calm, reassuring self. "We'll be ready for you in about an hour. I will be leading, Mr. Waring will perform your hysterectomy and then Mr. Shah from Moreton Grange will perform the reconstructive surgery. He is an expert in his field so you are in the best possible hands."

"How long will the operation last?" Paul asked.

"Difficult to say. Maybe four hours, up to six perhaps. Probably best if you go home and we will call you when Nessa is back on the ward. She will be very sleepy."

Maryam left us and minutes later, Joyce appeared with a packet. "These are your lovely stockings," she said, with heavy irony as she removed a pair of restrictive-looking, blue-green pressure socks. "They'll help your circulation while you're not terribly mobile."

She proceeded to tug them on.

"You need muscles for those," I said.

"It's all in the wrist action," she said and gave them a sharp yank over my heels, before rolling them up to my knees. "I guessed your size," she said, standing back and admiring her handiwork. "Spot on."

At least they didn't hurt but I certainly wouldn't have liked to try and get them off by myself. "I don't think they'll make the cover of *Vogue* anytime soon."

Joyce laughed. "Nor the *Nursing Times* either."

Two burly orderlies appeared in the doorway. Joyce acknowledged them. "You're on," she said. "See you when you get back."

A flurry of activity. A hurried kiss and hug with Paul and then I was being whisked away, lying in my bed, staring up at strip light after strip light as we glided down the corridor, into the lift, down, then out, through double doors, yet another corridor, culminating in a further set of double doors and finally into a waiting bay where another nurse waited to greet me.

The television was on. News. I can't remember what it was all about. I picked up a magazine from a small pile she had given me. Lurid headlines. 'My husband was a woman and didn't tell me until our wedding night.' 'I married a dwarf and gave birth to a giant.'

I pushed them away and settled for closing my eyes and trying to will myself out of my body. Between my legs the rash burned. *End of the road for you, sunshine. You're headed for a petri dish and a university research lab.*

The nurse returned. A lock of her blonde hair escaped from behind her ear and she pushed it back absently. "We'll take you down in a minute or two. They're finishing up a small operation and then the theater will be all yours for the rest of the day."

My levity gear kicked in. Humor always helped take my mind off the bad stuff. "I believe it's standing room only. I'm unusual. That's typical of me, you know. I can't get a normal cancer, can I? I have to get one that most people in the medical profession never get to see in their lifetimes. When they all publish their learned papers on me, do you think I'll get royalties?"

The nurse laughed. "You could always ask."

"I could sell my autograph." Behind the nurse, I saw an orderly approaching. My heart thumped its way half out of my chest, or so it seemed. But I had been given an ECG. Normal, I reminded myself just as I thought it was about to explode, and adrenaline pumped its way through me in a fountain of dread. Could I run away? Even at this late stage, I could hop off the gurney and make a dash for it. Over to my left, a set of fire doors. My legs twitched, my brain squealed at me to get out of there.

But where would I go? What about the cancer?

It had to be cut out of me.

And then it was too late anyway. And time seemed to speed up.

The nurse pushed open the double doors. The orderly wheeled me in and the two of them handed me over to the smiling team. Anita was there, ready to send me to sleep. Two scrub nurses smiled with their eyes, their mouths already covered in masks. Maryam said "Hello" and then something that didn't register, but I knew was meant to be reassuring.

Anita told me she was sending me off to sleep. She inserted a needle into my cannula. "Pleasant dreams," she said.

But not for me.

Instead of the boulevards and street cafes of Paris on a bright, warm spring day that I had willed my brain to dream about, I found myself back in the godforsaken tunnel.

Shadows closed in on me, whispering, cloying. I struggled to breathe, my lungs screaming for oxygen.

The light ahead pulsed in and out.

Breathe in…breathe out…in…out…in…out….

Two large almond shapes flickered. They seemed to be fringed, as if with eyelashes but on a giant scale.

I clutched at my throat. A furnace of pain burst through my body.

The shadows swirled and the almond shapes became more defined. They flickered again and again.

They opened.

I screamed. The glaring white of the sclera. The searing vermilion of the irises and the chasm-like black pupils focused on me, burning into my brain, yet freezing my soul. And the evil behind them. I could taste it, rotten, decaying, like eating a corpse.

The eyes had no face, no body and contained no soul. They came straight from hell itself. I screamed and struggled to break free but I couldn't move.

You're next.

* * *

"Nessa…Nessa. Open your eyes." The gentle, familiar voice pulled me back, bathed me in warmth. Sounds drifted into my head. People talking, a smell of clean linen. "Nessa. Let's see those eyes."

"Not the eyes." My voice croaked again as it had after the biopsies. My throat cried out for cold, refreshing water.

I opened my eyes. The light was quite dim. Joyce's smiling face looked into mine. Never had I been so glad to see someone. Despite my throat, I smiled. "Could I have some water please?"

Joyce held the sipping beaker for me. It had a lid on to stop shaking hands spilling the contents. I needed that.

"You gave us a little bit of a fright there for a second. Your blood pressure shot up. But it's all back to normal now. How are you feeling?"

I pointed to my throat. The water soothed it a little, but not much.

"It will be a bit sore for a few days. How's everything down below?"

I felt distant pain, throbbing but muted. "Not too bad."

"On a scale of one to ten where ten is unbearable and one is nonexistent?"

"Around five I think. I'm not sure. Everything feels a bit numb."

"That's the pain relief. We've given you a shot of morphine and you're hooked up to a morphine push. Just press it when you want some more. Don't worry, you can't possibly overdose. It won't let you."

"Thank you."

"You get some rest now." She took the beaker off me. "I'll leave this on your cabinet within reach and if you need a top up, let one of us know. Here's your bell and this one operates the morphine." She handed me the wired push buttons. "You're also hooked up to a leg massager. It will automatically massage your legs through the wraps we've put around them. It may seem a bit of an odd sensation at first but it's necessary to have them on for a few days until you're back on your feet. We have to make sure you don't suffer from embolisms, or blood clots. You can do without all that after what you've just been through. Oh, Maryam's here. I thought she would have gone home by now. Your husband's on his way."

Maryam touched my right hand. "Hello, Nessa. I wanted to pop in to see you. The operation went well and we have sent everything off for a histology report, which we should have back in a week or so."

"So everything is out and reconstruction done?"

"Yes. Mr. Waring and I kept Mr. Shah waiting a little. He has done a wonderful job."

"Thank you."

"And look at you with your sexy, husky voice."

"Bit sore."

"I know."

Paul arrived, paler than when I last saw him. The laughter lines had deepened, as if he had aged ten years. He looked anxiously at Maryam. She turned her winning smile on him.

"I have just been telling Nessa how well everything went."

Five years dropped off him. "Thank God. I was so worried. Over six hours…."

"Only five or so in theater. Nessa took a little longer to wake up. Maybe it was a lovely dream and she wanted to stay there a bit longer?"

I shook my head and wished I hadn't. I felt seasick for a moment. "Nightmare," I croaked. "Two huge eyes…shadows…a tunnel…." I shuddered.

For a second I could have sworn a look of recognition passed over Maryam's face, to be instantly replaced by her usual sunny smile.

"Anyway, you're back with us now. We'll keep you on regular observations overnight and see where we are up to in the morning. Don't wear her out now, Paul."

"I promise. I'll just sit with her for a little while."

"Take all the time you need."

"Thank you," we said in unison.

Maryam left us but the lingering memory of that shocked expression refused to leave me. I hadn't imagined it. Something I had said resonated with her.

CHAPTER TEN

The migraine started the following morning.

I'd suffered with them from the age of three or four but hadn't had one for a few years, yet it began in the same old, sickeningly familiar way.

Joyce had helped me have a bed bath, taking care with all the dressings and the temporary catheter. Not to mention the cannula, still providing me with measured doses of morphine for the pain. That hadn't been as acute as I had feared, but now, leaning back against the freshly changed pillows, a jackhammer began down the right side of my head, quickly rising to a crescendo before I even had time to press my buzzer.

Joyce was there within a couple of minutes. "How are you feeling?" she asked, frowning. "You've lost all the color from your face."

"Rotten all of a sudden. I feel as if I'm going to be sick. Migraine," I said.

"I'll be back in a second."

With the taste of bile in my mouth, I closed my eyes, swallowing hard. I heard the little trolley being wheeled in. It contained everything the nurse needed to perform the routine round of observations. She pressed a disposable bowl in my hands, just as I retched. I struggled to open my eyes, now leaden with pain. A thin trickle of bile dripped into the bowl.

She put the thermometer in my ear, and pressure cuff around my left arm, as my head thumped ever more painfully.

"Your temperature's a little high and your blood pressure is way too low. It's odd because everything came out normally a couple of hours ago."

I opened my eyes as Joyce pulled the sheet aside to get a better look at the urine bag attached to the catheter. She flipped through the notes and I closed my eyes against the pain, which was joined by the shimmering, flashing lights the migraine always brought on.

"I'll get you a couple of paracetamol," she said. "Do you still feel sick?"

"Not now," I said.

"I'll leave you a spare bowl just in case."

I could tell she was concerned, but at that moment I couldn't care less. All I wanted to do was sleep off the banging in my head.

It seemed only seconds later that I opened my eyes and Mr. Waring smiled down at me. "Right. Nessa, we're going to do a couple of tests to check your kidney function, so a couple of nurses will wheel you down."

The banging in my head had subsided a fraction but I still felt weak and listless. The morphine push had been removed. "That may have contributed to the migraine, although you used very little of it."

"The surgical pain isn't too bad, but this headache's awful."

"We'll soon have you fit again, don't worry."

It took Joyce and another nurse to heave me out of bed. I felt enormous, bloated and knives of pain sliced through me. I had no strength and, despite their reassurances that it was all perfectly normal, I felt as if my body was disowning me, getting its revenge for having so much scalpel work. At last, I flopped into the wheelchair they had brought, but I soon realized the extent of my surgery. I bit my lip. Hard.

Joyce stroked my hand. "Are you sure you're up to this? We can try again later if you prefer."

The thought of struggling again into the wheelchair, and of giving up now after all the effort it had taken me to get this far, felt worse than the actual agony I was in. "No, let's do it. It'll soon be over."

I floated on a sea of pain through a series of blood tests before they finally let me return to the ward.

Joyce tucked me in. "How's the pain now?"

I managed a weak laugh. "Which one?"

"Either. Both."

"Head banging again. Nether regions throbbing and stinging."

"I'll get you something."

She returned with a couple of white pills and poured a glass of water. My hand shook as I took it from her.

"Now lay back and try to sleep," Joyce said, placing a cool hand on my forehead.

Closing my eyes eased the pressure a little and I felt myself drifting. Maybe the effect of the pills. Maybe….

A noise roused me. I opened my eyes.

The room had grown dark. A few hours must have passed. Where was Paul? He was supposed to come at visiting time and that surely had to be now. But the other patients appeared to be asleep. Could it be that I had been out for hours? Had he come and gone?

A figure approached my bed. At first, it was in shadow; I couldn't make out any features. It appeared to glide rather than walk – one minute a few feet away, the next right by my bed. Still I couldn't distinguish the face and my eyes watered from straining to see.

Then it opened its eyes.

The gleaming white sclera, brilliant vermilion irises.

I screamed.

Pandemonium.

Patients woke, shouting out. Buzzers echoed down the corridor. The apparition had vanished, but I trembled and shook with fear.

A nurse I didn't know rushed in and over to me and dragged the curtains across. Other nurses soothed the agitated patients outside.

"Whatever's the matter?" the nurse asked me.

"I am so, so sorry. I must have been dreaming, but it felt so real."

"What did?"

"A face. A woman. But not a real woman. A ghost. Oh, I sound crazy. I must have dreamed it and now I've woken everyone up." Tears streamed down my face.

The nurse took my hand. "They'll be all right. Tell me what you saw."

"A sort of…woman…appeared. I couldn't see her properly

but I've seen her before. It's her eyes. They're enormous. No one's eyes could be that big. And the irises are a brilliant red color, with large black pupils that seemed to want to swallow me. It was frightening."

"It must have been. You're still shaking."

Mr. Waring put his head round the curtain. "May I have a word please, nurse?" He smiled at me. "I'll be in to see you shortly."

I lay back against the pillows, feeling stupid and foolish, not to mention guilty for having disturbed so many people's much needed sleep. Rapid whispering – words I couldn't make out – ended with both the nurse and the consultant returning to my side of the curtain.

The nurse smiled at me. "I'll go and make you a nice cup of tea. Sugar?"

"One please."

She left us. Mr. Waring crouched down by my bed. He spoke quietly. "Don't worry. You're not the first and you won't be the last to have nightmares in here. You're a bit of an enigma, aren't you?"

"I don't mean to be."

He smiled. "At least I have *some* good news for you. We have the results of your kidney tests and they're perfectly normal, but, on the flip side, your blood count is way down, so we have two options. We can either treat it over a period of days, maybe a week, to bring it up to speed, or accomplish that much quicker if we perform a blood transfusion. But I must warn you that you will never be able to donate blood again if we do. The decision is entirely yours."

"If you had to recommend though?"

"Blood transfusion. Simply because your recovery would be that much quicker."

"Let's do it. I had one before, years ago, after a car accident."

"Then you're an old hand. I'll get the consent forms for you to sign and we'll get it started right away."

"Thank you. Is Maryam all right?"

"Yes. It's her day off today so I'm covering for her. She'll be back to see you tomorrow. Now, get some rest and try to think happy thoughts."

* * *

A short time later, I was hooked up. Another needle punctured my skin and the bag of whole blood began to drip into me. My heart would need to work hard, pumping all the extra blood around my system. Exhaustion overwhelmed me and I drifted in and out of sleep. When I opened my eyes, it was daylight, the ward a hive of activity and Paul was smiling down at me.

"You've been in the wars, causing mayhem, haven't you?" he said with a grin.

Despite all the sleep, tiredness still enveloped me in its shroud. Even talking proved a burden and my words slurred. "Not... intention...ally."

"They've given you the good stuff I see. Forty per cent proof?"

"At...least." I drifted off again, awaking later to find that at some point Paul had left and Joyce was standing by my bed, attaching a fresh bag of blood to my drip.

"Last one," she said.

Once again I drifted off. Perfect, dreamless sleep. The rhythmic, strong beating of my heart lulled me. I stirred briefly to find my head no longer ached and I lay comfortably, free from anything other than a steady dull throb between my legs.

I awoke finally with a raging thirst. I pressed my buzzer and Joyce joined me. "You're looking much better. You've certainly slept. We did observations every two hours and you slept right through them. The night staff tell me the same thing. How do you feel now, apart from thirsty? Could you eat anything? The trolley will be around with lunch soon."

"Maybe some soup. My throat's still sore."

"I'll see what I can do. It's homemade tomato today. My favorite."

It was mine too. The thought of it appealed. At least that would slip down.

* * *

"Vanessa... Vanessa...."

The voice. Barely a voice at all. More like the softest of breaths, dusting my cheek, drawing me from sleep. I opened my eyes. A shadow moved past the end of my bed and a feeling of calm spread over me like a soft blanket.

"Who are you?" I whispered.

The shadow slid past. Sleep once again reclaimed me.

* * *

The following morning, I awoke with a clear head and felt refreshed. Joyce was on duty again. "We're going to get you up today. Take you for a shower and then, all being well, you'll be transferred to your own room."

I felt like cheering, especially as, since I had woken everyone up with my screaming, I could barely look anyone in the face.

I was still attached to a catheter, so showering was an awkward affair, but the feeling of cleanliness afterward made the effort worth it. The soothing spray on my tender parts provided a welcome relief too. A clean nightdress completed the overall feeling of wellbeing and when I emerged, Joyce was waiting to escort me. She steadied my arm as I took wobbly steps.

"No, you're not going back to the ward. We've got you all nicely installed in your room."

"That's fabulous. Thank you."

"You're doing really well, especially considering how poorly you were just a day ago. Maryam will be along soon. She's on her rounds now."

Joyce walked me down to the far end of the brightly lit corridor and opened the door.

My bed had been moved to a sunny room, painted in a pale lilac. A wall-mounted TV, bed table, chair, bedside cabinet, adorned with my things, and a door leading to my own bathroom sent a small thrill of pleasure coursing through my newly replenished blood.

"You'll be fine here, won't you?" Joyce asked.

"It's lovely. So calming."

"I think it's the nicest room of the lot. You've even got a reasonable view too."

She guided me around the bed and I glanced out of the window. Three floors up, my view took in the car park and extended over the treetops – with a few orange, red and yellow leaves still clinging to twigs. Parkland took over from there and a development of luxury flats where a friend of mine lived. A slight breeze sent more leaves fluttering through the air and floating to the ground.

Joyce helped me into bed but did not reattach the leg massage wraps. She picked them up off the chair. "Now you're going to be more mobile, you won't need these," she said. She produced a fresh pair of pressure socks from her pocket. "Sorry you're still stuck with these though."

I grimaced. Joyce proceeded to roll them on my legs with her expert touch.

"There you go. All ready for Maryam. I'll leave you to it."

"Thanks," I said and Joyce left.

Vanessa… Vanessa….

I jumped. The hairs on the back of my neck prickled. I couldn't have heard that, but it was right in my ear. That same raspy whisper.

The door opened at that moment and I gasped. Maryam came in, escorted by Joyce.

"Are you all right?" the consultant asked. "You look as if you've seen a ghost."

"No, I…. Sorry, I was miles away," I said.

"How are you feeling now? Mr. Waring told me about your problems, but we've sorted you out with some fresh blood, and your temperature and blood pressure are perfectly normal again."

"I'm much better now, thanks. Especially now I'm in here."

"That's good." Maryam pulled on some sterile gloves. "We'll just have a little look down below."

I assumed the position and she and Joyce inspected me. "That's coming on really well. See, Joyce, some of the stitches are already dissolving. You heal quickly," she said to me.

"Runs in the family. My mother had fast-healing skin."

"That's excellent. How about the pain?"

"Not nearly as bad as I thought it would be."

With a little difficulty, I rearranged myself and Maryam consulted my notes.

"I see we have you on Oramorph, paracetamol and codeine. And you are coping well with those?"

"Seem to be. The morphine push gave me a violent migraine so I was glad to get off that."

"The pain you experienced may have been down to your low blood count."

"And the nightmares? They were terrifying and always the same."

"Yes, I heard you woke up screaming. Tell me about them."

I described the tunnel, the figure with the frightening eyes. Joyce looked down at her hands. Maryam's eyes grew wider.

"That is so interesting." She turned to Joyce. "You remember the patient with the cervical carcinoma?"

Joyce nodded. She looked uncomfortable. "She described the exact same dream."

"Was that recently?" I asked.

"About a month ago, I think," Maryam said, looking at Joyce for confirmation. The nurse nodded but continued to look as if she would prefer to be almost anywhere but where she stood right now.

"She isn't still here, is she?" I asked, a nagging knot of concern planting itself in my stomach.

Maryam and Joyce exchanged glances. "No," said Maryam. "How is your appetite? Are you eating?"

That change of subject felt false somehow. What didn't they want to tell me?

"I don't feel hungry."

"Try and work on that. You need to eat, and drink a glass of water every hour. The nurses will monitor your fluid intake. Also try getting up and walking around a bit, keep those leg muscles working. No marathons, but a gentle walk up and down the corridor a few times a day should help. Can we get Nessa a leg bag? It'll make you more mobile," she said, addressing me. "During the day, you can attach the drainage bag to the catheter and strap it around your leg, rather than having to cart the stand around with you."

"When can the catheter come out?" I asked.

"In about a week. Best not to rush it. Apart from that, keep up the good work."

"Thank you."

They left. But the nagging question kept at me. Why hadn't they wanted to talk any more about the patient who had dreamed the same nightmares as me, and what had happened to her?

* * *

Getting in and out of bed hurt like hell. I girded myself each time. Sitting in the chair proved torturous, even with the special cushion Sandra supplied me with. I settled for little walks every three hours or so. The morphine in the Oramorph clogged me up so they gave me Movicol to encourage my bowels to produce, and that resulted in more frequent hikes to my bathroom the next day.

Paul came to see me at every visiting time. He brought fresh nightwear and took away my dirty washing. He brought me books and took away those I had read. I watched daytime TV for the first time in my life. Ancient reruns of *Columbo, McMillan & Wife* and *Bewitched* entertained me and, meanwhile, my body did its job and I carried on healing. Maryam continued to be pleased with my progress and, ten days after my operation, they took the catheter out.

I knew there was a chance the operation could result in urinary incontinence, but thankfully all went well and I was progressing in the right direction. They were even starting to suggest possible dates for my discharge. Another couple of weeks and I would be home.

Then, out of nowhere, the nightmares began again.

* * *

I had switched off the TV. The lights had dimmed in the corridor outside. The ward was in sleep mode and my eyes felt weighed down. I twisted myself into my best comfortable position, lying on my right side with my legs slightly drawn up. Half asleep, half awake, I heard the whisper and felt the cold breath on my left cheek.

"Vanessa...come to us."

Even though I told myself not to, I couldn't help myself. I pushed back the sheet and crawled out of bed, wincing at the now-familiar pain. My feet found my slippers and I tied my dressing gown over my nightdress. I made my way carefully to the door and opened it. At the far end of the silent corridor, there would be someone at the nurses' station but, almost opposite me, a door I couldn't remember noticing before silently opened. An indeterminate shadow crossed over the threshold and disappeared inside. Oddly, I felt no fear, just an irresistible urge to follow it.

The door was much older than the others in the hospital and had no glass observation panel. It closed quietly behind me. As it did so, I was thrust into a dark gloom with only sufficient light to see that I had entered an old and neglected corridor. Greenish yellow paint peeled off the walls and ceiling. I looked down at the floor. Filthy, mildewed linoleum in a nondescript shade of blue. The place smelled dank and musty. Cobwebs hung off old gas mantle wall lights. It was an incongruity. I must be dreaming and yet a part of me felt sure I wasn't.

"Vanessa...come...."

I knew I should turn back and get out of there but I couldn't. Something made me go on in the direction of that voice. A shadow flew across my field of vision. It could have been a woman. I wasn't sure.

"Who are you?" I asked. "I need to know who you are and what you want from me." I surprised myself at the firmness of my voice.

No answer.

I turned around. Behind me, I could see nothing, not the door I had entered by nor the corridor I had walked down. Ahead of me, nothing but the endless corridor, stretching apparently to infinity. It seemed familiar, but how could it be? I had never been here before in my life, yet.... A brief memory of the tunnel in my dreams swept across my mind.

A sudden movement in the corner of my eye distracted me. Unmistakably a woman this time.

I could only make out her silhouette, but she seemed to be dressed in a long cape. On her head, she wore an old-fashioned hat tied around her chin with a ribbon. A woman straight out of a Dickens novel. I must be dreaming this. Surely this couldn't be real.

I stared. She was weeping, her image clearer with every second. She didn't seem to notice me, as if we existed in two parallel worlds, but I could see her, even if she couldn't see me. I could tell the skirt she wore was of some cheap material, a muddy brown color and much mended. She also wore a jacket. This had once been red, probably quite a bright red, but now appeared faded and stained while her cape was muddied at the hem and also old. It had once been black but now looked almost rusty in parts. A straw hat of poor quality and riddled with holes perched on top of her unkempt pile of dirty-blonde hair. This was a poor Victorian woman and she didn't belong in this hospital in the twenty-first century. But then, in that particular corridor, neither did I. In that particular corridor the twenty-first century didn't exist.

Her weeping grew louder and she spoke, her words almost indecipherable through her choking sobs. "How could I come... to this? The workhouse.... I wish I was...dead."

She vanished, leaving an echo of her cries behind.

Behind me, the corridor had grown lighter, so that I could retrace my steps. I wanted to race out of there, but no way would my legs allow for that. My best motion was still a shuffle. Finally I made it to the door and turned the antiquated Bakelite knob.

Safely through, I leaned against it, relieved to smell the clean aroma of the ward corridor, while trying to collect my thoughts. A nurse I didn't recognize approached me.

"Whatever are you doing out here?"

Still trying to comprehend what had happened, I shook my head. "I went for a short walk, through here."

I stepped aside and pointed at…a blank wall. "But that's impossible. There was a door there. I went through it and down this derelict corridor. There was a woman…." I stopped. The nurse's incredulous expression told me that if I carried on, she would feel duty bound to report that Vanessa Tremaine, who had been progressing so well, was now certifiably insane.

"I'll go back to bed now," I said. "I must have dreamed it."

"That's quite possible. Come along, I'll help you." She took my arm and steered me gently but firmly back to my room. Tucking me into bed, she said. "If you want anything, just press your buzzer and we'll come and help you. Save your exercise for daylight hours."

"I will. Thank you. Sorry to be a nuisance, I didn't mean to be."

"You're not. Don't worry. Sleep well."

But I didn't sleep at all for the rest of that night. I knew what I had seen. Even if I couldn't have seen it.

CHAPTER ELEVEN

Somehow I had run out of reading material. Paul had been bringing me books every day but, once again, I seemed to not merely read them but devour them. As soon as I laid one down, I would pick up the next. My hospital life had developed its own routine. Up at six-thirty, gird myself for the struggle out of bed, mutter curses under my breath, hobble to the shower, perform the careful douching ritual on my rapidly healing wounds and emit gentle sighs as the warm water soothed and caressed the soreness.

I pampered myself with a rather expensive shower gel, which must not come anywhere near the surgically affected areas. I washed and conditioned my hair, dried myself carefully, ensuring I used some sterile pads for my nether regions. Only the gentlest of pats here, but I still needed to ensure I didn't leave wet skin, which could become sore only too quickly.

Once out of the shower, dressed in a clean nightie, with my dressing gown wrapped around me, I would switch on television or read until my morning cup of strong tea arrived. I didn't even have to ask – the staff knew me now. Builders' tea they called it; only a splash of milk and one sugar.

A few uneventful days had gone past and I had put my strange nocturnal experience out of my head. Almost.

This particular morning, having finished my breakfast porridge, I flicked through the television channels. A choice of news and current affairs – the usual diet of gloom and despondency, children's entertainment, reruns of old shows, talk programs.... Nothing fitted my particular taste at that time.

The door opened and a smiling face I didn't recognize greeted me. "Hello, would you like a book from the library?"

I could have kissed the bubbly young girl with maroon hair and a badge that proclaimed her to be a volunteer.

"What have you got in the historical fiction line? Or crime even?" I asked, perking up.

"John Grisham, Philippa Gregory…." She consulted her trolley out in the corridor. I could see it was pretty well overflowing. I finally settled on two books – John Grisham's *Camino Island* and Kate Furnivall's *The Italian Wife*. They would keep me going for a few hours at least. Paul had promised to replenish my stocks that evening.

After the volunteer had left me, saying she would return the following week, I inspected each book in turn. Deciding to start with Kate Furnivall, I turned the pages until I found the first chapter. As I did so, I became aware of a piece of paper lodged about halfway through. Maybe someone had used it as a bookmark. I retrieved it. It was a small scrap of old notepaper, folded once. I opened it and revealed a poem, or maybe part of a poem, written in small, neat and somewhat old-style handwriting and, by the look of it, using a fountain pen:

In darkness, shadows breathe….

I read the poem through twice. For some unaccountable reason, it sent shivers up my spine. I had never heard of the poet, Lydia Warren Carmody, which was a little strange as I had studied nineteenth-century poetry and prided myself on my familiarity with even the more obscure writers. I examined the notepaper in greater detail. It was good quality but looked as if it had been torn from a larger sheet. On closer inspection, the ink seemed a little faded, the white paper had taken on a yellowish hue and when I sniffed it, an odor of mustiness assailed my nostrils. The book did not have this smell so I could only conclude that this poem had been written or copied at some stage in the past and, for whatever reason had turned up at a time when its owner needed to mark their place in this book. As someone who had used anything from till receipts through to tissues to mark my place in my current bedtime reading, I didn't find this strange, but there was something about this poem that struck a chord with me. An uncomfortable one at that.

* * *

"Not the best poem I've ever read," Paul said, handing it back to me. "Never heard of the poet either."

"Nor have I, but there's something…oh, I don't know… something oddly familiar about it. I can't put my finger on it, but I had the weirdest feeling when I first found it."

"What sort of weird?"

"As if I was meant to find it. This will sound crazy, but it felt like someone had put it there knowing it would be me who read it."

"Yes, you're right. That *is* a bit way out there, even for you."

I smacked him playfully on the arm. "Stop it. I know it sounds mad but it really felt like that. Still does actually."

"Next time you see the library lady you had better ask her who had the book before you."

"If she remembers."

"Don't they make a list of who has what?"

"She didn't while she was in my room but she could have after she left I suppose."

"Bound to, or they would be losing stock all over the place."

"I'm going to donate some of my books, so you won't have as many to take home with you."

"Good, that will be a great comfort to the heaving bookshelves at home."

"You can never have too many books."

"Up to a point, but when you find yourself falling over the damn things to get out of bed in the morning, there comes a time when you say 'enough is enough, I must have a clear out.'"

"I don't think we're at that stage yet. There's a bit of wall in the living room that doesn't have any shelves on it."

"Yet," Paul added, grinning.

"Yet," I said and grinned back. "Ouch."

Paul's grin left his face to be replaced by a look of concern. "Does it hurt a lot?"

"Only when I move, sit, stand, lie down…. Same old, same old."

"Maryam's pleased with you. She told me you're healing remarkably quickly."

"It's in the genes."

"She remarked on that as well. Rarely, if ever, has she seen someone's skin heal as fast as yours. She reckons you'll be out next week if you carry on making such good progress. How's the walking going?"

"I'm about due for another little trot. Care to accompany me?"

"Sure. It would be my pleasure, ma'am."

Paul steadied me while I struggled out of bed, into my slippers and dressing gown and he put out his hand to help me up.

"Thanks, but I must do this myself." I gritted my teeth and Paul looked as if he was experiencing the same sharp pains as I was.

"That looked harrowing."

"Nothing a ton of co-codamol couldn't deaden. Trouble is they only allow me two every six hours."

"Still taking the Oramorph?"

"Yes, but I'm trying to do without it as much as possible. They won't let me have it when I leave here. It's the morphine. Addictive."

I tucked my hand into Paul's elbow and we made slow progress out of the door and into the corridor.

"Where to?" Paul asked.

"How about a nice stroll into town, dinner and a show?"

"I wish."

"So do I. Seriously, though, let's go down to the café on the ground floor and have a coffee."

"Sounds like a good plan."

I hesitated before we moved off.

"What's up?"

I was staring at the wall opposite, still half expecting a door to open up. "It's odd, because it was so real," I said and realized I had made no sense whatsoever.

"You'll have to explain that one to me," Paul said.

I touched the wall. "You remember I told you about the night the nurse found me standing outside here, convinced I had come through a door in this wall?"

"Ah, yes." He knocked on the adjacent wall and then on the

one that so intrigued me. Both sounded solid. Paul repeated the knocking with the same result. "Definitely no door there."

"At the time, it was like the past and present sort of merged. As if I'd stepped out of my world into a previous age."

"I wouldn't mind a bit of whatever they're putting in those pills."

"I'm serious, Paul. You had to be there. It felt so real." I touched the wall, almost willing the door to reappear. "How old is this building anyway?"

"Not that old. Twenty odd years or so. You know what used to be here, don't you?"

"Actually, I'm ashamed to say I don't."

"And you a historian too!"

"I know. Shocking. Go on then, enlighten me."

"The workhouse. Dating from the mid-nineteenth century I believe. They closed it in the 1930s along with the old hospital. Maybe they recycled bits of those buildings to construct this one, I don't really know. They do say that events can leave a sort of marker on the places where they occur. I read that somewhere. Can't remember where now."

That woman I was so certain I had seen in the corridor. She had mentioned the workhouse. Suddenly I felt cold. Shaky. My palms grew clammy.

"Maybe that walk isn't such a good idea right now," Paul said.

"No, come on, let's go. I could do with a decent coffee."

I nodded at the nurse on duty. "Won't be long," I said.

"I'm kidnapping her," Paul said.

The nurse laughed. "Don't go too far and don't get into any mischief now."

I rolled my eyes. "Chance would be a fine thing."

We opened the double doors at the end of the ward and stepped out into the main hospital corridor for that floor.

"They don't let me off the ward on my own yet."

"Still need your training wheels then?"

I smiled. "Something like that. I've been downstairs with the occupational health adviser and Sandra and I had an excursion to the far end of the corridor."

"Did you take a packed lunch?"

I giggled. "No, but a passing St. Bernard let me have a nip of his brandy."

We had reached the lift and Paul pressed the 'down' button. "Do they still do that, I wonder? You know, send St. Bernards with barrels of brandy round their necks off into the Alps to assist climbers in trouble."

"I have no idea. I always thought it was an urban myth."

A ping announced the lift's arrival; the steel doors slid smoothly open. It was empty. I pressed 'ground' and the doors shut with a gentle whoosh, while a woman's voice announced, "Doors closing, going down".

"She must get pretty fed up," Paul said. "Saying the same thing, day in and day out. Wonder where they keep her?"

"In the basement probably. Next to the Morgue."

"Ground floor. Doors opening."

"Thank you," said Paul as we emerged into the throng of staff, patients and visitors milling around, some looking lost, others purposefully striding along toward their destination.

The coffee bar was over half-full and I sat at a small table while Paul fetched us cappuccinos. I felt self-conscious of my left hand, with the cannula still attached. It was a mass of bruising. Livid blue, green, yellow and red marks aggravated by the anticoagulant they injected into my arm each evening. I hid it under the table, resting it on my left knee.

While I waited, I looked around. Every face I saw held a story trapped within. Some looked tired, weighed down by whatever was troubling them either physically or mentally, or probably both. Strange that, despite the fact I was engaged in a war with cancer, most of the time I hadn't felt scared about anything other than the operation itself and the thought of the pain and discomfort afterward. Except for a brief wobble, it never occurred to me that I wouldn't recover. Maryam had played a large part in that. Her positive, matter-of-fact way of dealing with my situation inspired confidence in me.

I caught the eye of a woman whose bald head proclaimed her to be a chemotherapy patient. She smiled and the radiance of that gesture warmed me. For a second I thought I recognized her but

I didn't know anyone going through chemo, so I dismissed the thought. I smiled back and she moved off, on her way to keep an appointment or to get home probably. Our lives had touched for maybe one second, perhaps not even that, but a little glow burned inside me.

"You look happier," Paul said.

"A patient smiled at me."

"That's nice of them."

"I smiled back. You had to be there. It loses something in the translation."

Paul's attention was distracted by something behind me. "Someone wants a word with you."

I turned to see the patient with whom I had exchanged smiles. Once again, I felt that warm glow. This woman had the charisma factor.

She spoke and her voice was soft. "I'm sorry to disturb you but I wasn't sure if you were aware of the little girl."

"Little girl?"

The woman nodded. "She's standing next to you."

A chill spread down my left arm. Paul paused in the act of sipping his cappuccino.

"I'm sorry," I said, my mouth dry. "I don't know what you mean. There's no little girl here."

The woman touched my right hand. "She doesn't mean you any harm. She is reaching out to you."

Paul coughed. "Thank you, but I don't think my wife needs to hear this right now."

"It's all right, Paul. I want to hear what she has to say." I turned back to the woman. "Who is she? Do you know?"

"Only that her name is Agnes and she has come a long way to be with you…Vanessa."

"How do you know my name?"

"She told me. She's going now, but she says she will be back and she will show you…."

"Show me what?" I heard the panic in my voice. Paul shuffled in his seat and stood up. I put a hand on his. "It's all right, Paul. Please."

"I won't have you being upset. You've been through enough."

"Forgive me," the woman said. "I don't mean any harm, but I had to speak to you. I can see what others can't. Sometimes it helps."

"Paul, I'm fine. Honestly."

Concern on his face, Paul sat down and pushed his cup away. He was frowning and his breathing had quickened a little.

I smiled at the woman. "Please tell me, what is it the little girl wants to show me?"

The woman shook her head. "I'm sorry. She left before she could tell me."

"Pretty convenient," Paul muttered.

I shot him a warning glance. He raised his eyes heavenward.

"Don't be alarmed. She only wants to help you. I must go now, but she will come back soon, I'm sure." The woman moved on and left me staring after her.

"There are some real nutters around," Paul said, standing. "Come on, let's get you back to the ward. I think you've had quite enough excitement for one day."

I stood awkwardly and accepted Paul's steadying hand. "You can say what you like about her, and maybe you're right, but that still wouldn't explain how she knew my name."

"You have it on your wristband."

I glanced down at my left arm. Sure enough, there it was. 'Vanessa Tremaine', along with my date of birth. Could she have seen it? I tried to remember how I had been sitting, and whether my wristband had been visible to her. It was a little loose so it could have turned round on my wrist. Right now, it faced inward.

We made our way back to the lifts. "Either way," I said as Paul pressed the call button, "you've got to admit it's odd."

"Don't think any more about it. She's probably having a good laugh now."

"Maybe." Once Paul helped me back into bed, I lay back against the pillows feeling weary. Such a short excursion yet it had sapped all my energy.

"You mustn't overdo it," he said, planting a light kiss on my lips. "Little steps. That's what the nurses told you and that's what I'm telling you."

I smiled. My eyes felt heavy and the effort to remain awake was proving a losing battle. "I think I'll have a little sleep now," I said.

"Then I'll leave you to it. I'll pop back this evening. You get a good rest."

"Thanks."

Another kiss and he was gone. I fell asleep almost immediately.

* * *

That night, after Paul had left, I sipped my last cup of tea of the day and picked up the poem, re-reading it. *In darkness, shadows breathe.*

It resonated so clearly with me. Those dreams I had experienced; the way the shadows pulsated, as if they were breathing.

Then I thought back to the odd encounter with the…psychic I supposed I should call her. I glanced at my wristband again. Had she seen it? Paul seemed convinced she must have but I had a nagging doubt about that, especially when I remembered that I had been sitting with my left hand under the table. A sudden jolt set my heart racing. That was it. She couldn't possibly have seen it, unless she had X-ray vision and could see through wood and metal.

The door opened and the cleaner came in. Over the past couple of weeks or so, Margie and I had become quite friendly. She was, I gauged, in her mid to late fifties, wore her impossibly black hair pinned up and brandished her cleaning cloths with scrupulous verve.

"You're late this evening, Margie."

She set about emptying the bin in my bathroom. "One of the girls called in sick so I've been covering for her. Nearly finished now though. I know you don't usually switch your light out for a couple more hours, so I left you till last. Hope you don't mind."

"No, not at all. Bet you'll be glad to get home."

Margie paused and straightened her back. "Me feet are killing me. I have a date with a long soak in a hot bath."

"Sounds good to me."

"How are you doing anyhow?"

"Not too bad at all, thanks."

Margie carried on in the bathroom and I finished my tea. When she emerged, she came over to clean my bed table and cabinet.

"Margie, how long have you worked here?"

"Since it opened. Over twenty years it is now. They'll be pensioning me off before long."

"Do you remember what was here before?"

Margie paused. "The old workhouse, asylum and hospital. It was derelict for many years."

"So I believe. My husband said they demolished it to build this and may have used some of the materials in the construction. Do you know if that's true?"

"Oh, I shouldn't wonder. I couldn't say for definite though. Why do you ask?"

"Idle curiosity. I have a lot of time on my hands at the moment."

"You'll soon be up and about again."

"I'm getting there. Have you…have you heard any stories about this place? Things happening that people couldn't explain, that sort of thing?"

"Oh yes. You always get people thinking they've seen ghosts in hospitals. Mind you, it makes you think when you hear the same story more than once from different people who couldn't possibly have met each other."

"Any in particular?"

"Well, yes, there was a lady in this very room about two years ago I think. She kept insisting that a little girl came to visit her every evening, stayed for half an hour or so and then left. Never said a word apart from telling her that her name was Agnes. She looked to be about ten or eleven and was dressed in clothes that could have come straight out of a history book. Very poor, threadbare and ragged. Other times she would turn up in only a thin cotton dress, maybe an undergarment, something of that sort. Time went by and I forgot all about it, and then not six months ago, another lady in this room told me almost the same story. Same description only she didn't know her name. Oh…don't tell me…. Have you seen her?"

"Not exactly. My husband and I were down in the café earlier today and a woman…I think she was probably a chemo patient because she had lost her hair…came up to me and told me a little girl was standing next to me. I couldn't see her. She said her name was Agnes."

"Very spooky."

"Do you know if there was a door in the wall opposite here at any time?"

Margie thought for a moment and then shook her head. "Not that I can remember. Why do you ask?"

"Oh, it's nothing. I had a…dream, I suppose. I went through an old door there into a derelict, dark corridor. At the time it felt so real I was convinced I had actually been there, but I couldn't have, could I?"

Margie shrugged but didn't reply. "I'll do your floor now and then I'll get going."

I nodded. Something bothered me about her response, or lack of it, but I decided now wasn't the time to pursue it. The poor woman wanted to get home to that hot bath she craved and didn't need me holding her up.

She finished her work, wished me good night and shut the door behind her. Soon after, the nurse came to check my blood pressure and temperature, both of which she pronounced to be fine.

An hour later, I put my book down and switched off the overhead lamp. Through the window in my door I could see they had dimmed the lights. I yawned and laid my head down on the pillow, wriggling a little to find a more comfortable position. I closed my eyes and tried not to think too much.

* * *

I don't know what woke me, but I had the impression of a noise or a sudden movement in my room. Reaching behind me, I switched on the light. For one fleeting second I saw something flash past me. Something? No, someone. A small, slight figure. Ankle-length flimsy dress, maybe an old-fashioned petticoat – the glimpse too brief to make out any other details.

Agnes.

It had to be, hadn't it? The woman in the café had been right. I lay there, heart thumping, breathing fast, for some minutes, not daring to move and certainly not daring to switch off the light.

I couldn't stay like this all night. I had to do something. The light had scared her off, but maybe if I called out to her, I could get her to return. What was I thinking? Who in their right minds would summon a ghost child? But I knew that was precisely what I was going to do.

"Agnes?" My voice cracked with fear and sounded more like a ragged squeak. "Don't be afraid." Who was I reassuring? Her or me?

Silence.

The door opened and I jumped. One of the nurses on night duty came in. "I saw your light on. Are you all right?"

"Oh yes," I said, a little too quickly. I sounded false. "Having a little trouble sleeping so I thought I'd read for a bit." I picked up my book from the bedside cabinet.

"I'll get you a cup of hot chocolate if you like."

"No, that's fine, thanks. A few minutes with my book should do it."

"As long as you're sure. You looked terrified when I came in. Like you'd seen a ghost or something." She laughed.

I managed a polite chortle and she left me alone.

Maybe if I did read, I could get so sleepy, I would actually drop off. It was worth a try.

I tried to read, but the words seemed to dance around wildly on the page. I took nothing in, which was annoying as, up until then, I had been enjoying the story. Half an hour later, I gave up and switched off the light, hoping that by some miracle sleep would grab me.

I lay in the darkness, the only sound my own breathing. I tried to concentrate on keeping the rhythm steady. In…out…in…out.

Something brushed my face. I snapped the light on. Nothing there. Not even a flash of a movement out of the corner of my eye.

"Agnes," I whispered. "Don't be afraid." I could hardly believe myself. I, who was terrified, telling a ghost not to be afraid!

Did I imagine the tiniest whooshing sound as of the lightest breath a human could take?

* * *

"Nessa. Come on, time to wake up now."

Joyce's gentle voice drifted toward me, invading my sleep. I forced my unwilling eyelids to open and blinked at the bright light overhead.

Her eyes peered into mine. "That's better. You've been asleep so long, at least ten hours by our reckoning."

"What?" I struggled to sit up. Joyce helped me. "I never sleep that long."

"Well, you just did and it's taken me a good few minutes to rouse you. How do you feel?"

I put my hand to my head. "Better. I must have needed that."

"Time to get into the shower now. I'm afraid you missed breakfast, but the mid-morning tea trolley will be along soon. Grab some biscuits."

"I will."

She left me to move at my own slow pace, which I punctuated with the odd "You bugger", whenever something smarted, stung or pulled. Under the soothing warm water, I stared down at my belly, still distended from the operation, although I could swear I now had a better view of my feet than I had since before my surgery. My legs and ankles had also lost their disfiguring swelling and were pretty much back to normal. That, at least, was a relief.

Dried – or in the case of my nether regions, well blotted – I changed into a clean nightie, relishing the sensation of being cleansed and sweet-scented. After ten days with a catheter I didn't think I would ever take such personal freshness for granted again.

Returning to my bed, something caught my eye. The poem. Lying on the bed. I was sure it hadn't been there when I went for my shower but now, here it was.

And something had changed.

Someone had written on it. Scrawled more like. Not the neat handwriting of the original. I deciphered the almost illegible scribble and my blood chilled.

'You're next.'

I threw the paper down as if it had burned my fingers. Hastily I opened the top drawer of the bedside cabinet and tossed it in there. I slammed the drawer shut, my heart pounding and my breath coming in short gasps. I grabbed my dressing gown off the chair and wrapped it around me before tugging the door open and stepping out into the corridor, grateful for the chatter and sounds of patients and nursing staff going about their normal daily business.

"Off for a walk?" Joyce said. "You'll miss your cup of tea."

"I'm just going to the end of the ward and back."

"Good idea." She went into the next side room.

I felt someone close up behind and turned my head. No one within six feet of me. Then why was it I could feel breathing on my neck? Why had the clean, antiseptic smell of the ward been replaced by a stench of unwashed human skin that couldn't be emanating from me?

A strong smell of halitosis preceded the familiar, unpleasant, female whisper. "I told you. You're next. Don't forget. She's coming for you."

I stopped. Paralyzed with fear.

"Are you okay?" Margie paused in the act of mopping the floor.

I improvised. "Sorry. Yes. I just remembered something."

She carried on with her work. I turned and made my labored way back to my room. Down the corridor, the tea trolley rattled closer. I reached my door and turned the handle.

Something skittered out of sight.

But on the bed, the disfigured poem was back.

* * *

"I agree. This is strange." Paul handed the sheet of paper back to me. "If I didn't know better…if this wasn't a hospital, where they generally take things seriously, I would swear someone was playing a game with you. Have you spoken to Joyce or one of the other nurses about it?"

"Not yet. Do you think I should?"

"Definitely. If it's a prank, it's most likely one of the student nurses and they need to be put right straightaway."

"I'll talk to Joyce later."

"Or I can, if you like?"

"No, it's okay, I'll do it."

"I'd chuck it away after that if I was you. Or give it to Joyce as evidence. I mean it's hardly Shakespeare, is it? The poem I mean."

"Oh, I don't know. It has a certain charm."

"Goodness alone knows who the poet is. Couldn't find anything about her on the internet and I really searched."

That nagging doubt that wouldn't go away tackled me again. "I saw something odd today too. As I came back to my room, a figure raced out of my line of vision."

"What was it like?"

"It was too brief a glimpse to tell, but I did think it was human. Small, thin. That's all I can say and I'm not even sure that's entirely accurate."

"It couldn't be a hallucination caused by the painkillers, could it? I know morphine is supposed to induce vivid dreams."

"Surely not in the form I'm taking it, and the doses are strictly controlled. I'm down to just one in the morning and one at night."

"What about the other stuff?"

I shook my head. "Co-codamol is only codeine and paracetamol. Nothing hallucinogenic about that."

"Then we're left with the conclusion that you really *did* see something today and maybe on one or two other occasions as well. Unless you were sleepwalking when you returned to this room?"

Somehow the realization that Paul was apparently prepared to give credence to what I was now certain I had seen with my own eyes came as a mixed blessing. Relief, certainly, that he believed me, but also fear because if he believed it had happened, then I really did have something to worry about, apart from the obvious challenges of my medical condition.

* * *

My sleep was disturbed that night. Every time I dropped off, swirling images of creatures half concealed by shadow taunted me, reaching out tantalizingly close and then withdrawing right at the moment I was sure they would grab me.

Eventually I gave up the effort and hauled myself out of bed for a visit to the bathroom, instantly aware of the chill in the room. Strange because, if anything, the room was usually a little too warm.

When I emerged a few minutes later. I heard a sound coming from the corridor. A knock, followed by a thump. I opened my door and peered out. The corridor was deserted, the lights dimmed as always at this time. I glanced at my watch. Three forty-five. I stood listening.

Thump.

As clear as it could possibly be and it had come from somewhere inside the wall opposite. The wall where the impossible door had been.

The wall where the door, once again, appeared.

My mouth ran dry. I put out my hand and clasped the antique round doorknob. As before, it was dark brown, made of Bakelite, the sort of doorknob that had been on my grandmother's front door all those years ago in Halifax. It felt smooth under my fingers. I turned it. It moved slickly and the door opened without a sound. A rush of cold, dank air made me shiver and I pulled my dressing gown tighter around me.

I stepped over the threshold onto the old linoleum, noting the flaking paint of the walls and ceiling and the flickering gas mantles along the walls which cast an eerie, uneven glow. All seemed still. My breathing sounded loud in contrast to the silence all around me. Silence so complete it was tangible. It was *too* quiet.

My heart thumping, I took one uncertain step after another, all the while my brain screaming at me to turn and go back to the safety of my room. But I had to keep on. I had to know what was in here.

A woman moaned, shattering the stillness. I caught my breath.

It came again. A long, low keening of someone in abject despair. I stopped next to the source of the sound. Another door. I put my hand out to turn the handle and opened it.

I peered inside. A smell of disinfectant and something unpleasant. Something like urine. Slightly fishy.

A loud moan. Right in my ear. I cried out. The noise of people bustling around grew from a murmur into a clamor. I turned back from the room to see the corridor milling with semi-transparent figures, all in Victorian dress. Women in long white uniforms with starched aprons, wearing identical and quite elaborate white cotton bonnets, strode purposefully along, ignoring my existence. An old woman, her hair in an unkempt bun, hobbled toward me. She was dressed in an ankle-length smock over an old, much-mended dress. Behind her, three more women of indeterminate age, similarly attired. None paid me any attention as they moved past. I could hear their footsteps but their bodies were ethereal. The woman I had seen on my earlier visit to this corridor drifted past me, this time dressed like all the others, her expression blank and hopeless.

I stood in the doorway, seemingly unable to move, riveted by the spectacle playing out in front of me. As if a projectionist had hit a fast forward button, the scene sped up, slowly at first then faster and faster as the figures raced back and forth until they became a blur.

Out of nowhere, a solitary figure emerged, more tangible than the rest, moving at normal speed through the speeding apparitions. A woman. Maybe my age or perhaps younger – and I read something in her eyes I had seen in no other.

She could see me.

Her eyes were cold, gray, staring at me. Almost through me. Her gaze sent shivers through me.

"You're the one, aren't you?" I said. "You wrote that message on the poem."

She stopped in front of me and said nothing. She stared at me. Unblinking, unwavering.

I noted she wasn't dressed like the others. Already I knew who they must be. I had stepped through some kind of portal back into the old workhouse. The women in the dresses, aprons and bonnets were staff and the other inmates. None of the women I had seen looked quite like this one though. She appeared the same, although her body was much less transparent, her dress was black and her hair severely dressed in a bun. I felt if I reached out and touched her I would feel a living person beneath my fingers. She did not belong in a workhouse. And she certainly didn't belong here.

"Who are you?" I asked.

Still she didn't speak. Now we were alone in that strange place and she began to fade until she disappeared. I glanced over my shoulder, but the door that had been open was now shut. I looked for the handle but it had vanished.

I should have been terrified but, for some reason, I felt calm. My need to find answers overwhelmed my trepidation and fear. The corridor to my left grew dim. To my right, back where I had come from, the gas mantles continued to flicker as before. I had to get back to my room. But who was the woman and why was this happening to me?

Retracing my steps, hoping and praying I would be able to get out of there, I was within inches of the closed door when it slowly swung open, revealing the welcoming sight of the Gynecology ward corridor. I raced through it and immediately looked back over my shoulder. The door had gone.

* * *

Margie was in a talkative mood later that afternoon. She chattered to me about her son and his latest girlfriend, her plans for Christmas, and I was happy to listen. She was a good storyteller with a keen sense of humor.

"There'll be twelve of us for Christmas dinner. Twelve! We've only got six chairs. They'll have to be fed in shifts. I'd better be more careful about the turkey this year as well. Last year I got such a big 'un I had to chop its legs off to get it in the oven…."

She had just finished the bathroom and was starting on my

floor when I decided the time was right. "Do you believe in ghosts, Margie?"

Margie paused, and leaned on her mop. "Well, let's say I don't *not* believe in them, if that makes sense. Like I said to you a few days ago, I have heard some strange stories about this place and some more than once. Like the little girl I told you about."

"Agnes."

"Yes." She wrung her mop out in the bucket.

"Have you heard anyone say they found a door in the wall outside here? A door that was only there now and again?" She hadn't responded last time I had tried to raise this subject and I wondered how she would react. Last time, she had simply changed the subject, but this time she would have to *really* ignore it, or else answer me.

"Once. A long time ago." Why did she look so uncomfortable talking about this? All her earlier humor and good spirits seemed to have evaporated.

"What happened?" I asked.

"I hadn't worked here long and a woman came in. She was really sick. Cancer. She didn't have long. They put her in this very room and she was drugged up on goodness knows what, so she used to ramble a bit. Sometimes she would get up, although how she managed it no one could imagine. The cancer had spread all through her body by then and usually she couldn't walk at all, but somehow she would get herself out into the corridor and they would find her, always in the same place, slumped against the wall opposite. She said there was a door and she had gone through it and found herself in the old workhouse. She saw all these people from, like, a century or more ago. I found her once and she said the same to me. It actually scared me. Mind you, I was a lot younger and more impressionable then.

"I helped the nurses put her back to bed. She couldn't get there by herself even though she'd managed to get herself out there. I remember, we settled her down and tucked her in and she stared straight at me. Then she said something really weird. I have never forgotten it because it didn't make any real sense, but she said it with such conviction...." Margie shook herself as if trying to rid herself of something unpleasant and unnerving.

"What was it? What did she say?"

Margie hesitated. "She said, 'In darkness, shadows breathe.'"

CHAPTER TWELVE

"The same as the title of that poem," I said to Paul as he sat next to my bed that evening.

He said nothing for a few moments, before inhaling deeply. "You've certainly had a busy day," he said at last. "I haven't been idle either. I've been doing some research and I think I've located a history of the workhouse. I had a chat with that friend of yours, Joanna, at the university and she recommended it, so I've ordered it online and it should arrive within a few days. Judging by the preview, there's a blueprint of the layout of the building so we may be able to work out where it lay in relation to this hospital."

"No more joy on Lydia Warren Carmody?"

Paul shook his head.

"I can't help thinking she's tied into this in some way," I said. "Maybe she's the one I saw today."

"You seem incredibly calm for someone who's had the sort of encounter you've had."

"I've just had major cancer surgery. You get a different perspective."

Paul looked as if he didn't know whether to believe me. In truth I had surprised myself. I had always thought I would run away screaming if anything remotely supernatural came my way but then, I had experienced many a sleepless night when I was a child, worrying about getting cancer. I couldn't imagine myself ever being able to cope with *that,* yet here we were.

* * *

Maryam's smile was not quite as broad as it had been last time I had seen her, and a pang of fear curled in the pit of my stomach.

"How are you feeling today?" she asked as I assumed the now-familiar position for an examination of my wounds. A gentle series of prods between my legs followed and her smile grew brighter. The ball of fear settled into a corner and went back to sleep.

"I'm feeling fine," I said.

"Everything looks well down there," she said, peeling off her surgical gloves and throwing them in the waste bin. The metal lid slammed shut as she released her foot on the pedal.

Joyce stood by.

Maryam gave a light cough. "Your blood pressure has been a little erratic for a couple of days. Mostly at night and first thing in the morning. The rest of the day is fine. We'll keep monitoring you regularly and it's nothing to worry about at this stage, but is there anything you are doing in the evenings that you are doing differently to any other time of day, apart from sleeping, of course?"

There was only one thing I could think of. I swallowed. "I've had some strange experiences."

She looked at me questioningly. I had to continue now I'd started. "In the early hours of this morning for example, I couldn't sleep and I heard a noise outside my door…." I carried on with my strange tale while Maryam and the nurse exchanged glances but said nothing.

When I had finished, Maryam spoke. "That's quite some story and yes, your BP was up this morning." She thought for a moment. "I think I would like you to have another MRI. I know you've had a couple of these recently but I just want to rule anything out that could be the cause."

I looked from one to the other. Their faces gave nothing away, but…. "You think I'm imagining this, don't you? I can understand it. I know this must sound crazy but I also know it happened and that I'm not the only one in this hospital that's ever experienced the same things I'm now experiencing."

"Who told you that?" Maryam glanced at Joyce, who shook her head.

"I don't want to get anyone into trouble so I would rather not say," I said.

"Probably Margie. The cleaner," Joyce said. "She does like to chat about the ghost stories patients have told her. I keep telling her she shouldn't because most of the time they're probably induced by the morphine they're on."

"But not in my case," I said. "I've only been on Oramorph and not even as much as I used to take."

"It's still morphine," Maryam said. "And Joyce is right. It can cause distressing dreams."

"These aren't dreams," I said, desperate to keep my temper under control. Nothing I hated more than being disbelieved. "You know when you're awake and when you're dreaming. It's two different things altogether."

Joyce piped up. "Not necessarily. I have known patients on morphine who have sworn they've been out of bed and running up and down the corridor when, in actual fact, they've been fast asleep the whole time."

I shook my head. "Not in my case. I promise you."

"Nevertheless," Maryam said, "let's get that MRI done, just to be on the safe side."

"Fine with me," I said, trying not to feel irritated.

"We should be able to squeeze you in tomorrow, all being well."

They left shortly after, leaving me unhappy and annoyed. Why wouldn't they even entertain the possibility that all wasn't normal in this hospital? That somehow, for some unknown reason, a portal opened up between the world of the present and the world of the past? I was sure it would happen again before long and, when it did, I would once again venture down that corridor.

Only, this time, I would bring something back with me.

* * *

"We've managed to get you in right now." Joyce handed me my dressing gown and waited as I put it on.

"Cancellation?" I asked. Maryam had been gone less than an hour.

"I think so, anyway best get it over and done with." She had brought a wheelchair and helped me into it. I eased myself down gently. Sitting was still my most uncomfortable position, mainly owing to the pressure it put on the area of my body where the skin had been harvested to create the flaps that had recreated my vulva. I clenched my teeth against the stinging pain.

"What's it like, on a scale of one to ten?" Joyce asked.

"About a seven at the moment," I said.

"When we get back, you'll be able to have some co-codamol."

"I could do with some."

"It's too soon after your last dose. Give it another hour."

I nodded, concentrating hard on trying to push the pain away. If I told myself it didn't hurt, it wouldn't, right? Mind over matter. I had read screeds of worthy advice before I came into hospital. Right now I could have cheerfully strangled all those who had beamed at me on my computer screen, with their perfect white teeth, no doubt basking in the sunshine of their Miami mansions bought with the proceeds of their bullshit. *You should try sitting where I am, in my body, sometime.*

We arrived outside the room where the scan would take place. I was an old hand at this now and it was a relief to stand up. The raging stinging settled down from feeling as if a hundred hornets were simultaneously attacking me to a dull burn. From inside the room I heard the familiar rhythmic clanking of the MRI machine.

"Won't be long now," Joyce said.

Joyce handed me over to the radiographer. She looked vaguely familiar, but I had seen so many members of staff over the past few months.

Inside the room, I saw the doughnut shape of the scanner, with a hard bed waiting for me to occupy it. I had gone in feet first previously but this would be a brain scan. Head first. I shivered. Not that I was normally claustrophobic, but the thought of being enclosed by this sophisticated piece of equipment suddenly terrified me.

"Are you all right, Vanessa?"

My face must have betrayed my fears because the radiographer was giving me a look of deep concern. "Do you want to take a minute?"

I shook my head. If I was ever going to do this it had better be now. I put my watch in the pocket of my dressing gown, took it off and laid it on a nearby chair, wishing my hands would stop shaking.

With a nurse's help, I lay down on the uncomfortable bed and closed my eyes. At least then I wouldn't be able to see my prison. Another nurse positioned a pair of headphones on my head. They would blot out the worst of the noise.

The radiographer spoke softly through the speaker. I could tell her at any time if I panicked and they would get me out. The whole procedure would only take a few minutes. I should relax.

I felt a sharp tug and then a slow progression as the machine drew me into itself. Slowly.... I screwed my eyes tightly shut. I didn't want even one chink of light to seep through. I concentrated on lying perfectly still, barely breathing. The machine started its relentless mix of clanking and a sort of incessant hum. In a weird kind of way, the rhythmical noise was soothing. I tried to concentrate on thinking happy thoughts but the only image that kept repeating itself was the face of that ghostly woman I had seen in the old corridor. She dominated my mind, so real I actually felt I was looking at her. I seemed to float out of myself, not aware of the machine, the tube I lay in or even the hospital. I existed in a state of limbo, only for a few seconds, but in those seconds my reality was far from where I knew I must be.

The clanking stopped. The voice came through the speaker. "All done. We'll get you out now. You can open your eyes."

I suppose everyone closes them, but I certainly wasn't opening mine until I was sure I was well clear of the machine's confines.

"That wasn't so bad, was it?"

I was about to shake my head. Then I caught a glimpse of what was standing behind the radiographer and gasped.

"Whatever's the matter?"

"There's someone behind you."

The radiographer spun round. "Where?"

There was no one there, but she had been. I would swear she had. The little girl. Agnes. And she had pointed to me.

* * *

All I wanted was to return to my room, but Joyce kept me waiting in the wheelchair while she had a word with the radiographer. I knew from the hushed whispers that the nurse was being regaled with details of my sudden outburst. I tried to keep my face non-expressive. Next stop Psychiatric Ward if I wasn't careful.

Eventually Joyce pasted a smile on her face and came to wheel me back, which she did mostly in silence, beyond making some light remarks about how the weather had turned a lot colder.

"We'll be getting snow by the weekend," she said.

I murmured some form of agreement and tried hard not to panic about what I had seen. That someone – or something – was trying to communicate with me was, in my mind at least, certain, and their need to do so had clearly risen a notch. The questions remained as to why, and for what reason I had been chosen.

Another blow came when Paul rang to tell me he couldn't come to see me that evening. Some crisis at school threatened to keep him there for hours. After a few mouthfuls of a mild chicken curry, I couldn't eat anything else and gave up the effort, concentrating instead on vanilla ice cream.

Television proved its usual mix of game shows, soap operas and films of varying quality. A daft little comedy kept me mildly amused for a couple of hours until the evening cup of tea arrived and it was time for me to get ready for bed. I read a little but found it difficult to concentrate. When I eventually turned off my overhead light and shifted into as comfortable a position as my body would allow, my eyes had grown heavy with sleep.

I must have drifted off straightaway because when I awoke, it was with a jump. Surely I had only lain down a couple of minutes previously. I listened. Silence.

Then it came. That thumping I had heard previously. This was my chance.

I didn't even stop to think what I was doing. I grabbed my slippers and dressing gown and made my way to the door. I opened it quietly. A glance at my watch told me it was two-fifty. I watched the retreating form of the nurse on duty as she made for the far end of the corridor. Hadn't she heard the noise? It was loud enough, but evidently I was the only one permitted to hear it.

A movement in the corner of my eye distracted me. In the wall opposite, the door had reappeared. Once again, it stood ajar. I pushed it open wider and stepped in.

The familiar musty smell hit me and the gas mantles flickered as before. I cursed myself for forgetting to put my phone in my pocket. Snapshots of this corridor would surely have provided the proof I needed. I could go back to my room but that would risk coming back to find the door gone. Nothing for it, I would have to find something else.

For a moment, the corridor was deserted. Then the murmur of voices reached my ears. Figures materialized all around me. The same ghostly apparitions I had seen before, all ignoring me as if I, and not they, didn't exist. The scene swirled before my eyes at a nauseating speed.

The woman with the piercing gray eyes appeared, her gaze once again boring into me.

"Who are you?" I asked again. But still she wouldn't answer. She put out her hand, but not in a friendly way. Her fingers clenched into claws. I shrank from her icy touch and an unpleasant smile spread over her face. A look, almost of triumph, lit up her eyes.

"You're next," she said and vanished, along with all the others in the corridor. Still I had no proof. But this time, she had made physical contact. Her fingers had brushed my arm – the lightest of touches, but where she had made contact felt grazed.

She had said those words again, the same voice I had heard whispering them in my ear. All my instincts told me I had to get out of there fast, but I had to take something with me. Something that couldn't possibly have come from the present-day hospital.

I looked around me. A piece of linoleum perhaps, or scraps of the peeling paint. I tried to bend, but a sharp pain warned me to stop, so I settled for some larger scraps of paint hanging off the wall and slid them into my pocket. The color was a dirty yellowish white, completely unlike the soft pale gray of the present hospital walls, and the texture felt strangely granular. I hurried back along the corridor to the door leading to my ward.

The door that was no longer there.

Panic set in. I must have taken a wrong turn somewhere. But how could I? I had walked in a straight line. Pressing my hands against the wall, I willed the door to reappear, even pushed at it in the hope the wall would somehow give and let me through.

Behind me, voices struck up again. Chattering, their conversations indistinct. Smells of disinfectant and human sweat mingled and swam around me and, all the while, one voice sounded above the rest. The woman's voice repeated over and over, "You're next…you're next…"

A hand tugged at my dressing gown. I looked down at the little girl's face.

"Agnes?" I asked.

She nodded. "You can't be here. You mustn't stay and you mustn't come back. She wants you here too badly."

"Who is she, Agnes? Who is that woman who keeps appearing to me in this place? What do you know about her?"

The little girl blinked a few times and bit her lip. "I don't know her name. No one knows her name. She gets inside people and makes her home there. Then they die and she finds another. She found my ma. And took her. They told me so."

"Took her where?"

"She took her body."

"Is it your ma that I see here? Does she have gray eyes?"

Agnes shook her head and lowered her eyes.

"Agnes?"

She looked back up at me. "You have to go now. It's not safe."

"I'm trying to leave but the door's disappeared. Do you know another way?"

Agnes continued to look at me, her eyes wide. She slowly shook her head. "I'm not allowed. I have to stay here. The only time I can leave is when *she* lets me."

"Do you want to leave?" I asked.

She nodded. "But I know I can't. Not yet. It isn't my time."

Something about Agnes's appearance today had been bothering

me. Then I realized. Her dress. Before she had looked as if she probably belonged in the Victorian era, the same as the others that inhabited these corridors. But this time she looked different, her clothes belonging to an age far earlier than that. The collar of her dress would not have looked out of place during the English Civil War, and neither would her bonnet. "How old are you, Agnes?"

"I think I'm ten now."

"How long have you been here?"

She shrugged. "Always."

"And this is…was…the only way in and out of here?"

Agnes shrugged again.

"There must be another way. A main entrance."

The realization that I would have to go farther into the building in order to get out of it frightened me, but who knew when, or even if, the door would appear in this wall again?

"Will you come with me, Agnes? You don't have to leave here, but I would welcome your company."

What was I doing speaking to a ghost like this? But somehow it made sense. If she knew enough to know the woman wanted to keep me here, maybe she could also help me evade her clutches. Any straw, however fragile, was worth clinging to at this time.

Agnes slipped her cold hand into mine. It was like being grasped by a snowflake.

With one last, desperate look at where the door should have been, I started down the corridor.

CHAPTER THIRTEEN

It felt strange moving among ghosts, especially when it seemed none of them could see me. Only Agnes. I glanced down at her, to find her gazing up at me through pale, almost colorless eyes. She was only a child – a strange one, even in these most peculiar of circumstances, seeming out of place and time wherever she manifested herself – but those eyes seemed to hold knowledge more appropriate in a much older person. They were old eyes in a young body. And her apparent concern for my welfare did not ring entirely true although, for the life of me, I couldn't think why. I pushed the thoughts away. They took my already frazzled nerves into overdrive.

I also noticed Agnes seemed not to need to watch where she was going, but then she had walked these corridors for so long she probably knew every inch of them blindfolded. Not only that, I was becoming more and more convinced that Agnes was as much out of time here as I was. Apart from her current mode of dress, she was too young to be with the rest of the women.

There were no men among the constantly changing collection of faces. I knew from history that workhouses had been segregated. No family life here. Women and young children in one block – but kept separate – men and older boys in the other. The faces showed few smiles. Most looked tired, worn down by poverty and the hopelessness of their situation. Here, if I was to believe the evidence of my own eyes, even death would not part them from that.

I felt an overwhelming sense of sadness, a huge sense of loss. And then I heard the scream.

We froze. The scream came again. "Did you hear that?" I asked Agnes.

She nodded. Why didn't she seem scared? As if she had read my thoughts, she spoke.

"It's the madwoman. They tie her up when she makes too much noise."

A door opened and a well-dressed male strode out. "Keep her sedated."

One of the nurses spoke. "But what about the relatives, Dr. Franklyn? Surely we must let them know."

"There are no relatives, Nurse. Not here. Not now."

The nurse nodded to the door, which still stood slightly ajar. The woman's screams had died down to long, low moans. "She shouldn't even be here. She should be in the asylum. How can they say she's not insane? You only have to look at her."

"Nevertheless," the doctor said, "she is here and we have to contain her behavior as best we can. She's been quiet recently. Today was an unfortunate lapse. I'll increase her dosage and she will cease to be a problem. Alert the orderlies and the morgue, and you'll need the key for the corridor. We don't want to alarm the inmates by dragging a corpse through the building."

The nurses and doctor moved away, seeming to have forgotten all about the open door.

I moved closer. Agnes tugged on my arm.

"Don't go near. She'll kill you."

I couldn't help it. I had to see for myself who this woman was. Besides, she was sedated.

I crept into the room and up to the meager bed. Leather restraints secured the woman's wrists and ankles where angry sores had suppurated and oozed blood and stinking pus. What remained of her strangely modern-looking nightdress was little more than rags, filthy like the rest of her. Tentatively, I leaned over and looked into the woman's face. I recoiled both from the smell and the shock. Her eyes flew open. Her lips pulled back over her teeth in a snarl. Her voice was no more than a croak, but each word chilled me.

"You're next."

I raced out of the room, my heart thudding. I had to get out of that place. Agnes was nowhere to be seen. The corridor was empty and I had been trapped out of my time and space with no idea how to get back, and a strong sensation of being watched.

I tried to run but the best I managed was a hobble. Pain surged through me. I held my distended belly and prayed for help. Someone moved up behind me and I glanced over my shoulder, letting out a cry as I recognized the woman from the bed. She was gaining on me.

Her voice echoed. A thin, dry cackle. "You're next. She will have you. She has decided."

How could she have freed herself from those restraints? *She's a ghost. Of course she could get free.* The specter floated, some inches off the ground, her feet bare, straggly hair gusting behind her. She was maybe thirty feet away, but I knew she was making up the distance fast.

The corridor swung round to the right and sheer terror fueled the adrenaline that kept me going. Ahead, a Victorian-style door with glass panes through which daylight streamed. I prayed it wasn't locked. When I turned the handle and it opened, I dragged myself through and slammed it behind me. I leaned against the wooden panels, panting, my eyes closed.

"Are you all right?"

I opened my eyes, relieved to find I was back in the hospital in my own time, but not my ward. An unfamiliar nurse dressed in blue scrubs peered at me anxiously and I forced a smile on my face. "Yes, thanks. I seem to have got myself a bit lost. I should be in the Gynae Ward."

She smiled. "I'll take you back. You're only a little mislaid." She took me down past bays and individual rooms, out through double doors and into a familiar corridor. To my left I saw the sign 'Gynecology Ward'.

"There you are. Not too far from home."

"Thanks," I said. In familiar surroundings once more, I managed to regain my composure enough to be able to saunter – well, my version of it anyway – back onto my ward.

Joyce met me at the Nurses' station. "You were up early. Breakfast hasn't even been served yet. Been for a walk? Go anywhere nice?"

I pasted a smile on my face. "Oh, just into town, quick bit of retail therapy."

She laughed and I made my way back to my room, where I sank onto the bed, exhausted. I didn't even remove my dressing gown but did shrug my slippers off. Painfully, I bent down and picked one of them up. The sole was filthy. Was that evidence of my claims to have been somewhere other than the clean wards of this hospital? Hardly. It would only prove I had stepped outside.

Remembering my precious cargo, I reached into my pocket. Sure enough the flakes of paint were still there. I extracted them one by one and laid them on the bedside cabinet. They didn't look much. Just some old whitewash and paint layers in small insignificant chips. Better than nothing, but not much.

I took a tissue from the box and carefully wrapped them before placing them in the top drawer of the cabinet. I would show them to Paul later. Meanwhile, sleep was all I craved.

It wasn't to be. The door opened. Time for my usual checks. This was swiftly followed by my morning cup of tea, shower and breakfast.

It struck me around then. I had been out of my room for maybe three hours, since before dawn, and no one had missed me. Those who had noticed had merely assumed I had gone for an early walk – even though I must have broken the cardinal rule of telling someone when I left the ward. Supposing I had come to harm in that strange place, how long would it have been before anyone had realized I was missing?

* * *

Paul's anger showed in his rapidly reddening face. "I'm having a word with someone. This is disgraceful."

"No, Paul, don't. Please. I'll only have to try and explain where I was and no one will believe me."

He hesitated. "Look, I understand that, but anything could have happened to you and they wouldn't have known. I'll only promise I won't make a complaint this time if you promise me you won't go looking for trouble again. Stay away from that… that…whatever it is."

"Okay." I sighed. Frankly, after my last experience I didn't much fancy repeating my visit or even my encounter with Agnes. "Let's go for a coffee."

"Are you sure you're up for it?"

I nodded, then pointed to the flakes of paint lying in the tissue. "Do you think you could get someone to analyze those?"

"I have contacts," Paul said, carefully wrapping the tissue into a tight wad and tucking it into his jacket pocket.

"I wish I could have found something more tangible."

Paul was looking at my feet. "You need new slippers. I'll bring some tomorrow and I'll get the old ones analyzed as well. You never know. Maybe you've picked up something on them that couldn't possibly be here in this day and age."

"Thanks. They look as if I've been for a ten-mile hike."

* * *

The cafeteria bustled as usual. A patient limped by, wheeling a portable drip. Others lounged in dressing gowns talking to their visitors. Children chattered and played. Nurses grabbed coffees and sandwiches on their breaks.

I nursed my cup of mocha while Paul sipped a flat latte.

"Do you think you'll still be coming home next week?" he asked.

"I hope so. Maryam hasn't said anything different. I should be getting the MRI results through soon. Meanwhile, I'm keeping quiet on my experiences. I don't want to give them any fuel for thinking I need psychiatric assessment."

His attention was drawn to something over my shoulder. "Your friend's back."

I blinked. Paul nodded behind me. I struggled to my feet.

"Hello, Vanessa."

Hearing her voice without seeing her brought a shock of recognition. It held a distinctive tone. How had I missed that in our earlier encounter down here? I took a deep breath and turned to face her. She stood, smiling at me. *That* was why. The voice and the facial expression didn't match and I had previously allowed myself to be taken in by the warm smile. It was in evidence today, but much altered. This time, her mouth smiled, but her eyes were a different matter. Gone was the aura of friendliness. In that instant I knew I was right and another piece in this impossible jigsaw slotted into place. "Hello," I said, my mouth dry.

"You're looking tired. Are you getting enough sleep?"

"Not entirely." I was aware of the chill in my voice.

"I'm sorry to hear that. I hope you'll sleep much better very soon. In fact, I know you will."

She smiled, nodded and moved away. I sat down.

"You were almost rude to her," Paul said. "You defended her to me last time. What's happened? Something you haven't told me?"

I avoided his eyes for a second while my thoughts raced, but there was no point in hiding my suspicions. "It's *her* voice I heard whispering to me in the corridor when I went through that wall. I didn't register at first but now I'm certain. Somehow she can materialize here and go back in time. She looks different there but I'm certain. *She's* the one who tells me I'm next. But next for what? She's some sort of link between the two…worlds."

Paul stared at his coffee. "I think we need you out of here. Get you home or transferred to another hospital."

"No, Paul, no. I'm getting the best treatment here, I can't go anywhere else. This is the right hospital for my cancer."

He drummed his fingers on the table. "I'm not happy about this." He stood, pushing his chair back.

"Where are you going?"

"To have a word with that woman. Which way did she go?"

I looked wildly round. Still the milling throngs, but no sign of the woman.

"Damn it!" Paul sat, scraping the chair noisily across the floor.

"It won't do any good," I said. "Just leave it."

"I can't just leave it. That woman threatened you."

"When? She hasn't actually said anything threatening at all, apart from 'you're next', and I have no idea what she was referring to when she said it. It could be something completely innocuous."

"But you don't think so. And then there's that little ghost girl. Didn't she warn you about her? She actually said that woman would kill you."

"Maybe I got that wrong. Maybe Agnes got that wrong. Maybe she didn't even mean her or it could simply be my own paranoia."

"You're not paranoid. I've known you too long, Nessa, I'd notice."

I drained my coffee. "I think I'd like to go back now. I'm feeling really tired." I didn't tell him about the strange feeling I was experiencing. Something in my head didn't feel right.

Paul took my arm as we made our way back to the lift. No sign of the woman.

Back in my room, it was a relief to sink into my comfortable bed, even though the area between my nonexistent waist and the top of my thighs stung and burned until I got myself comfortably settled.

"Better?"

"I will be. It'll die down in a few minutes."

"Do you need some more painkillers?"

I shook my head. "It's too early. They'll come round with them later."

Paul glanced at his watch. "I'd better get off now. I've still got some notes to write up for tomorrow's staff meeting."

"Thanks for coming and for putting up with me."

Paul smiled and kissed me lightly on the lips. "No wandering into strange places. Remember you promised."

"I know. I won't."

The door closed softly behind Paul as I leaned back against the pillows and closed my eyes.

* * *

I felt a breath on my cheek, opened my eyes and stared straight into the face of the woman from the café.

She smiled down at me as I shrank back in bed.

"Who are you?" I asked.

"My name's Hester," she said. She had opted for the natural look today. No scarf. The light glanced off her bald head.

"How did you find me?"

"I told you when we first met. I can see things others can't."

"But why me?"

"Because you have been chosen."

"Chosen for what?"

"You have a special purpose."

I clutched the sheet tightly up to my chin, my knuckles white from the effort. "I don't understand what you want from me."

She laid her hand over mine. Icy cold, white, bloodless. I shivered.

The woman's eyes held me in their gaze. She said nothing. Tension mounted inside me. "My husband just left," I said. "You must have seen him. Did he speak to you?"

"No."

Scared as I was, I needed confirmation. I moistened my lips. "You know about the corridor, don't you?" I said.

Her eyes held a questioning look.

"Please don't pretend you don't know what I'm talking about, Hester. The door that appears sometimes and not others and when it does it takes you into an older building. A different time…."

"There have been many buildings on this site over the centuries. Some have left their mark."

"The workhouse. The last building to be here. There's some sort of portal outside this room."

"There are many portals."

"I believe you know what's going on. I believe I have seen you there and you keep telling me I'm next. What am I next for? Why are these things happening to me and what's your involvement?"

"I have already told you all I can. For now. Has the little girl been back? Agnes?"

"Yes. You told me she wanted to help but I'm not sure that's true."

Hester smiled. "She has…let's say she has her own agenda. I think that's the correct term. Yes. Her own agenda."

"I'm not going back there. Not after last time. I couldn't get out of that place. And you threatened me. I'll ask you again. What did you mean by 'you're next'?"

Hester smiled but it was a smile that could freeze boiling water. "You can always come back. There's always a way, you simply have to find it. As for threatening you.... No, I didn't threaten you. I merely stated the truth. You *are* next. Time is a strange medium. The past, present, future, all exist simultaneously. You only have to know where to look and sometimes your destiny finds *you*. Sometimes others help you find your destiny, and sometimes others are sent to bring you to your destiny." She picked up my book and the folded sheet of paper containing the poem fluttered to the floor. She bent and retrieved it, opened and read it.

A wave of anger dissolved my fears as it swept through me. "What the hell are you talking about?"

A slow smile spread across her face as she refolded the paper and tucked it back into the book, noting its author. "John Grisham. I am unfamiliar with his work. Is he any good?"

"Yes. He writes great suspense novels." Surely even a non-reader must have heard of one of the world's bestselling authors? Apparently not this one. "Are you going to answer my question?"

"The poem. Where did you get it?"

"It fell out of another book. I got it from the hospital library."

She nodded. "You should heed the words."

"Heed them? In what way?"

"Because they apply to you."

"I don't understand. Will you please stop talking in riddles and explain yourself?"

"It will all become clear, but I must go now."

"But hang on a minute. Wait—"

The door closed behind her only to be opened a few seconds later by a nurse I hadn't met before.

"Hello, I'm Nancy. I'm on duty this evening."

"Hello, Nancy. Did you see a woman come out of my room?"

"When? Now?"

I nodded.

She shook her head. "I probably missed her. I was with another patient next door until a few seconds ago."

I let it go. She took my temperature, blood pressure, enquired after the state of my bowel movements, fluffed my pillows and left, promising a dose of Movicol the next morning unless I had managed to 'perform'. Movicol always did the trick all right.

The problem was it did it too well and every time I went to the bathroom I had to douche my lower parts afterward to ward off any chance of infection. Maryam was strict about that. Last time I had 'performed' five times in as many hours. That's an awful lot of douching. It would certainly keep me out of mischief the next day because I wouldn't dare stray too far from my bathroom.

I fought to keep Hester and my experience down that corridor out of my mind. I made myself as comfortable as possible with the television on. I caught the last half of *Back to the Future*. I had lost count of the number of times I'd seen all three of the series, but it was what I needed that night. Forcing myself to become absorbed in it gradually relaxed tense muscles. By the time the credits rolled, I had almost convinced myself that Hester was a crazy eccentric who enjoyed playing mind games. Almost. But a weird feeling in my head wouldn't go away. A sort of probing sensation. My eyes grew heavier and I may even have drifted off.

The scream blasted through my semi-conscious state. I struggled out of bed and grabbed my dressing gown. From outside I heard the sound of running feet, a gabble of voices, a woman sobbing hysterically.

I pulled the door open and saw a fellow patient – a young woman in her twenties, I guessed. I had seen her before. Her face had looked troubled then and she had seemed wrapped up in dark thoughts. She was lying on the floor in a heap, her feet under her, clutching at her hair while two nurses and a couple of patients tried to calm her. There were pale reddish marks around her wrists as if they had been bound for some reason.

She looked directly at me, her eyes red with crying. "They hurt me. They're using me like a guinea pig...."

One of the nurses called to a colleague who was hurrying up the corridor. "Page the doctor on call. Get him here now."

The young student nurse needed no further telling.

"What happened to her?" I asked.

One of the patients replied, "I don't really know. Maybe she was sleepwalking."

"Wasn't...sleepwalking. She told me...to come with her." The woman on the floor continued to direct her responses directly to me. "*You* know, don't you? You've seen her too. You've been there. I can tell by the look on your face." A patient handed her a tissue and she blew her nose and attempted to sit up. All eyes turned to me.

"The little girl or the woman with the bald head?" I asked. The women glanced at each other. I must have sounded crazy to them. But not to the patient on the floor.

"The woman. Hester."

I nodded.

The woman pointed at the wall. "You've been there too, haven't you? To the other place."

Inwardly I thanked every being I could imagine. I wasn't alone now. Even though I knew Paul was prepared to give me the benefit of the doubt, not to mention Margie, it wasn't the same as meeting someone who had shared my experience and been frightened by it.

"What's she on about?" one of the other patients asked. The other one shrugged, while the nurses looked from one to the other of us, their faces incredulous.

"Did she hurt you?" I asked.

The woman shook her head. "Not her. Not Hester. Arabella Marsden, and Dr. Franklyn. They're evil. They're experimenting on people. They drilled a hole in my head.... And they tied my legs and wrists. You can see." She shifted her position, the effort etched in her face. At the sight of her ankles, even the nurses looked shocked.

Suppurating reddish-purple weals showed clear evidence of bonds that had been tied too tightly.

The doctor hurried up the corridor. "What's going on here?" He bent down to the patient on the floor. "That looks nasty, Carol," he said, gently touching one ankle.

The girl winced.

"How did you do that?" the doctor asked.

"You wouldn't believe me. No one would. Except her." She pointed at me. "She knows because she's been there too."

"She's not lying," I said. All around me, disbelief led to shaking heads, even a muffled giggle from one of the patients.

The doctor stood up. "I don't know what's going on here, but I think it's best if we get Carol down for an X-ray on those ankles to make sure nothing's broken. They're both quite swollen, but I think it's soft tissue damage. The rest of you, back to bed."

The nurses nodded and the other two patients reluctantly dispersed.

"We'll talk tomorrow," I said to Carol, who nodded.

The student nurse reappeared with a wheelchair and Carol cast a glance back at me as she was taken away. "In darkness, shadows breathe," she mouthed.

That poem. Shocked, I nodded and gave a little wave. I went back to bed but couldn't sleep. What had Carol seen and experienced on the other side? Whatever this was, it seemed to be stepping up its actions and who knew what it would do next?

* * *

I had showered, breakfasted, taken my Movicol and was preparing to make my way down the corridor to see Carol when the door opened to admit Maryam, accompanied by Joyce.

"Hello, Nessa. You've been having some adventures I hear."

I grimaced. "I'm not the only one."

"So I've been told. All very mysterious."

"You could say that."

Maryam gave me a curious look before plowing on. "I have some news. We have had two lots of results back. Firstly, the histology has come back on the tissues we sent following your operation. It showed primary vaginal cancer but only at a microscopic level. The good news is there is no evidence it has spread and everything points to us having caught it early enough, but the next course of action is radiotherapy when you've recovered. This cancer isn't known for traveling too far but we need to make sure it hasn't wandered into the lymph nodes."

I squirmed. "I still have to have radiotherapy even though you've caught it all?"

"It's advisable. I mentioned during our consultations that we needed to allow a surgical margin around the affected area and that led us to have to remove part of your urethra, but in that area it was difficult to ensure the safest margin, so radiotherapy is the best way to ensure we catch anything that might be lurking there. The thing to focus on is that it is curative in your case, Nessa. We've caught it early enough."

"So the burning vulva was a good thing then?" I managed a smile.

Maryam gave a light laugh. "You could put it that way. I'm not sure I would. It highlighted the problem though, even if it presented us all with an enigma. All sorted out now of course. We'll be sending you home in a few days if you keep making good progress. Then it will be checkups in the clinic every four months, which we'll run in conjunction with Moreton Grange so we're covering all angles. I have more news as well. The results of your MRI are in and that's good news. There is nothing to indicate anything abnormal is going on inside your brain."

"Thank goodness for that." The strange, unwelcome sensation in my head seemed to swim around a little, making me feel momentarily nauseous. I swallowed hard and chose not to mention it. A minute ago, I had been told everything was fine. I must have been imagining the odd feeling.

"It was better to be cautious." Maryam performed her usual physical examination, pronounced herself delighted with the way my skin was healing and left me.

I promptly had the urge to visit the bathroom. The Movicol was doing its job.

Twenty minutes later, freshly douched and dressed in a caftan Paul had brought in for me the previous day, I even managed to put on a little makeup. For a woman who rarely went out without at least a bit of lipstick, eyeshadow and foundation, it made me feel more like me. Carrying a light shoulder bag, I made my way down the corridor to the bay containing six beds, one of which I knew must be Carol's. Three of the beds were unoccupied. Friday. Kicking-out day. Those beds would probably remain empty until Monday when a new influx of patients would arrive.

Joyce had just finished tending to a patient.

"Do you know where Carol is?" I asked.

"She's been moved to another ward in the main hospital, I think. I'm not sure really."

Damn.

I made my way to the elevator, intent on going down to the shop next to the cafeteria.

But never made it.

CHAPTER FOURTEEN

The lights snapped off, plunging me into darkness while the entire elevator shook once and stopped.

"Vanessa...Vanessa...."

The whispers were all around me. More than one voice, overlapping each other. I clapped my hands to my ears to shut them out but they invaded my mind and came from within me.

"Vanessa...Vanessa...."

"Stop it!" I screamed out into the darkness. Not one chink of light anywhere. No sound except the interminable, infernal whispering. Female, male, child. A whole throng of people all whispering my name.

"What do you want from me?"

No response. More murmuring.

The blackness bore me down. Its weight crushed me. I tried to curl myself into a ball but the pain refused to allow me. I sobbed louder, trying to drown out the spectral sounds.

"This isn't real. It isn't happening."

When all the while I knew it was.

"Vanessa...Vanessa...."

"Who...are you?" I was choking. I couldn't get my breath, every gasp a supreme effort of will. "Let me out of here." Frantically, I scrabbled along the wall, trying to find the control panel. My fingers found only smooth metal and then...buttons. I pressed one after the other. Nothing worked. One was larger than the rest. I had found the alarm. That *had* to work, didn't it? I pressed it once, twice, again and again. Either it was out of order or I was pressing the wrong one after all. I ran out of buttons. Nothing.

I cried out for help until I thought my lungs would burst.

Without warning, a dazzling white light lit up the compartment.

It blinded me and I shielded my eyes. Something grabbed my arm but I couldn't see who or what it was. Were they taking me to safety or…? The door opened.

I allowed myself to be propelled forward until I was clear of the elevator and back in the old corridor of the workhouse. This time, the women milling around could plainly see me. And they weren't ethereal anymore, but as solid as me.

A tug at my arm. I looked down. Agnes. She seemed a little older today. Taller. And she was wearing a dark brown Victorian dress.

"Was that you?" I asked. "Did you just get me out of there?" I nodded to where the elevator was…or rather, had been. Now there was a solid wall of peeling paint.

"She says you are to come with me," Agnes said.

"Who says?"

"Miss Marsden."

I let Agnes lead me past the questioning faces. I must have looked completely out of place in my green and blue caftan, compression socks, and slippers. They were all dressed the same in drab brown dresses with aprons. Their eyes bored into me.

An officious-looking woman in a smart uniform of a navy-blue dress, buttoned up to her neck and extending to her feet, topped off with a starched snowy-white apron and bonnet, marched up the corridor clapping her hands. "To your work. To your work. Idleness has no place here."

She cast me a quick, almost angry glance and promptly ignored my presence as she continued to chivvy the women along. She didn't seem to see Agnes at all. No one did, apart from me.

"Where are you taking me?" I asked Agnes.

The child did not answer. We had rounded the corner I remembered from my earlier visit and now passed the door I had exited through. This part of the building was quiet. Presently, Agnes stopped in front of a door and knocked.

A strident female voice called from within, "Enter."

Agnes reached up to the door handle and turned it. She half pushed me in and closed the door, leaving me alone with a woman dressed in black from head to foot.

She stared at me and I blinked. Her eyes. I had seen them before. Pale gray, seeming to penetrate deep into my brain. The hairs on the back of my neck bristled and I would have given anything to get out of there. The woman radiated evil.

She spoke. "My name is Arabella Marsden and I have waited a long time to meet you."

"What is this place? How am I even here?"

"Questions. Always questions. This is Waverley Workhouse and you are here because I sent for you."

"But I don't belong here."

"You're wrong. You belong here every bit as much as you belong in your own time."

"I don't understand."

"You will."

"What did you do to Carol?"

"That is none of your concern."

Strange that I had lost all sense of the peculiarity of the situation. That I could be here, so far out of my own time, talking with…a ghost. She had to be, didn't she? Or was *I* the ghost here?

The woman continued to stare at me. She clasped her hands in front of her and said nothing.

"The poem," I said at last. "*In darkness, shadows breathe.* What do you know about it?"

"It was written for you."

"How could you know that? It was written over a century before I was born, and who is Lydia Warren Carmody anyway?"

"You have a limited sense of time and space. You see time as linear but it is not. It is fluid. I knew about you long before you were born. We too are linked, as you are to Lydia Warren Carmody. All of us are linked to the spirit that sought us out long ago. The One and the Many. Old as time itself. Older even, since time does not exist as you know it."

My back ached from standing. "I need to sit down."

"Ah yes, your operation." She indicated a chair and I lowered myself into it, trying not to wince.

I tried again, calmer this time. "There was a woman here…."

Last time I came. Agnes called her the madwoman. She was screaming and they sedated her, but the way the doctor was talking, she wouldn't be sedated for long. I'm certain he was planning to kill her. Somehow she escaped from where they were restraining her and followed me. She spoke to me and said, 'you're next'. And there's another woman who I've met in my time and this. Her name's Hester and she claims to be psychic. She also keeps telling me I'm next. I need you to tell me what's going on here, and what your role is in this."

This time I did get a reaction. "Hester is a transient spirit. To put it in language you might understand, she moves across time as easily as you move from your time to this. It is she who brings you here. As for the other…. Her name is Susan Jackson. Unfortunate case. She could have been so much more, but we learned a great deal from her and her soul will soon be free." She closed her mouth. I would get nothing more out of her.

She turned back from me and I felt an overwhelming tiredness. My eyelids grew heavy and I could no longer keep them open. I tried to speak, but my mouth wouldn't obey and I slipped into a half-conscious world where phantoms moved silently along endless hallways and the woman's eyes stared at me from every angle. Silent, unblinking, waiting.

* * *

I came to in my bed. Margie was bustling around with her cleaning cloths.

"Had a good sleep?" she asked.

It took me a second to realize where I was. I looked down at myself, still dressed in my caftan, my slippers on the floor beside my bed. I sat up, glanced at my watch and found it was almost lunchtime.

I shook my head. "I had another one of those…I don't even know what to call them. Experiences, I suppose."

Margie paused, cloth in hand. I noticed my bag, perched on the visitor's chair – something I never did. For reasons of security I always put it in the bedside cabinet, but I ignored it for the moment.

"What happened?" Margie asked, her attention firmly diverted away from her work and onto my story.

I told her, watching her expression change from curiosity to something like familiarity. "You've heard all this before, haven't you?" I asked.

Margie nodded so vigorously her hair threatened to escape the clutches of the loose bun.

She hesitated as if uncertain whether she should say anything, then made up her mind.

"You need to leave here." Her voice was low, as if she was scared someone might overhear her. "You need to ask them to discharge you. Tomorrow. Today if you can. It's too dangerous for you here. Someone else—"

The door opened. Joyce popped her head around the door. "Margie, when you've finished here could you pop next door with your mop and bucket?"

Margie nodded and Joyce shut the door.

"What do you mean it's too dangerous?" I asked. "Besides I can't leave until next week. Maryam said so."

Margie came closer. "Look, I don't know everything, but there have been instances over the years when women have simply disappeared from here. Every time, just before it happened, they had a story like yours to tell. The last time I heard it was yesterday evening."

"You don't mean…Carol?"

Margie nodded. "After she had that funny turn, they took her to X-ray and the next anyone knew she was bundled off to another ward, except she never arrived. It's all being hushed up at the moment, but she is officially a missing person and she's not the only one. A woman called Susan Jackson has also disappeared. Same ward as Carol."

"Susan Jackson?" I didn't tell her that I very much feared I knew exactly what had happened to her. "What about the families? They must be going crazy with worry."

"I don't know anything about Susan but Carol hasn't got any. There's a friend, I believe, but that's it. No one to kick up any kind of stink as far as I can see. The official line is that she simply walked out, but I have my doubts, especially with her ankles so sore and bandaged. These past few days Carol has had a similar story to tell as all the rest of them. As you have. And now she's gone. When your husband comes in, get him to help you pack and then discharge yourself. Please. It's for your own good. You're a nice person and I don't want them to get you as well."

"Who, Margie? You said 'them'. Do you know who they are? Apart from Hester, I've only seen ghosts of people from the old workhouse, a doctor, Agnes and a woman called Arabella Marsden." I didn't mention Susan Jackson.

"That's her. Arabella Marsden was in charge of the workhouse at one time, along with a man, a Dr. Franklyn. My great aunt knew of them because she spent part of her childhood there. They were praised by the medical world for pioneering work in the field of mental illness, but they were evil, cruel. They terrorized the female inmates, conducted experiments on them, treated them worse than animals. Great Aunt Florence used to say the Marsden woman was the devil in person, without one ounce of compassion or humanity in her. But she was clever. Very clever. She could be your best friend one minute and your murderer the next. She had some plan. I don't know what it was but she swore she and the doctor had discovered the source of the soul. She said the truth had been revealed to them and they were guided by the hand of another. Something supernatural. My aunt didn't believe any of that but there was someone else she used to speak of. Oh, what was her name? Double-barreled surname, Warren something."

"Lydia Warren Carmody?"

"That's it. Aunt Florence said it was rumored that Arabella Marsden was in league with a she-devil who had possessed a patient in the asylum – a woman who had tried to commit suicide. Then there were rumors about this Warren Carmody woman, who was a convicted murderer I believe."

"I need to show you something."

I removed the poem from the book and handed it to Margie. She read it and handed it back to me. I read it again.

"It makes you shiver, doesn't it?" Margie said. "That's the woman's name all right. Not long before she died, Arabella Marsden went mad. This was after Dr. Franklyn passed away in strange circumstances. The story goes that he and Marsden were conducting some experiment where they summoned the she-devil that possessed the woman who wrote this poem. They wanted immortality and they said the demon could grant it to them in return for all they had done for her. They were arrogant as always. Anyway, there was a strange fire one night. Staff heard the Marsden woman screaming hysterically from the laboratory and they had to break the door down to get to her. That's when they found the doctor. Incinerated on the floor. Not much more than a pile of ash. Great Aunt Florence called it a load of stuff and nonsense, but my grandmother – her sister – wasn't so sure. She'd read some folk story about a wandering wrathful she-devil called the One and the Many who possessed the bodies of women, heightening their emotions of anger and revenge. It was her belief that the doctor and Arabella Marsden had overstepped the mark and the demon had struck out. Arabella Marsden spent the rest of her wretched life in a padded cell."

"That's quite some story." I pointed to the poem and read it aloud.

"In darkness, shadows breathe
Though the earth be still, with graves,
The mourning yearn for solace
And the dead shall hear their cry,
Sending spirits on winged flight,
To comfort and console,
But one among them bides behind,
Her soul of ebony and granite,
The fires of life long since quenched,
Replaced with voids of emptiness.
In darkness, shadows breathe
And death their only reward.

"You know, the first part is quite gentle," I said. "But I'm seeing the rest of it differently now. It's as if she's talking about something evil that will triumph over the innocent, who can now only look forward to an eternity in death."

The door opened again. Joyce didn't look happy. "Margie. Please could you go next door? There's a big puddle there and Kerry's going to go mad if she sees it."

"Coming. Sorry." The apology was to both of us. Joyce left again. "Don't stay here any longer or you *will* be next."

I nodded at Margie. "Thank you for telling me all this."

She gave me a quick smile and left.

My thoughts tossed themselves around my head. None made much sense unless I completely abandoned every rule of the natural world I had ever grown up with. The questions grew until my head felt as if it would explode at any moment.

I decided to take myself off for a short walk. Maybe I would stand at the main entrance of the hospital and get some air. Perhaps that would help unclog my overloaded brain.

It didn't.

* * *

"I'm not happy about letting you go quite so soon," Maryam said. "You've had such a big operation, I would prefer we left it a few more days. Just to be sure there are no more complications. You've been through such a lot, Nessa. I don't want us to undo all the good work by making rash decisions now."

"I really want to go home, Maryam. I promise I won't do anything stupid."

She hesitated. "I'm a little concerned as to why you want to leave us so suddenly."

"I'm feeling much better and I just feel ready."

"Give it another three days. Providing your temperature and blood pressure remain steady and there are no further setbacks, I think we can look at that."

Not the immediate discharge Margie had urged, but at least I had something to work toward. Only three more days. Then I would be home.

Safe at last.

CHAPTER FIFTEEN

I don't know how I ended up there.

After Maryam left I drifted off to sleep. A combination of relief that I would be able to escape Margie's predictions and the fear I had been under for days rose to the surface and left me exhausted.

A fusty smell invaded my nostrils and I opened my eyes. The noise of women milling around outside wafted through the keyhole of the solid metal door. I didn't need to wonder where I was. I knew. The only questions were how and why.

My heart plummeted. I was alone in a filthy room, lying on a bed that consisted of a bare board partially covered with a moth-eaten and threadbare gray blanket. Another bed lay empty beside me and there was plenty of evidence of Victorian medicine all around – white china or porcelain bowls of varying shapes and sizes, a trolley with vicious-looking instruments laid out neatly and covering the surface. Stands, rubber tubes, bottles, machines for goodness alone knew what purposes. A galvanized bucket stood in one corner. No prizes for guessing its purpose.

Despite the horror around me, I felt strangely calm. Then I heard a scratching sound. Someone turning the key in the lock. The door creaked as it was pushed open.

Arabella Marsden strode in, her mouth twisted in a half grimace.

"What do you want with me?" My voice sounded strong. I was glad of that because I certainly didn't feel that way.

"You will see." She turned to her sidekick – a thin woman with a pinched face. "Bring the other one in."

I recognized her as soon as they wheeled her in. "Carol!"

The orderly dragged her out of the wheelchair. Her nightgown was torn.

I struggled off the bed and tried to help her. The Marsden

woman thrust me to one side and I scrabbled for the bed to stop me falling.

Carol collapsed in a sobbing heap on the floor at my feet.

"You can't do this. It's inhuman," I said.

Arabella Marsden threw back her head and laughed, a low, vile guttural sound. "I haven't yet begun."

I put out my hand to Carol, who struggled to her feet. I steered her as best I could to sit down beside me as I glared at our captor. Her eyes mocked me and I had never felt such abject hatred for anyone in my life. The woman spun on her heel and, with a swish of her dress, left us. A key scraped in the lock of the door.

Carol raised tear-stained cheeks and reddened eyes to mine. Her shoulder-length hair looked matted and in dire need of washing and brushing.

"I…know…you," Carol said. "I'm sorry, I know we've met somewhere but I've forgotten your name. I can remember so little these days. I even have trouble remembering who I am."

"I'm Nessa. What's happening here? Do you have any idea?"

"A little. Not much. How do you know me?"

"The doctor referred to you by name when we found you on the floor outside my room, and Margie, the cleaner, told me you disappeared on the way to the general ward."

Carol blinked a few times, clearly searching her mind for some relevant memory. "I don't remember any of that." The effort of trying to recall showed in her face. "A nurse was with me…and then it all changed…. Darkness…. I was lying in a heap on the floor of the corridor out there." She nodded toward the door.

"The same thing happened to me. Not this time. Another time."

"You've been here before?"

"So have you. You told me so when we first met, and you guessed I had been here too."

She shook her head. "I'm sorry, it's all so hazy, as if it's been happening to someone else. A long time ago. Someone else in my body. But that doesn't make any sense."

"It makes more sense than you realize. When I last saw you, you said something about Arabella Marsden, Dr. Franklyn and some kind of experiment. You said they had drilled a hole in your head and they had restrained you. Your ankles were pretty messed up."

Carol looked at me as if I had suddenly grown another head. "I don't understand any of that. My ankles are fine. Look."

Apart from the grubbiness of being in contact with the filthy floor, there was no trace of bruising, swelling or weals on either ankle. Her wrists no longer showed evidence of being bound either. Carol tossed her hair forward and I peered at her scalp. No trace of any lesion there but, then, I hadn't seen one on our first encounter.

"You really don't remember being on the floor outside the ward? That's when I met you."

Carol frowned and shook her head. "I know we've met before, but I don't remember when or where and I do know that time has been playing strange tricks on me. I can remember less and less each day. When I try to recall where I live…or work…I can't. It's all a blur, like a heavy fog in my brain."

"Time isn't linear."

Carol's eyes snapped open. "What did you say?"

"Time isn't linear. Well, it's a theory anyway. A friend of ours kept us entertained at a dinner party once, regaling us with this idea that we humans have invented time because our brains can't cope with the truth that there is actually no such thing. There is no past, present or future as we choose to interpret it. That woman, Arabella Marsden. She said time did not exist as we know it. It put me in mind of it."

"It's just I heard someone say that very same thing once. 'Time isn't linear.' I can't remember…." She tapped her forehead harder and harder until I had to pull her fingers away to stop her hurting herself. I was struck by the iciness of them.

"You're freezing," I said.

She looked at me vacantly as if trying to remember yet again who I was. "Am I?"

"You realize that we're not in our own time, don't you?" I said. "Maybe that's how you're here now, without the injury I saw you with a few days ago. Maybe it hasn't happened yet. Or maybe it has, but long enough ago to give your body time to heal." The sheer unfathomability of what I was saying hit me. I shook my head. "All I know for certain is, we're in the same place – the Royal and Waverley – but as it used to be many years ago when this part was a workhouse."

Carol blinked a few times. "Now you've said it, I can accept it, even though it seems impossible."

"Do you know why they've brought us here? According to Margie, there have been other disappearances like ours over the years."

"I do know she seems restless. Arabella Marsden. The others seem scared of her as if she has some kind of hold over them all, not that I remember having much to do with anyone else. They seem to keep me apart from any of the inmates."

"Do you see them as real, or ghostly?" I asked.

"The inmates? Almost transparent."

"I don't think they see us at all most of the time. It's as if they exist in a different dimension."

Carol touched my hand. I felt the chill almost freeze my blood. "Are you scared? I know I am."

"Terrified, but we mustn't show them that. Somehow we have to get out of here."

"But how?"

We both stared at the door. How could we get through six inches of iron or steel or whatever that thing was constructed out of?

The door rattled as its key turned. It opened and the orderly motioned us to follow him. I helped Carol up and we followed him down the corridor. Our progress was slow, irritating our escort, who kept looking back over his shoulder and frowning at us, gesturing to us to speed up.

"I'm going as fast as I can," I said. "Can't you see I'm in pain here? I had major surgery a couple of weeks ago."

The man resumed his strident gait until he stopped in front of another door. A wooden one this time. The orderly knocked and a strong male voice answered. "Enter."

The orderly turned the door handle. "In here."

I hobbled inside, Carol at my side.

This room looked freshly whitewashed. An oil lamp burned on a polished desk behind which sat a man. A doctor by the look of him. He wore a smart, dark brown suit, high starched collar and tie. His beard was neatly trimmed and, as we entered, he removed wire-framed spectacles, which he folded and positioned neatly in front of him.

"Please sit." He indicated the two chairs in front of his desk. "That will be all, Withers." The door closed with a click.

"Now, ladies, I expect you want to know why you are here."

"You have no right to kidnap us," I said.

He gave a hollow laugh. "Kidnap? Yes, I suppose to you it seems like that. I think a more accurate term would be... repossession."

The arrogance of the man. "Repossession?"

"Exactly. You belong here."

"I have a husband. A life," I said. "And it's not here. Carol has a life—"

"Does she? Do you, Carol?"

The girl stared down at her hands, which were twisting together in her lap. Why didn't she speak up for herself?

"Carol?" I prompted.

She looked up, panic filling her eyes. "No...I don't. I can't remember when I had a life. That's the problem with me. I don't belong anywhere."

The doctor looked at her steadily. I couldn't believe what I was hearing. "But you have a home?" I asked. "A job? Friends?"

Carol sighed, tears filling her eyes. "Not really. I live... somewhere. I'm not sure where at the moment. It's lost to me somehow. As for a job. I don't remember anything about that, and friends.... Do I have friends? Are you my friend?"

"Carol, what *is* this?" I glared at the doctor. "What have you done to her? This woman has a life in our time. I know she has friends because someone told me. Someone at the hospital, which is where we should be right now. My husband will be coming to see me this evening. My life is *there*, not here."

"Interesting," the doctor said. "Carol hasn't been with us long but already she is assimilating to her environment. She knows, deep down, that she belongs here, in this time and space. Soon you will feel the same way, Vanessa."

"I most certainly will not. I can't speak for Carol. I only really met her today, although I've seen her before, in distressing circumstances thanks to something that happened here…or that *is* going to happen here. But, for myself, I have a husband. I was a lecturer in Modern History at the university and Paul and I live in an apartment overlooking the Irish Sea. I remember every inch of my life and none of it belongs here or in this time."

"Nevertheless." The doctor opened his hands expansively. "Here you are and here you are meant to stay."

I struggled to my feet. "No," I said, my voice firm, even though the surgical pain once again asserted itself.

"We'll see how you feel tomorrow."

"I don't intend to be here tomorrow. In fact, I don't intend to stay here one minute longer."

"You don't have a choice in the matter."

I made it to the door, gritting my teeth. "We'll see about that." I could get back, couldn't I? I had done it before, more than once. Find that door, the one that led outside. Then I would emerge in the ward adjacent to mine.

The doctor made no move to stop me. Carol sat, still staring down at her hands. I couldn't leave her there. For all she seemed to be suffering from some form of amnesia, probably brought on by the shock of all that was happening to her, she didn't belong here any more than I did.

"Carol?"

She raised her eyes to meet mine.

"Come with me. It's time to go back."

Slowly she shook her head.

"But you can't stay here."

"Maybe it's where I belong."

How could she think that? "But you don't. You don't belong here and neither do I. If you stay here, they'll operate on you. They'll put you into restraints so tight they cut into your skin, and drill a hole in your head. I know. I saw you after they had done it." At least I thought I had.

"Is that true, Doctor?" Her voice was lost, barely audible. "Why would you do that? Is there something wrong with my brain?"

The doctor ignored her question and gave a light cough. "She doesn't know what you're talking about, Vanessa. She won't come with you, so you either go alone or not at all."

I hesitated. Part of me cried out to get away. Carol was an adult. I wasn't responsible for her. Hell, I didn't even know her. But who knew what they had done to her in the time she had been here before our paths crossed? Whatever it was I felt certain she faced much worse to come.

"Carol, please. Don't listen to him. Come with me."

She shook her head.

I turned the handle, opened the door and once again stared into the face of Arabella Marsden. I took an involuntary step backward. Her eyes drilled into me. Behind her, mists swirled and darkness descended. Shadowy figures pulsated like heartbeats. Images flashed into my brain. Memories that didn't belong there, fighting with those that did, stripping away the real and the precious, imposing stories from another age. Someone else's stories. Someone else's memories. I struggled to push them away. A young, vibrant girl laughed and danced in my mind, in a meadow of spring grass and early flowers, and I knew who she must be. Lydia Warren Carmody as she had been many years before, skipping through the tall grass. Innocent, free. I could almost believe....

It wasn't me. I couldn't be remembering this. I had never lived this life. These were *her* memories. *Her* life, before something happened to change her.

The happy girl vanished from my mind. Dark shadows swept in, pulsating, throbbing. Breathing. In the blackness...I could sense something. Another presence. Menacing. I couldn't make it out. I didn't *want* to make it out. The epitome of evil, its presence grew with every breath and it meant me harm. It had already taken Carol, but she was not enough. It wanted more. The extra pulse that had grown in my brain kicked in.

Outside my own personal anguish, the world had faded into oblivion. I was living entirely in my own head, unaware of anything around me. I heard a scream. Was it me? I had no idea, only that it was close. Too close.

The…thing…inside my head weighed me down. I was sinking; the walls of my mind closed in on me, the shadows overpowering my senses.

Another scream. Then another and another.

A child shrieked. "Nessa! Nessa!"

A face penetrated the blackness. Pale eyes scythed through the swirling mass.

The child. Agnes. The woman. Lydia. Inextricably joined and reaching for me.

"Now you begin to understand." A voice I knew had to belong to Lydia Warren Carmody drifted toward me and each word seemed to dispel a little of the shadow. The mists parted, grew paler. My vision slowly returned until I was once more face to face with the woman I recognized as my nemesis. The woman who was hell-bent on transferring Lydia Warren Carmody's soul – and with it the evil that had possessed her in life – into my body.

Arabella Marsden stepped to one side and the shadows I had seen so clearly in my mind filled the corridor. Fear welled up inside me as I felt a tugging at my insides. I fought to stand my ground but the force proved too strong. It drew me toward the blackness of the pulsating mass ahead. Shadows enveloped me. I couldn't breathe as my nostrils filled with acrid smoke, as if I was somehow standing in the middle of a smoking coal fire with no flames and no heat.

Agnes appeared and spread her thin arms wide. Her eyes shone with vermilion fire. Lydia appeared by her side and took her hand. In unison they spoke and the words echoed around me:

"But one among them bides behind,
Her soul of ebony and granite,
The fires of life long since quenched,
Replaced with voids of emptiness.
In darkness, shadows breathe
And death their only reward."

A scream rose up inside me and I gave it full vent as the air expelled from my lungs. I took an automatic breath and choked on the evil smog.

Then I was through it. The blackness fell away and I found myself in the workhouse. Ahead of me, at lines of long tables, women dressed identically in the same drab brown dresses and aprons I had witnessed before sat eating something out of bowls. The only sounds, the clattering of spoons and the slurp of the diners. Some sort of thin soup. Cabbage probably. The air was rank with it.

I looked down at myself and found that I too was dressed the same as the other women.

On the wall, framed homilies reminded the inmates to, 'Avoid idleness and intemperance', 'Be thankful for God's great mercies' and a clearly strictly enforced, 'No Talking'.

Female staff patrolled up and down. One approached me and I recognized the thin-faced woman I had seen before. She pointed a long, skinny finger at an empty seat and, seeing no immediate alternative, I sat down. The woman next to me pointed at the meager slices of stale-looking bread on a plate in the center of the table. I shook my head. I couldn't have eaten a morsel of anything, let alone something I guessed would probably taste like sawdust, and might even contain some.

As each woman finished her meal, she silently waited, head bowed. The noise of spoons clattering against cheap pottery bowls died away as more of the assembled finished their sparse meal.

I caught the eye of the thin-faced woman, who glowered at me. Evidently I should have lowered my eyes and remembered 'my place'. Some part of me rebelled. I continued to meet her eye to eye.

She turned her head away in disgust, scanned the room and nodded to her colleagues. As one, they clapped their hands loudly and a general scraping of stools echoed around the room.

I stood as well. Not a word had been spoken.

"Back to work," the woman called.

My former neighbor took my arm. Once we were out of the dining area, she spoke. "You're new. I haven't seen you before."

She was probably less than half my age but she hadn't a tooth in her head, her hair hung, dull and lifeless, and her hands were scrubbed red raw. "Have they given you your job yet?"

I shook my head.

"I work in the laundry. It's not so bad. A bit hard on your skin, but there's worse jobs. You can come with me if you like."

"Thanks, but I shouldn't be here. Something's gone wrong. I'm supposed to be—"

She stared at me intently, but how could I explain I was from a different time?

"I'm supposed to be somewhere else, that's all." A lame finish but the best I could manage.

"You've got something wrong with you, haven't you?" she said, tapping her head and then apparently changing her mind. She frowned and pointed at my stomach. "Something wasn't right in there and they took it out, didn't they?"

How could she possibly know that? I nodded.

"They think I'm touched but I'm not. I see things." Her face clouded over. We had reached the door to the laundry. "This is where I work," she said. Her voice changed, as if someone else was speaking through her. "You must get out of here. They're going to get you. You're next."

The door slammed shut behind her. From the other side, voices, steam, and the smell of soap wafted through the gaps in the doorframe.

I looked wildly around me, with no clue as to where to go. This corridor was unfamiliar. The whitewash looked white, fresh and clean. No one milled around. Everyone had gone back to their designated jobs. All except me. I had no job. I didn't belong.

Sadness threatened to overwhelm me. Sadness and despair. I longed for almost anything from my own time but most of all Paul. Would he be wondering where I was? I didn't even know how long I had been away, or more particularly how much time would have elapsed in my own world. A few minutes? An hour?

"You're next."

The now-familiar voice of Arabella Marsden startled me. I spun around but there was no one there.

"You're next." It was Hester's voice this time. Behind me. No, nothing there.

A door opened farther along the corridor. Two burly men dressed in navy uniform advanced toward me, their faces serious. Each grabbed one arm and they manhandled me back down the corridor. I squirmed and protested but I couldn't break free. Their hold was too strong.

In a room, a wooden chair complete with restraints for wrists and ankles. The men sat me down roughly and pain shot up from between my legs. My ankles were thrust into the braces and my wrists roughly secured with leather straps that cut into my skin and threatened to stop the circulation.

The men stood back and the door opened again. This time, Marsden and the doctor entered.

The doctor spoke first. "Now then, Vanessa, it's time you joined us properly. Carol is waiting for you. She'll be your friend once you've learned your place."

"Why are you doing this to me? You know I don't belong here. I was in hospital. I had a serious operation."

"Yes, you did. And, you see, that really should never have happened. It's not possible for it to have happened because that type of surgery doesn't exist here."

"But I'm not from here. I belong in the twenty-first century."

Marsden let out a laugh that was close to a snarl. "You belong wherever the One and the Many says you belong."

I struggled but the bonds cut deeper into my wrists.

The doctor moved out of my field of vision and returned momentarily with a hypodermic syringe in his hand. It was nearly full of a colorless liquid.

"You can't use that on me. I haven't given you permission."

The woman laughed again. "Permission? We don't need your permission."

A sharp stab in my left arm. The doctor plunged the contents of the syringe directly into a vein. A rush of heat swam through me. I caught my breath and came to in an unfamiliar room. Everything looked big to me. A solid wooden dining table loomed above me and I realized I had regressed to a child of no more than three years old but, a second later, I had grown so that I was standing next to it, resting my hand. A mirror on the wall behind the table reflected a young woman with dark blonde hair arranged in a bun, and dressed in a cotton gown sprigged with small flowers. It buttoned up to the chin. I felt my own neck, and the hand in the mirror did the same.

"Lydia." The voice belonged to an older woman with graying hair, smartly dressed in a dark blue tunic and skirt typical of the last quarter of the nineteenth century. "Come along now or you'll be late. You know Mr. Carmody doesn't like to be kept waiting."

"But I don't…."

The woman flicked her gloves impatiently. "You don't what?"

I shook my head. My thoughts were too jumbled to decipher. Part of me hadn't a clue who this woman was and another part recognized her. My mother. Not Nessa's mother. Lydia's. And now Lydia and I were one and the same. In another flash, an image of a young man with black hair and a neat moustache. His lips were set in a line and his eyes held a harshness and contempt that made my flesh shrivel.

Lydia didn't like this man. In fact, she was scared of him, and so was I.

I followed the woman – Mother – out of the room. I glanced down at my feet, shod in black leather buttoned boots with a small heel. In contrast to the room, which had been over-stuffed with furniture and knick-knacks, the light and spacious hall led to a wide front door with stained glass panels.

Outside, the street consisted of mainly Georgian buildings, painted creamy white. Horses, carts, horse-drawn buses and carriages all jockeyed for position on the dusty roadway. A policeman in his Victorian uniform stopped to admonish a young boy who was playing with a whip and top, dangerously close to the traffic. After delivering a cuff to the lad's ear, the constable strode on. The boy blushed deep pink and sped off down the street.

"Come along, Lydia. Don't dawdle." Her mother ushered me into a waiting carriage pulled by a bored-looking black horse. The driver tipped his hat to me as I managed awkwardly to mount the steps. I sat down inside and closed the door, realizing that the awkward maneuver hadn't kicked the pain off. I fidgeted a little, much to the older woman's disdain.

"Oh do stop that, Lydia. It is most unbecoming. Sit still."

I said nothing.

"And answer me when I speak to you."

"Yes," I said.

"Yes, what?"

I looked at her questioningly.

She sighed. "Say, 'Yes, Mama', not just 'yes'. It's rude. Honestly, Lydia, I don't know what's got into you recently. You never used to be so willful and awkward."

"Yes…Mama," I said quietly.

"And sit up straight. You'll end up hunched over like poor Mrs. Feathers."

Some flicker in my mind told me Mrs. Feathers was the family's cook/housekeeper at one time.

The horse clopped steadily on, occasionally veering to the left or right in order to avoid a collision. I stared out of the window at a constantly changing scene that was both familiar and unfamiliar. It was as if my brain had been neatly sliced in two. Memories from both the personalities that now inhabited my body vied with each other, but the Nessa that remained in me was losing the battle to Lydia and the darkness within her. Maybe it was because we were in her time. Nessa's memories simply didn't fit here. I felt disoriented and confused, being tugged this way and that like an elastic band stretched too taut.

The carriage stopped and we got out. Lydia's mother – *my* mother I suppose – handed over the fare and I stared up at a much grander house than the one I had so recently found myself in.

A tall, smart butler let us in, answered the door before the sound of the bell had faded. He led us into a large room with floor-to-ceiling bookshelves crammed with leather-bound volumes. A fire crackled in the hearth and the leather Chesterfield looked inviting.

A man my Lydia-self recognized as Roger Carmody stood and came toward us, hand outstretched.

"Good afternoon, Mrs. Warren, Miss Warren. A pleasure as always."

But he didn't make it sound like a pleasure. His patronizing tone was that of a master to an underling.

All my senses told me he was everything I hated most and, as yet, I hadn't a clue why.

CHAPTER SIXTEEN

"Nessa, Nessa. Come on, wake up."

Joyce's voice wafted into my nightmare and broke it. I opened my eyes, the memory of that awful dream still so real to me I could barely take in the comforting sight of the nurse's smiling face. "Goodness, when you sleep you really sleep, don't you?"

Right now, I could have thrown my arms around her and kissed her. Never had I been so relieved to see anyone I barely knew.

I hoisted myself up into a comfortable sitting position. "What time is it?"

"Just after eleven. Maryam's on the ward. She'll be coming to see you in a few minutes."

She poured a glass of water from the jug, which I noticed had been replenished and topped up with ice. I took the beaker from her and drank it down.

"I must have fallen asleep straight after breakfast. At least…." But was it a dream? One thing had to be true though. "Have you heard anything about Carol…or Susan Jackson? The patients who went missing?"

Joyce's hand shook as she was setting down the jug. She took a breath. "Missing? I don't know any Susan, and Carol Shaughnessy didn't go missing. She discharged herself."

"Really? When did she do that?" I still couldn't come to grips with the way time was working. The last time I had seen Carol had been in the past, evidently before she had endured being the victim of Dr. Franklyn's more hideous experiments. In this time Carol was no longer missing but had turned up and discharged herself.

"She went home. Against medical advice, of course. Her ankles were really bad, but…." She made an expansive gesture with her hands.

The door opened and Maryam entered, accompanied by another nurse I didn't know.

"I'll leave you all to it," Joyce said and closed the door behind her.

Maryam pulled out a pair of disposable gloves from the wall dispenser and proceeded to put them on. "Right, now, let's take a look, shall we?"

Maryam's touch was gentle and soft, but I still flinched slightly.

"That's looking better and better. You're doing really well, Nessa." She pointed out some finer points of my newly reconstructed anatomy to the nurse, who murmured in appreciation.

"The flaps have taken well. No sign of any problems there. Mr. Shah did a marvelous job."

"I can go home tomorrow, can't I?"

Maryam exchanged glances with the nurse. "I need to talk to you about a development. Something has shown up in your most recent blood tests and we need to investigate a little."

My heart gave an extra beat. "What is it?"

"An anomaly. Something that isn't possible but we need to rule everything out, so I need to arrange for you to have a scan. This time, on your abdomen."

"It isn't—"

"No, no. I'm quite sure it's not the cancer, but I want to make sure nothing else is going on there."

"But what showed up in the blood tests?"

"This will sound a little crazy. In fact, a lot crazy, but the results showed the presence of a hormone called HCG. It's a hormone secreted during pregnancy."

I thought there must have been something wrong with my hearing. "What?"

"Now you can see why we need to do a scan. Quite obviously you cannot be pregnant, so we just want to check if anything else is causing this."

"Like what?"

"I wouldn't like to speculate at this stage. Don't worry about it. There will be a rational explanation and, whatever it is, we will be able to deal with it."

* * *

"*Pregnant?*" Paul's face blanched ivory.

"Clearly I'm not, so something is giving a false reading."

"Could they have mixed your blood up with someone else's?"

"I very much doubt it."

"I don't know how you can remain so calm."

I didn't either but he didn't have to know that. "I've been through so much worse, I really don't rate this on a scale of one to ten at all. It's some daft anomaly, that's all. Anyway, we'll find out the results in a day or two."

"But meanwhile, you can't come home."

"Not unless I discharge myself and that would be crazy. Especially now."

"I'm not happy about you being here. Too much is going on that neither of us can explain."

And it was that fear of his, which I echoed, that made me decide not to tell Paul about my latest experience.

* * *

At least I didn't have to wait more than a day for the results of the latest scan.

"I'm pleased to tell you that nothing showed up." Maryam, accompanied by Joyce, looked uncharacteristically serious for one delivering good news.

I struggled to get myself more comfortable in bed. "So what caused the presence of that hormone?"

"We simply don't know. As you know, we took more bloods this morning and the result was the same. In fact the level had increased slightly which would be expected…in a pregnant woman."

"Well, we know that doesn't apply to me and there's nothing untoward going on—"

"Nothing that shows up on the scan. But clearly something is causing it. We simply don't know what yet and, until we do, I am not happy about discharging you. We need to conduct more tests.

I am meeting with my colleagues later today and we are going to put our collective heads together."

"Maryam, I need to go home. I really do."

She must have read the fear in my eyes. "What's the real reason you want to leave so much?"

Joyce was staring up at the ceiling.

"You know, don't you?" I said to her.

She looked at me. "I'm sorry…I—"

Something snapped inside me and I had to fight for control of my temper. The words came tumbling out in an unstoppable flood. "There's something not right in this hospital. Something that happened way back in its history before it even *was* the Royal and Waverley. People who have worked here for any length of time know about it. There have been too many incidents of patients reporting seeing things they couldn't possibly have seen. Things *I've* seen. That portal out there. The door that's there sometimes and then disappears. I've been through it. Carol and Susan, the patients who disappeared, they went through it. It takes you back in time. To the workhouse. There's something evil there. A woman. Arabella Marsden and a Dr. Franklyn. And there's a little girl…Agnes. And it's all linked to a woman called Lydia Warren Carmody, who wrote a poem I found. I haven't worked it all out yet…." My voice trailed off as I saw Maryam's expression change from sympathy to concern to outright disbelief.

Joyce touched my hand. I withdrew it as if I'd been stung, then chastised myself. She was only being kind after all.

The nurse spoke. "You've been through a lot, Nessa. And you've had some pretty strong pain relief."

"Is she still on Oramorph?" Maryam asked. Joyce nodded. Maryam looked back at me. "I think we had better stop it altogether now, Nessa. In rare cases, Oramorph can lead to hallucinations and I think this may be happening to you. It would explain why you are having strange visions. At the very least, if we stop the dosage we can see if the symptoms cease, but, I'm afraid, I really can't send you home yet. It would be irresponsible of me. If you are experiencing hallucinations, we don't know which direction they might take. You could be at risk of unintentionally harming yourself."

I said nothing, I wanted to insist they weren't hallucinations, but could I really be sure? As far as I could remember I had never experienced a hallucination in my life until I came into this hospital. I was still convinced Maryam and Joyce knew more than they would admit to, but what else could I do? I nodded my agreement.

Maryam squeezed my hand. "Good. I'll pop back and see you tomorrow. By then I hope to have a plan on what we should do next to get to the bottom of the HCG phenomenon."

* * *

Paul was accompanied by a large bouquet of colorful flowers. Chrysanthemums, dahlias, roses, carnations, a burst of reds, oranges, yellows, pinks and blues. "From your friends at the university. They're missing you." He handed me a card.

Margie popped her head around the door. "Shall I get a vase for those? They're beautiful, aren't they?"

"Yes, please. They're lovely. I never expected anything like this."

The card was signed by pretty much every person in the department. Tears sprang into my eyes. "People are so kind," I managed, around the lump that had settled in my throat.

Paul kissed my forehead. "They love you. And so do I as a matter of fact."

Margie returned with my flowers in a large glass vase, which she now placed on the bedside cabinet. I set the card next to it.

When she had gone, Paul said, "You're not going home yet I hear."

"No, they think that what I experienced may be down to the Oramorph but they can't be sure so they need to monitor me now I'm off it. Then there's the small matter of the hormone that can't be there but still is. Maryam's coming back with a plan of action tomorrow."

"How do you feel about that? Staying here I mean." Paul's tone made it all too clear how he felt about it.

"At first, not happy, but I can see her point. Hallucinations are a rare side effect of Oramorph and what I experienced was so vivid and real…." If there was even an outside chance that all of this was in my head, I had to grab it.

"And what about the woman in the cafeteria?"

"You mean Hester?" Paul gave me a surprised look. "Long story, but I found out that's her name."

"Hester. Was she a hallucination? I saw her as well, remember."

"And you thought she was a nutter. Plus, you didn't know her name. My mind could easily have stored the real woman we spoke to away and hallucinated about her later. She was a bit weird. Perfect for a ghost. Oh…." A memory flashed through my mind. The last walk I had taken before I had the operation. The storm. And the stranger all bundled up in the parka….

"What's the matter, Ness? You've lost all color in your cheeks."

"That woman. Hester. She didn't just make contact with me when I came here. I think I saw her before. When I first saw her down in the cafeteria I thought for a split second that I had seen her somewhere before but I didn't make the connection. It was the last time I went out for a walk along the promenade. A woman approached me. She was so wrapped up against the weather, I could barely make out that she was even female. She spoke to me. And told me I should go home. Then she walked away, but I got the distinct impression she said something else. I'd forgotten all about it until now."

"What did she say?"

"That's the thing. She said, 'You're next.'"

Paul inhaled sharply. "And you want to stay here?"

"I've got no choice, have I? Maryam is dead against discharging me and I'm scared to go it alone yet. What if she's right and it *is* the Oramorph?"

"But you're not taking it anymore, are you?"

"I don't know how long it lingers in your system. It could be a few days before I'm totally clear. And that's before we consider this bloody HCG business."

Paul looked around the room. "What if I stayed here? I could sleep in this chair. It's comfortable enough."

"No, it's out of the question, Paul. You've got work. I won't hear about it. I shall be fine."

"I need to speak to Maryam."

The door opened before I could respond. Margie breezed in. "Do you mind if I do your room now? Only I'm on my own again today and I can't be too late leaving tonight."

Paul stood. "I'll get out of your way."

"Oh no, don't do that," Margie said. "I can work around you."

"Actually," Paul said, "can I ask you something, Margie?"

"Fire away."

"Paul—"

He raised his hand and I closed my mouth.

"You know something about the strange things that go on around here, don't you?"

Margie threw a quick glance at me. I cast my eyes down. "If you mean the ghost stories then, yes, I've heard some good ones down the years."

"Do you think this place is haunted?"

She nodded. "Yes. I do. Definitely, and I think Nessa should get out of here as soon as she can."

"Thanks, Margie. That's what I think too. You think she's in danger from whatever exists in these walls, don't you?"

"Oh, I know it." She lowered her voice and came closer. "Look, I know they told you that Carol Shaughnessy discharged herself, but she didn't, and neither did Susan Jackson. They're still missing and no one has a clue where they went."

"How do you know this?" I asked.

"Because I overheard them talking. All the bigwigs on the top floor. One of the advantages of being a cleaner is that no one really notices you. Especially the higher up in the pecking order they are. I carried on mopping the floor outside the meeting room and there they were with the door wide open. Jabbering away." She shook her head. "Anyway, they're worried sick it's going to leak out. They've had every inch of this place searched from top to bottom and then all over again. No sign of them."

"In which case, I may know exactly where they are," I said. "The only problem is I can't get to them either."

Paul's phone rang and he answered it. His expression clouded as he stood up and left the room.

"I'm sorry you've got caught up in all this," Margie said.

"If I only knew why and how to stop it."

The door flew open and Paul dashed back in. "That was the school. I have to go back in. Some parents have been kicking off. It's the new teacher we hired to take over from Kristin while she's on maternity leave. He doesn't seem to be coping, and now a posse of them are demanding to see me. Are you going to be all right, Ness? I'll be back tomorrow, but call me if anything happens. Promise?"

"I will. Now, go on before they lynch you." I shooed him away, doing my best to sound lighthearted. I don't think he was too convinced but he left anyway.

Margie finished cleaning and pretty soon I was alone again with my gremlins.

Sleep wouldn't come that night, no matter how hard I tried. I gave up, switched on the light, read until my eyes dropped, switched the lamp off and immediately my brain kicked in with all sorts of random and frightening thoughts. Then the knocking began, and I knew things were about to get a whole lot worse.

CHAPTER SEVENTEEN

It started in the corner of the room. A movement. Like a breath of smoke at first, then slowly taking form as I watched, horrified but unable to tear my gaze away. A pulsating shadow of charcoal mist, writhing, twisting in on itself, gradually developing definition.

Spectral arms, legs, a head. I scrambled out of bed and watched the figure emerge from its cocoon of smoke. It – no, *she* – dressed in charcoal gray from head to foot. A Victorian woman, her eyes fixed on me, and it seemed I shouldn't be able to see her at all in the murkiness of the room, but a strange half-light illuminated the shadows all around her and gave them life. Behind her, the wall faded into the room that was no longer a room, but a familiar corridor. The woman looked straight at me and drew me into the deep pools of her eyes. Lydia Warren Carmody. I took a step to the side and she mimicked me. I raised my hand and so did she. Her dress had changed and she wore the same nightgown as me. On her feet, *my* slippers. I was staring into a mirror. I put my hand out and met hers, only it wasn't flesh I touched but a cold, hard surface. Glass. The whole wall in front of me was made of it. One gigantic mirror reflecting me and the swirling shadows behind and around me.

In darkness, shadows breathe.

They breathed and my own breath mimicked them. In…out… in…out….

Another figure emerged from the darkness behind me and I saw her reflected in the mirror. I spun round to face her.

"Carol!"

"So sorry…Nessa. So sorry."

I looked at her, confused, but then realization dawned.

Carol came closer and lightly touched my face, her touch cool, soothing. But there was something badly wrong with her. Her head was roughly bandaged and the whole of her left side seemed damaged, paralyzed. She dragged her foot as she stumbled away from me.

"What have they done to you?" I called to her.

She hesitated and spoke with difficulty. Every word fought for. "They…have…shown…me…who…I…am…."

She moved away, appearing to slip through an invisible wall so that I could no longer see her.

I turned back to the mirror. My reflection spoke, but I didn't. The shadows echoed the words with pulsating spasms. "You are ours now. You belong to all of us."

Fear and anger coursed through my veins. I looked down at myself. I was dressed in the workhouse uniform with no recollection of how that had happened.

Lydia Warren Carmody stretched her arms wide and suddenly I was back. In her body. In her time, and I was standing over the body of a man I knew was her…my…husband. In my hand, a letter opener dripped blood. His blood.

I killed him.

I threw the weapon on the floor and recoiled from it.

Footsteps. Fast. Echoing down the corridor outside the over-stuffed parlor I found myself in.

The door flew open and a uniformed policeman dashed in, truncheon raised. A stranger in civilian clothes accompanied him. "Lydia Warren Carmody, I am arresting you for the murder of Roger Carmody…."

The policeman clapped a pair of handcuffs onto me. They cut into my wrists. I cried out, protested my innocence, but the part of me that had become Lydia Carmody knew I was guilty… *she* was guilty. As for me, I no longer knew who I was anymore. Time flashed forward. I was pregnant. No, I had been pregnant. I had given birth. They had taken it straight off me. I never even saw its face. Never knew if I had a son or a daughter….

A mist descended and I stood in the prisoner's dock. A judge placed a black cloth on top of his wig.

"The sentence of this court is that you will be taken from here to the place from whence you came and there be kept in close confinement until a date to be determined for your execution, and upon that day that you be taken to the place of execution and there hanged by the neck until you are dead. And may God have mercy upon your soul."

"No!" I...Lydia...had been judged a murderer and, as another veil lifted in my mind, I knew why she had come to this.

The beatings, his drunken rages. Women flaunted in front of me. More beatings. Black eyes, bruises and always lies. I had tripped, fallen down stairs, knocked myself out. The catalog of untruths spilled so easily from his lips as, over the years, he glibly explained away my more obvious injuries to anyone who saw them. And I – the Lydia part of me – said nothing. The anger built inside me until one day, my fury exploded and he paid the ultimate price. The problem was, so did I.

* * *

Time passed. It meant nothing. I lay in the confines of a damp cell as night became day, became night and then dawn.

The sixth day. The day I would be put to death. They came for me at dawn.

A priest followed me, almost chanting with familiar words of the 23rd Psalm.

They put a bag over my head. It smelled fusty, old. I could hear my breath, shallow, too quick. My heart beat too fast. Soon I would breathe no longer. Soon my heart would stop.

A coarse rope cut into my neck....

* * *

"Nessa. Nessa. Wake up." Paul's voice.

I opened my eyes, saw his concerned face looking down on me.

I burst into floods of uncontrollable tears.

"We're leaving. Now."

I couldn't protest. Didn't want to. Couldn't even speak. It had seemed all too real. I knew one thing for certain. If I stayed, it would *become* real.

Joyce dashed into the room. Through my sobs, I could hear the argument. She protested I wasn't well enough. Paul insisted I would never get well if I stayed there.

Maryam came in and my hysteria reached fever pitch. I clung to Paul as he promised to bring me back to the outpatient clinic, the next day if need be, but he would not let me stay.

Eventually they brought me a form to sign. Paul wouldn't back down and I somehow managed to sign something vaguely resembling my name. More argument. I had signed the wrong name.

"That's the problem," Paul said. "That's why she can't stay here."

"Lydia Warren Carmody…." Maryam read out loud.

I had signed the form with *her* name. It didn't even look like my handwriting. *Her* signature, *her* handwriting.

"I have to get out of here," I said, forming the first lucid words I had managed since I woke up.

Paul clasped me to him, held me tightly. "Don't worry. They'll bring you another form. But you must sign your own name. Vanessa Tremaine, remember?"

I nodded, my whole body shaking with the effort of trying to stave off another wave of hysterics.

"…Psychiatric assessment…."

"…Danger to herself…. Sectioned…."

Words I never thought I would ever hear applied to myself, now being spoken in serious terms by Maryam and Joyce. Paul protesting that all I needed was to get out of there.

"Please," I said, "listen to him. Why won't you listen to him?"

Exhaustion took over. I blacked out. When I came round, I was still in bed, Paul at my side holding my hand. I gripped his fingers so tightly he winced. "I've got to get out of here. She's coming for me. Lydia. Something evil took possession of her and it's trying to get inside my body. The spirit that haunted… possessed the real Lydia Warren Carmody. It's called the One and the Many and now it wants me."

"It's going to be okay. I'm taking you home. Now you've woken up, we can go. I'll help you up."

"It's all sorted out now?"

Paul nodded. "Eventually they agreed with me. You can't stay here. I can tell you something else too. I believe Maryam and Joyce both know more than they're letting on. They caved in remarkably quickly when I filled in the details of what you had experienced. And I've been doing a little digging of my own. The flakes of paint you brought back are consistent with the type used in the nineteenth century and not found anywhere in the modern hospital. It's true they built this place using reclaimed material from the old workhouse, asylum and hospital, especially the bricks. Joanna has been doing some research of her own and she's found some old plans hidden away in the university archives. When construction got underway, they were digging the foundations and came across a mass grave. A couple of thousand bodies, all thrown in together. Then workmen started seeing things. People dressed in old-style workhouse uniforms, walking through walls. Unexplained accidents started happening. They closed the site down for a month while the Health and Safety people undertook a thorough inspection. Modifications were made and the work resumed but, until building was finally completed, accidents kept on happening. Ladders collapsed when they had been firmly secured. Scaffolding fell down when every precaution had been taken. Most of the injuries were relatively minor – cuts, sprains and bruises mainly. But the turnover of labor was incredible. The men wouldn't stay. The average length a bricklayer spent on this site sank to as low as two weeks. Then, as soon as the place opened, more things started happening."

"He's right, I'm afraid." Joyce was framed in the doorway. I had no idea how long she had been there. She came closer. "I'm sorry I didn't say anything before, but you can appreciate, no one wants a panic. None of us is supposed to say anything about what we've seen, but I had only been here a month when a patient told me of her experience, walking through a wall and going back in time. Then Maryam was approached by someone in Victorian dress who disappeared as soon as she spoke to her. There are so many stories, but yours is a bit different. Whatever it is has targeted you for a special purpose. Maryam confided in me that she's sure that's why the HCG is showing up in your blood."

"But if that's the case, why didn't she encourage me to leave here instead of putting obstacles in my way?"

Joyce sighed. "Because she doesn't believe that will save you and she wants you to be where she can keep an eye on you and be on hand should you need urgent medical help. I hope she's wrong. I truly do. I hope that when you come back to Clinic and we take more bloods we'll find the HCG has disappeared. But, in all conscience, I can't guarantee it."

"Thank you for your honesty, Joyce," I said. She gave me a half-smile and left.

Paul helped me dress in a long skirt and sweater, wrapped me in my coat and handed me a large pharmacy bag, stuffed with small boxes of drugs.

Joyce greeted me at the nurses' station, her normal demeanor and air of efficiency restored. "Plenty of rest, light exercise. No housework and definitely no lifting. Maryam will see you in Clinic next Wednesday."

Other nurses waved and smiled. Margie blew me a kiss and mouthed, "Good luck."

Normality. The hysteria of a short while earlier seemed forgotten. As if it had never happened. This was the way they dealt with the impossible at the Royal and Waverley – the hospital they shouldn't have built here.

I said little in the car. My thoughts were so jumbled I couldn't be sure what I was remembering and what I had dreamed.

* * *

When I got home again, Paul settled me into a comfy chair where I could look out over the sea. Gulls soared over the gray waters into the sky, itself heavily overcast with a blanket of clouds.

He brought me a cup of strong tea and sat with me.

"Thank God they let me go."

"You can start putting all that behind you. You're safe now."

I looked at Paul. He truly meant every word. "I wish I could be as certain as you are," I said and sipped my tea. Outside, the clouds turned gunmetal and a wave of heavy rain swept in from the sea. I watched it lash against the windows and thought of Carol. What was the truth for her?

* * *

My first visit to Maryam went well. My body was healing nicely and she had some good news.

"We still don't know what caused the anomaly but everything is back to normal again. There is no trace of HCG in your blood."

"So I'm definitely not pregnant then?" It was a mark of how much I had recovered that I could even joke about it. Maryam saw the funny side and laughed too. We would simply have to put that one down as 'one of those things'. I felt a massive weight had been lifted and the strange, pulsating feeling had vanished from my brain. The sheer fact that something so bizarre could exist inside me had worried me more than I realized.

The rest of the appointment progressed well. Maryam prodded and poked in my groin. "Everything seems fine there but I still don't think it's worth taking any chances. We'll start radiotherapy in a few weeks just to be sure. Are you happy with that?"

I nodded. It wasn't a prospect I relished. Having my already beleaguered body pumped through with radiation was hardly a lifestyle choice, and I knew I would be in for some serious discomfort from irradiated skin, which would blister in the course of treatment and for a while after.

"They will give you moisture cream to soothe it and they'll monitor you carefully so you have no need to worry."

I did my best to smile and focus on the good news I had received.

When I came out, Paul was waiting for me.

"How did it go?"

"Well. You can stop knitting baby booties. We won't be hearing the patter of tiny feet after all."

He clapped his hand to his forehead. "It's gone?"

"Every last trace. As if it had never been there apparently."

"Weird."

"As is so much of all this. But it's gone, that's the main thing. Radiotherapy in a few weeks' time and then regular monitoring for around four years. I can get on with my life at last."

Paul cuddled me close. "We'll get a bottle of champagne on the way home. It's time to celebrate."

* * *

Gradually, everything returned to normal. Well, my new version of it anyway.

Three weeks later, I realized I still had the two books I had borrowed from the hospital library and asked Paul to hand them in for me when he was passing.

"An odd thing happened when I returned them," he said when he got back. He rummaged in his pocket. "This dropped out of one of them."

I reached for the scrunched-up piece of paper but he held on to it.

"In a second. Let me tell you what happened. I saw the librarian and I asked her who had borrowed the Kate Furnivall book before you. She searched her records and, guess what? Susan Jackson returned that book the same day you took it out. The girl said she usually went through the returned books before lending them out again, checking for anything that had been left in them. She said she found all sorts of things, even paper money used as a bookmark. On the day you borrowed the book, she was in a bit of a rush and simply marked the returns off and stuck them straight back on her trolley." He handed me the paper without opening it. I unfolded it, guessing what I was about to find. It still came as a shock. I gave an involuntary exclamation and hurriedly tossed it into the waste basket.

Almost immediately, I retrieved it and handed it back to Paul. "Burn it, please. I don't want that thing falling into anyone else's hands."

Paul nodded. "Sorry. Stupid of me. I should have done that when the thing fell out of that book. What was I thinking of?"

"The important thing is we get rid of it now."

I followed him into the kitchen and watched him grab the box of matches. Over the sink, he lit one end of the paper and the flame quickly caught.

Paul blew out the match. "Do you think that's how the link was made between you and Susan? Did that woman, Hester, put it there for each of you to find?"

I shrugged. "I have no idea. I never spoke to Susan, but I do think the poem itself is a significant factor between us. For one thing it links us all, Carol included, to Lydia Carmody." I pointed to the ashes in the sink. "I certainly welcome *that* sight."

Paul washed them away.

A wave of relief swept over me. From somewhere I heard a woman sigh. "Did you hear that?"

"What?"

"I thought I heard.... Oh, never mind. Nothing. Probably air in the pipes."

Paul looked at me curiously. "What did it sound like?"

I could see no point in lying. "Like a woman sighing. It sounded familiar."

"But they couldn't get you here surely?"

Could they? The old fears, the muddled memories, all came flooding back to me, but we weren't in the hospital or on any of the land that had housed those old buildings that seemed reluctant to give up their dead spirits. But if I had been right about seeing Hester on the promenade.... Then I thought of our friend, Joanna. She lived in Waverley Court and Paul had promised to consult her. She had access to so much archive information at the university. "Did you speak to Joanna?"

"Certainly did. She rang while I was at the hospital. She's going on holiday for a couple of weeks but when she returns, she has invited us round for a meal. We were chatting and you're not going to believe this, but she lives in the same block as Carol Shaughnessy."

"Really? She knows her?"

"Not terribly well, but...okay. It's a lot to process, so brace yourself. She told me she took Carol back to her flat from the hospital and hasn't seen her since. But, get this. Joanna told me

Carol had two stints in hospital. The first was for an appendectomy and the second was shortly afterward, following an incident at her home. That resulted in her being admitted for medical treatment and then being transferred to a Psychiatric Ward, in the same hospital. She was there for three weeks before being discharged. She never went missing and she never discharged herself. Jo knows nothing about any injuries to her ankles, so basically, the episode you remember so clearly is not something she knows anything about and she was in daily contact with the hospital. Okay, they didn't go into detail about her because Joanna isn't family, but there was never any question about where she was at any time, or what she was in for. The referral for psychiatric care was because she had a breakdown, which had led to the incident at her home. When she was discharged, Joanna took her home and that's the last time she saw her. When I told Jo about your experiences, she wasn't in the least surprised. Apparently in the short time she lived there, a lot happened in that apartment to Carol, and even the actual owner of it, who is abroad at present, had told Jo about being frightened there. Joanna believes something latched on to Carol and either she has run away to try and escape it or…."

"It's got her. Trapped her."

"It has to be a possibility, hasn't it?"

My head felt as if it was going to explode. "When did Jo say all this happened with Carol? Something doesn't seem right about the sequence of events here."

"I picked that up too. Jo said the last time she saw Carol was over a month ago."

"What? But that means we were never in hospital together."

"I know. But Jo is adamant."

"But I know I saw her collapsed in the corridor. The other patients saw her…the doctor…. Margie said she and Susan had gone missing, but Joyce told me she had discharged herself."

"It seems you and Carol were never actually in hospital at the same time, but you were inextricably linked by that spirit, so time had to be manipulated to bring you together."

"'Time isn't linear.'"

"That's what Joanna said. She reckons it's quite possible no one else but you will now remember having met Carol at that time. As for Susan Jackson.... Her family have reported her as missing. She appears to have vanished off the face of the earth."

I shook my head. The thought of Carol doomed to spend the rest of her life in some kind of thrall to the evil pairing of Arabella Marsden and Oliver Franklyn revolted me. But I had to face facts. There was nothing I could do for her or Susan Jackson for that matter, or any of the poor hapless women who had found themselves victims of that she-devil and her henchmen.

* * *

I awoke to a perfect early spring morning a mere week away from my first date with the technology that would ensure any lingering trace of cancer had been eliminated from the lymph nodes in my pelvis and groin.

In the mail, a letter arrived, advising me that my application for early retirement on the grounds of ill health had been accepted. I felt strong, alive, and a bit of a fraud as I didn't feel the slightest bit unwell. I did know I wouldn't be so great in a few weeks, though, as the effects of the radiation kicked in.

What better time to make the most of the sunshine, early blossom and fluffy white clouds? I donned a light jacket and headed out for the beach.

I didn't pay any attention to the woman at first. She was leaning over the rail, watching the seagulls bickering and screeching, chasing other, smaller seabirds away. I took up position a few yards from her. Within moments, I sensed her looking at me. I turned and caught her eye as she pushed her hood back off her face.

Instant recognition. She moved toward me and I must have looked stupid, standing there, my mouth partially open in surprise and shock.

"Carol?" I asked at last.

She nodded. "Yes, it's me. As you see me anyway."

I had no idea what that meant, but my relief at seeing her overwhelmed my need for answers at that point. "I never thought

I would see you again. Thank God you escaped from them." I would have loved to be able to tell her how well she looked but, truth was, she looked awful. Her skin had a grayish unhealthy tinge to it and looked almost granular.

"You're going back there, aren't you?" she said. "To the Royal?"

"Next week. For radiotherapy."

"They'll put you in a room on the other side of the wall from where you were. That's where you'll have your treatment. The corridor you and I both remember runs between the two. That's when *they'll* take you and that's when the she-devil they serve will take over your body for the rest of your life. The One and the Many will possess you and live through you. Already a part of her is there inside you – the part of her you inherit from your forebears. It has been this way for millennia, only this time she is stronger. Lydia's daughter absorbed some of her spirit while she lay in her mother's womb."

"Lydia's dau— ? None of this is making any sense to me, Carol. I'm sorry."

A sad smile flicked the corners of her lips. "When the spirit that lies within you was Lydia, your husband, Roger Carmody, raped you. Oh, they didn't call it rape in those days because you were married to each other and the law permitted him to do whatever he wanted to his legally married wife. But you took your revenge and they called it murder. They waited for the child to be born before they hanged you by the neck until you were dead. Lydia's body was buried in the grounds of the workhouse and still lies there, moldering away under the foundations. They never found all the bodies, you see. And those they did find…. There was no way of knowing who they were. They were all dumped together in their thousands. Criminals, the insane, or those whose only crime was to be poor. They reburied the ones they dug up, and they built their hospital, but things started to happen. The fabric of time had been disturbed. That was kept quiet, but these things have a habit of leaking out, and your admission to the Royal and Waverley stirred it all up again. The One and the Many needed a new host and reached out through time to you. Your fate was sealed the moment you were admitted to the hospital. That poem, *'In darkness, shadows breathe'*? You've had it in your possession, haven't you?"

"It was in a book I borrowed from the hospital library. But how—?"

"It's a link. In my case, it was brought to me. Left where I would find it."

"Who brought it to you?"

"A child. The ghost of one anyway. One with whom you too are linked."

"Agnes, you mean. Are you saying that I'm being possessed?"

Carol nodded. "The One and the Many transported from me to you, back in the other time, and brought the memories of all those it has possessed before and after. You will only be aware of the more recent ones. As I was."

"But why me?"

"It had to be you. The One and the Many long ago chose your family and that was one reason I proved unsuitable. Dr. Franklyn and Arabella Marsden got it spectacularly wrong with me and then they made it worse by attempting to use Susan Jackson. The One and the Many rejected her, sent her screaming mad back to Victorian times and then batted her back and forth through time until there was nothing left of her. Nothing sane anyway. You saw the result. Marsden and Franklyn ultimately paid the price for their evil, but the spirit brought them back to do her bidding one more time. *You* are Lydia Warren Carmody's direct descendant, through Agnes. The doctors found that pregnancy hormone inside you, didn't they? Even though there was no possible way it could have been there. Lydia had been through pregnancy and, to ensure the transfer was perfect, you had to be pregnant too. The hormone has gone now, hasn't it?"

I nodded slowly. "This is insane."

Carol shrugged. "Insane or not, you are about to forfeit your life for it."

I shook my head, closing my eyes for a moment. When I opened them again, she had gone. I looked all around me at the deserted walkway, and along the beach. No sign of her.

I wandered back home. How could I tell Paul that all the horror had merely been put on hold? And how could I stop myself from being the next victim?

Then I reminded myself. If what Carol had told me was accurate, it was too late anyway. The demon had already taken up residence, somewhere in the recesses of my brain. That extra pulse I hadn't felt since I left the hospital started up again and I knew I was no longer alone in my body. I should tell Paul about it and my latest encounter with Carol, but what good would it do?

I told myself radiation was a powerful weapon and even found a reference to some scientist who had successfully cleansed his home of a horde of evil spirits by bombarding it with radiation. Surely the One and the Many wouldn't be able to live inside me after my treatment.

It is strange how tenuous your hold on reality can become when you're desperate. Besides, I told myself, I wouldn't be alone for one second when I was in the radiotherapy suite. They had shown me a treatment center and walked me through the procedure. Unless an entire team of specialists was in on Carol's theory of my abduction, it simply wouldn't be possible for this evil spirit to get to me.

* * *

Paul handed me a cup of tea from the vending machine. "You're very quiet, Ness. Are you okay?"

"Just a bit nervous, that's all." I didn't mention the bombardment of butterflies performing aerial acrobatics in my stomach.

"Vanessa Tremaine."

I jumped at the sound of my name and nearly spilled my drink. I handed it to Paul.

"Good luck," he said.

I followed the smiling nurse down a short corridor into the treatment suite. A chorus of greetings welcomed me and I said "hello" back to everyone. The nurse led me to a curtained-off area.

"Just take your skirt and shoes off and pop the gown on. Come out when you're ready."

She left me alone. *Alone. I mustn't be alone.*

The lights flickered so quickly as to be barely noticeable but *I* noticed and so did the team on the other side of the curtain. Next to me, the wall seemed to undulate. Again, only for a second. A dark shadow appeared, growing, seeming to absorb the wall behind it. I dragged my skirt down and kicked my shoes off. I was back through the curtain in under a minute, panting hard.

The nurse looked up from what she was doing. "Hey, it's okay. No need to rush. Take all the time you need."

How could I explain to her that I didn't have time? Certainly not time to be alone even if there was only a curtain separating me from them. *They* could still get to me.

And then I realized. They already had.

It was that time-shift phenomenon. The demon's ability to bend and shape time. To me and to the team of radiographers and specialist nurses, a minute or two had elapsed, but I knew. I had gone through that curtain as Nessa Tremaine, albeit Nessa Tremaine with a dormant evil spirit inside her. But I had emerged fully integrated with the One and the Many. She had taken hold of me and claimed me fully as her own.

* * *

And now, I am lying here in a room in the Radiotherapy suite. They've positioned me, lined me up and, in any second, I will hear the sound of the machine delivering its first destructive, yet necessary pulses.

I close my eyes. The sound of the machine fades away until I can no longer hear it.

In the distance I can hear voices calling me. The voices of my ancestors.

And the voice of the spirit who controls us all.

CHAPTER EIGHTEEN

"What do you mean, you can't find her?" Paul stared in disbelief at the pale, scared-looking nurse who had been all smiles when she had escorted Nessa in for her treatment. Now she stood opposite him in a consulting room off the main waiting area.

"I'm sorry, Mr. Tremaine. I can't explain it. Nessa had her treatment—"

"I know. I heard the machine."

"She went behind the curtain to get dressed and when she didn't come out, I went to check on her. But she wasn't there."

Paul flopped down onto a chair, his head in his hands. "This can't be happening."

"We've alerted Security and a search is being made right now."

"Somehow, I don't think they'll find her. And it wouldn't be the first time it's happened."

"Sorry?"

Paul couldn't bring himself to even begin to try and tell a story so fantastic he could hardly believe it himself.

He had reported Nessa missing to the police and they took a statement. A part of him still clung to the hope that she had simply panicked and run away from the treatment even though he knew that made no sense.

"I need to know my wife is all right. I'm going out of my mind here." Paul had meant every word as he sat in his living room opposite a man young enough to be his son.

The police constable tucked his notebook in his pocket. "I assure you we're doing everything we can to trace her. Maybe she simply needed a little time on her own."

"But she knows she can't do that. She must compete the full course of treatment. Now she's missed two appointments."

The police officer moved toward the door. "Let us know if you hear from her. Meanwhile we'll do all we can to find her."

Paul let him out, locked the door behind him and sank down onto the settee.

* * *

An hour later, Joanna held an old brown leather book out to Paul as they sat in his living room. "I've bookmarked the relevant entry. It's Lydia Warren's diary from 1874. It makes for interesting reading and it'll probably mean more to you, given what you've told me of Nessa's experiences and now her disappearance. So much like Carol."

Paul opened the diary and read the entry silently to himself.

'May 5th

What strange thoughts I have been having. They are not mine. They belong to someone else. Someone in the future, speaking words that mean nothing to me. Radiotherapy. What is that? Something about a woman called Nessa and a child called Agnes. I don't understand any of it. Who are these people? Yet I feel I should know them. That, in some way, I do know them.

I am seated at a battered wooden desk. Dr. Franklyn is sitting on the other side of the room, writing something in a large book. I look down at my hands. I am writing too. My penmanship is quite good. It never used to be. No, that's not right either. This is not my memory but that of another. I was taught to write neatly, as I am now.

I turn back a few pages and find the poem I was working on yesterday. Was it only yesterday? It seems longer ago somehow, but I've only been here a short while. I never thought I would work in a place like this. An asylum for heaven's sake!

I am not supposed to be writing in this diary, I am supposed to be reckoning figures. Income and expenditure for the past month. All these receipts. Each one must be entered and tallied. Any shortfall will have to be accounted for.

The doctor gets up and leaves without saying one word to me. He is like that. Most of the time he barely acknowledges my existence. It is a strange place, this building. So much whispering and I can never see who is speaking. Most of it is in the walls. I hear odd sounds. Like machinery, but none I can recognize. Sometimes I think I see shadowy people. Women dressed like men with thin trousers and matching shirts. Others are dressed like doctors. And the lights. They are so bright, sometimes they dazzle me with their brilliance.

In a couple of months none of this will matter anyway, for I am to be married to the awful Roger Carmody. I can't abide him, but Mama says I must. He wants to marry me and he has money. I should be grateful she says. I, Lydia Warren, am most fortunate he still wants to marry me after the disgrace my father brought to us. Married to Roger, I will never have to turn my hand to work ever again. Mama has secured herself a position, her needlework skills being put to use working for a high-class milliner. She used to buy her hats there before Papa gambled everything away and left us penniless. I know I should not think such a wicked thought, but I am almost glad he killed himself. The strychnine did what I wanted to do myself. I have these peculiar rushes of excitement when I think what I would have done to him. It is as if something triggers in my brain. An odd sort of pulse. I would have used a knife probably and plunged it into his worthless, feckless heart, but he settled for the strychnine. The ferocity of my thoughts frightens me sometimes. It is as if I am experiencing the passion of another who shares my body.

Papa left Mama virtually destitute. I fear for her eyesight as she works so long into the night, producing tiny, perfect stitches for rich society women to ignore. Sometimes I want to kill them too.

I have just looked back at what I wrote at the beginning of this entry and it makes no sense to me. It is as if someone else wrote it. Someone who would feel at home living deep within these walls in the company of the other strange people and things.

I must finish my work for today now or he will be after me.

Maybe I will write more tomorrow.'

Paul Tremaine closed the battered diary and returned it to Joanna. She took it from him.

"Where did you find it?" he asked.

"In the apartment where Carol was living. I still had the spare keys, so I thought I would have a look for anything that might give us an inkling of where she may have gone or a clue as to what's happened to Nessa. This was tucked away at the back of a drawer in the bedroom. I'm not even sure who it belongs to. I asked Adele – she and her husband are the owners of the flat – but she said it wasn't theirs, so I suppose it must be Carol's, but it doesn't *fit* somehow and surely she would have mentioned it to me.... Ah well. Another mystery. I'd better get going." She stood and Paul showed her to the door. Joanna put her hand on his shoulder. "Take care of yourself, Paul. Let me know if...when you get any news."

Paul nodded. His own welfare was the last thing on his mind and as for news....

After he closed the door, he angrily wiped yet more tears from his eyes and moved over to the window. Outside, a stiff wind was whipping up the sea. White horses. Nessa loved watching this kind of weather. She had chosen this apartment for the view alone.

"Where are you, Nessa?"

The doorbell buzzed.

CHAPTER NINETEEN

"Oh my God, *Nessa.* It's really you." His wife half fell into his arms. He drew her inside and closed the door. She leaned on him until they were safely in the living room and he deposited her on the settee.

"What happened to you? I've been going out of my mind."

Nessa's clear eyes met his. Considering she had been missing, God knows where, for two days, she looked remarkably well. Almost youthful, and rejuvenated.

She smiled at him. "I can't tell you because it's all hazy, but the important thing is that I'm back and I'm stronger than before."

"You don't remember where you've been? Not any of it?" How could she have forgotten?

Nessa shrugged. "I'm more settled now. Isn't that the most important thing?"

She certainly seemed calm, but there was something different about her. Paul tried to quash the uncertainty. He was looking at his *wife.* This was Nessa, who had been through so many life-changing ordeals recently. It was bound to have a lasting effect on her.

"Have you eaten, or slept?"

Nessa nodded. "I think so. I'm not hungry and I don't feel tired, but I would like a shower." She stood and Paul watched her walk steadily out of the living room, with no trace of the stumbling gait of a few minutes earlier.

He heard the noise of the shower running and called the police.

* * *

Nessa combed her hair and examined herself in the mirror. She blinked and a flash of vermilion reflected back at her. She smiled and part of her enjoyed the sensation of seeing the world through new eyes. The eyes of the One and the Many. The eyes of Agnes, daughter of Lydia and Roger Carmody, who was daughter too of the spirit that chose them. Agnes, who lived in every generation and every century and who could take the form of another. At once the innocent child, holding out the hand of friendship, only to transform into Hester, the handmaiden to her real devil mother.

Reflected in the mirror, the eyes of all who had gone before and all who would come in the future looked out, as time – never linear – looped and curled over itself in sinuous waves. Together they formed the One and the Many as she – and they – raised their silent voices in unison.

How strong we are. Together we shall continue to grow, for all eternity.

* * *

On the beach, the woman stopped in her tracks. The wind whistled off the sea bringing salty grittiness that coated her dry lips. She stared across at the apartment block, a slight smile on her face. Her life, and that of the devil who had shared her body for a time, passed through her mind. A series of snapshots and short movies. Of murder, suicide, retribution. Jonah, the Sinclairs' rapist son. She had killed him all right. He lay, where she left him, for fifty years. Maybe more. Until the site was cleared and his chained-up skeleton found. One more unsolved murder.

She knew the real Carol Shaughnessy didn't exist. Hadn't existed for over a century. Not since Oliver Franklyn and Arabella Marsden had killed her, in the name of the One and the Many. Carol should have been the perfect host – an empty vessel for the spirit to fill with hatred, lust for vengeance and sheer evil, but Franklyn and Marsden had said her brain was too damaged. It was because nothing real existed within her anymore. They had seen to that. Their incessant quest to find the source of the soul had been successful, but they had gone too far and destroyed it.

So the spirit had moved on to Nessa's body and now Carol could no longer exist in any form in this time and space. As she looked down at her hands, she could see them fading, taking on a semi-transparent, granular appearance.

In *this* time, she only lived in some small memories possessed by other people. For now, they had recollections of her touching them briefly before passing through their lives. Soon those memories would fade until they wouldn't even remember her name. In that way time healed itself.

Someone was looking down at her through the window of Nessa's apartment. Paul Tremaine. He wouldn't see her of course. There was no longer any need for anyone to see her. She wished she could help him, but no one could. He alone would have to fight the devil in his home.

A shape moved into her line of vision. An elderly woman. There was something familiar about her…. A flash of memory. In *this* time, in a supermarket. The woman dropping her money all over the floor. Carol had helped her. The woman had been grateful…tried to give her cash…and then another piece of her life's jigsaw slotted into place and she recognized the entity that had been with her all her life. Her familiar. Not powerful enough to ward off the One and the Many but here for her now.

The familiar shimmered and nodded, raised a hand and beckoned to Carol. "It's time…."

Carol turned into the wind, felt it whip across her face one last time. She smiled and gave herself up to it, becoming one with the grains of sand on the beach and the salt in the air.

ACKNOWLEDGMENTS

It is fair to say this book would not even exist without the inspiration of friend and fellow Flame Tree author Hunter Shea. His incredible novel, *Creature*, gave me the courage to confront some of my own demons, which I then handed to poor old Nessa to deal with.

My eternal thanks and admiration go to the (British) National Health Service (NHS), without whom this book would not exist, because neither would I. I am forever indebted to the amazing skill, expertise and care of the team of oncologists, specialist nursing and support staff at Liverpool Women's Hospital, the radiographers and everyone at Clatterbridge Cancer Centre – and everyone at Broad Green Hospital who successfully operated and steered me through a further battle (one which Nessa escaped. I thought she'd suffered enough!).

I also want to say a huge 'thank you' to the Macmillan Cancer Nurses (macmillan.org.uk) who provided me with such vital support. They are too often the unsung heroes, work so hard and see us at our worst.

Going through cancer is a team effort and my husband, Colin, was there with me every step of the way. Thank you so much for your love and support, Colin. In some ways, it is harder for those who have to watch their loved ones suffer. For them, there's such a feeling of helplessness, which the patient doesn't experience in the same way. We have our medical team keeping us busy.

Julie Bridson and Flora Macdonald – friends and former colleagues from the University of Liverpool's School of Health Sciences – supported me with their friendship and their own medical expertise for which I am ever grateful.

This was not an easy book to write – for a number of reasons – and, thankfully, Julia Kavan was there, as always, homing in on the impossible, the inconsistent, the farfetched and the incongruent. As I always say, every writer needs a Julia!

Massive thanks to Don D'Auria for his faith in me, his knowledge, expertise and legendary editorial skills. Where would the horror genre be without you, Don? I dread to think.

To everyone at Flame Tree – you are brilliant to work with, so supportive and professional. It is a privilege and an honor to be included on your roster.

And to you, reading this book, thank you for spending time with me. I hope you'll come back and join me on another adventure into the darkness….

FLAME TREE PRESS
FICTION WITHOUT FRONTIERS
Award-Winning Authors & Original Voices

Flame Tree Press is the trade fiction imprint of Flame Tree Publishing, focusing on excellent writing in horror and the supernatural, crime and mystery, science fiction and fantasy. Our aim is to explore beyond the boundaries of the everyday, with tales from both award-winning authors and original voices.

•

Other titles available by Catherine Cavendish:
The Haunting of Henderson Close
The Garden of Bewitchment

Other horror and suspense titles available include:
Snowball by Gregory Bastianelli
Thirteen Days by Sunset Beach by Ramsey Campbell
Think Yourself Lucky by Ramsey Campbell
The Hungry Moon by Ramsey Campbell
The House by the Cemetery by John Everson
The Devil's Equinox by John Everson
Hellrider by JG Faherty
The Toy Thief by D.W. Gillespie
One By One by D.W. Gillespie
Black Wings by Megan Hart
The Playing Card Killer by Russell James
The Portal by Russell James
The Sorrows by Jonathan Janz
Castle of Sorrows by Jonathan Janz
The Dark Game by Jonathan Janz
Will Haunt You by Brian Kirk
We Are Monsters by Brian Kirk
Those Who Came Before by J.H. Moncrieff
Stoker's Wilde by Steven Hopstaken & Melissa Prusi
Stoker's Wilde West by Steven Hopstaken & Melissa Prusi
Creature by Hunter Shea
Ghost Mine by Hunter Shea
Slash by Hunter Shea
The Mouth of the Dark by Tim Waggoner
They Kill by Tim Waggoner

•

Join our mailing list for free short stories, new release details, news about our authors and special promotions:

flametreepress.com